ALSO BY S.J. KING

Where You Belong

To my mother and my daughter.
Thanks to you, I am both.

When truth is buried underground, it grows, and it gathers such a force that the day it burst out, it explodes everything with it.

Émile Zola – *J'Accuse...!*, 1898.
Translated from his open letter.

PROLOGUE

Memory is a fragile thing for you as well as me. I know I was born, though I can't remember it, and after there are fragments, like shop windows I might have glanced at in passing. Vignettes, perfectly framed, random objects and room settings. Mannequins dressed as my mother, my father. Laughter. Tears. A family, of sorts.

Then there are snippets. Little things I cut out and kept. A scrapbook of disjointed moments that hinted at what was coming for us. Or rather, for her.

Those spots of blood on the kitchen tiles. Mum's hand striking someone's cheek, a sound like ice cracking. My nanna on her deathbed with eyelids as thin as tissue. The scent of Mr Colson, too close and too wrong. A boy who rolled joints and sang songs he'd written, the light of a bright young future in his eyes. The smell of lasagne baking in the oven; the flickering of the TV in the background; my father's briefcase waiting in the hall. Had he just arrived, or was he just about to leave?

And then I remember the velvety petals of a yellow rose. How they looked on a stone step in the snow on the night that she went out and simply never came home.

When I lay them out like that they all seem so connected. Like dots that could be joined to form a picture. Or an exam question I might not fail:

Life is a timeline. C follows B, and B follows A.

Discuss.

But there is no picture emerging. No answer on the page. It is still all so unclear to me.

And Lauren is always missing.

ONE

JANE

Today

Jane bustles in from the car and slings her handbag onto the kitchen counter. She throws her coat over the back of a chair where it hangs like a slumped body. She's annoyed; that *bloody* doctor. So condescending!

She's thinking how warm today is for January, how quiet the house is. That it will start to get dark in an hour or so, and the Christmas lights are all packed away; no kids coming in from school to look forward to. Dan will eventually arrive in from work, grumpy no doubt, rummaging in the cupboard for crisps or nuts. Her hamster husband with his increasingly chubby cheeks and a small paunch.

She crosses to the Belfast sink to fill the kettle, needing a cup of tea. The clinical, cloying scent of the doctor's surgery still lingers in her throat. She can taste it. But when she reaches the tap, she feels momentarily disorientated and glances out of the window, searching for something.

Later she'll tell the police it was as if she already knew something – or *someone* – was out there.

She leans over the sink to look at her garden which, like everything, she loves a little less in winter. The skeletal bushes, a few scavenging crows, the unused wooden seat where she takes her coffee in spring. That delicious puddle of sunlight that always spills up the side of the house, like stepping into a warm ray of happiness. Nothing there today.

The garden is naked. The trees and shrubs leafless. If they weren't, she might never have seen what she sees.

What is that...?

It's too big for a bird, too dark for a fox. A stray dog perhaps? Or a person, hunched over by the rose bush.

She retrieves her glasses. She'd set them on the counter when she came in. Vaguely recalls lifting them, rubbing her eyes; not crying, just tired. Well, maybe a bit tearful. Her body cold and achy despite the unseasonable day. Hot one minute, cold the next; the doctor's disinterest, despite the effort and resolve it had taken to get the appointment in the first place. Instead, she'd been tarred with broad brushstrokes – *menopause* – the peri kind. He'd almost laughed as he'd mansplained that menopause was just one day, but the *peri* part could last for years. *Lucky her.* High blood pressure too, some of that for good measure. 'Try to relax,' he'd said, as if that was all it took.

With her glasses on, Jane can see a little better... there *is* someone crouched under her rose bush, their back to the house. What on earth are they doing there? Someone stooping and rising. She sees a clod of soil thrust out. Digging...? They're digging for something.

The idea incenses her.

Is it a girl...?

Jane doesn't think it's one of the neighbour's kids... *Suzy... Sally... whatever they're called...* They wouldn't come over after the incident with Dan and the hose pipe. Besides, there's something unsettling about this girl. Taller than a child, thinner too. Long, matted hair – *is that hair...?* – hanging down her back. Even with her glasses, Jane can't quite make it out. Damn it!

She needs a new prescription; fifty doesn't love eyesight anymore than it loves muscle strength or skin tone, or a good night's sleep. Or sex, for that matter. She doesn't care what Amanda Holden says, all braless and frisky in a silky blouse and flashing her bum in a bikini. Fifty is not all that for Jane.

She reaches the kitchen door; grateful she hasn't yet changed out of her shoes. She takes the key from the place where she hides it on the shelf behind a photo of her family. Dan and the kids: Alice and Aidan, grown up and left home. She can't quite accept they no longer live under her roof. Yet she loves this frozen moment, Aidan's fourteenth, is it five years ago already? Him ruffle-haired and ruddy, caught mid-laugh. His older sister, Alice, gazing at him with a genuine look of love. He'd been fanatical about wanting lemon drizzle cake, and in the weeks after he'd asked Jane to bake it twice more. She lingers here often, back in this moment, almost tasting lemon zest, reminding herself of who she has been. Hard to believe she's out the other side of motherhood. She misses them both with a sting. She'd step back into the chaos in the blink of an eye, if given the choice. But that's not how life works. It only moves on. And you only miss things when they're gone.

Now she unlocks the kitchen door, steps out. 'Hey there... hello?' she calls, a wave of her arm. The sudden thwack of crows' wings as, startled, they take flight.

But the girl doesn't turn. She hunkers, even if Jane knows she heard. That stilling. That watchful waiting. Jane's heartbeat climbs a notch – *beating, beating* – the cold invading her jumper, forcing her to shove her hands into opposite sleeves. The January day not as warm as she'd thought.

The steps are slippery as she hurries down, and after that fall last summer, she needs to be more careful. Another sign that ageing is here for keeps, not like a brief visit from her kids. It doesn't just pop in to do laundry and have a home-cooked meal.

Jane half expects the girl to be gone when she looks up. But she's still there, hasn't moved a muscle. The girl cowers further as Jane approaches, her face intentionally turned away.

'Can I help you?' Jane asks, as if approaching someone in a shop. She has never worked in one, and it's more prim than she'd like. 'I'm sorry, but this is my—'

Her words snag then, wedged in her throat. The girl turns, just enough for Jane to see things that she wishes she hadn't. Dark eyes, gaunt cheeks, a look of feral fear. Older than a girl and younger than a woman, and something wrong about her. Bruises, scars, a patch of skin buckled like melted plastic. Jane's hand rises to her mouth, stifling a scream. She scans the girl's clothes; a jumper with holes, an oversized man's shirt, jeans that are washed out and patched, like a Sarah Kay doll.

'Are you all right?' Jane falters. But she could answer that herself: *Not all right. Not OK.*

The girl is clutching something to her belly as if her life depends on it. Jane has a fleeting sense of horror, then realizes it is some kind of book. Was she burying it, or digging it up?

'Who are you? What are doing here?' Jane asks. So many tangled questions.

But the girl doesn't speak. No hint of who she is, or how she came to be here.

In fact, she's as silent as winter.

TWO
RENE

Before

In the dark, in my head, before I even open my eyes, I make a happy list. What it is I want to feel before my day is done. Today's list is quite simple:

- *Warmth*
- *Happiness*
- *Freedom*

Now I open my eyes, seeing the muted pink glow of my bedroom, the rose velvet curtains at my window. Fingers of morning light trying to prize their way in.

On my wall, there's a collage of photographs and magazine pictures stuck up for fun and inspiration; little things to stop me from falling into a pit of despair. And that's where I see her, there on the wall amongst all the other images: *Lauren*. Her hair glowing like fire; catching light from the sun. How ecstatic she is as she streams downhill, her hands only loosely on the handlebars of her bike. How tanned her legs, gold-tinged and slender, outstretched as she flies along. She looks like she knows all about warmth, happiness, freedom. She's thirteen in this photo. By fourteen, she was gone.

I trace my finger lovingly along her outline.

'Thank you,' I tell her, because at least now I know what I'm going to do today, on my day off. Bike ride, down at the canal. She'd have liked that.

But my sister, Lauren, went missing eight years ago. Disappeared from this life, left mine in her shadow. Because I am the one my family were left to love, who went to school in her footsteps. To find endless hobbies to keep me busy and sane, a job I might one day make a difference at. Yes, I am the one who got to grow up. All the while wondering who she would have been, or might have truly become.

Don't think of me, she whispers.

So, I dress. A light dusting of pink blusher, a circle of fruity cherry lip gloss, hasty tugs on my long blonde hair. It dances with static before settling down over the slogan of my favourite T-shirt: *Don't be a Zombie. Own Life*, it says. I always said that if I came back as anything, it would be a zombie. It's a joke. But to be honest, zombies are pretty kick-ass, and their life seems mindless and simple: *Chase. Kill. Eat. Repeat.*

In the mirror, I see my almost – dare I say it – pretty reflection. My green eyes are brighter than Lauren's, my teeth straighter – after all, I got to wear braces. There's a dimple in my chin, it looks like pressed dough. Around my face, tucked in the frame, there's a circle of old Polaroids. A friend has written on one in eyeliner: *Rene is all that, and a bag of chips! xx*

I haven't seen those friends in a while.

I force a smile, tucking my hair behind one ear, pinning it with a clip with the words *Go Girl* in glitter. It's a bit childish, but I like it. We could talk for hours about stunted emotional development, but let's keep things bright and glittery, shall we?

I glance back up at the walls to check that Lauren is still there. Yup, still happy, still bathed in light, still racing endlessly downhill on her forever bike. Her hair, her face, her legs, everything glowing. I long to feel that, even for just a moment. The sun tumbling over every inch of my skin, right down to the tips of my... bright yellow boots.

I don't own yellow boots...!

Should I stop off in town and buy some? If I do, perhaps something significant will happen. Is that why I've noticed them today? Maybe the boy in the shop will know something about Lauren. He'll slip me his number, we'll meet for hot chocolate. He'll tell me a secret, a clue... something we missed, something vital. Maybe he'll say that he'll help me to save her; he doesn't believe that she won't be found either.

He'll ask me to see a movie, and I'll accept, because something about him reminds me of a boy I used to like. We'll sit side-by-side in the movies, his arm resting just above my shoulders, eating buttered popcorn from the same tub. Hands accidentally touching. The small white popcorn blooms finding their way down my top and into my bra. Afterwards he'll walk me home, we'll kiss goodnight on my doorstep, his hands worming their way inside my clothes, finding those salty-sweet puffs of corn... pushing me against the door, more firmly, more forcefully. Telling him to stop. Telling him I don't want that—

No!

That's not how today should go. I can't let things head off in unexpected directions. I tuck the strand of hair behind my ear, reclip the clip. *Click click.* Nervous tic.

My mobile phone jitters across the bedside table, saving me from my own thoughts. I pick it up and see a message from David, my boss, editor in chief at the *Local Chronicle*.

Enjoy your day off

That's not much for someone who once wrote novels I devoured as a teen, which was part of the reason I went to work for him. Part of it, though not the full story.

I try to think of a million funny, sassy, cryptic replies. In the end, I just write *Thanks* and click send.

Perhaps I *should* go to the office after all. Because there's safety in numbers, comfort in the mundanity of what I already know. David will give me a new assignment, a person to interview, a tale for me to unfold. 'Everyone has a story,' he'll say, tapping his pencil against his top lip, reading my latest submission. 'This is good,' he'll reassure me with a thin, impressed smile. 'Really good.' He always tries to encourage me. Well, nearly always.

But I can't become too dependent. Don't want him thinking that I'm too desperate. Got to keep it safe and professional.

So, no David. Not today.

I tug on a mismatched pair of socks. Somehow, I've convinced myself that that is lucky. Today it's taco cats and pizza slices. Then I hesitate. Two food items. I switch out the pizza slice socks for unicorns. That's better.

Then I head into the kitchen.

I open the fridge and take out a box of sugared donuts I bought on my way home yesterday; the ones I absolutely *love*, especially for breakfast on a day off. I tingle with excitement.

From the neat rows of Coke cans, I take one, cracking the ring pull and washing down a big old bite of donut. Then I rearrange the cans to accommodate the missing one. There's a dusting of white powder on my lips, on the handle of the fridge, and a clot of blood-red jam that dollops out on the counter. Messy, but delicious.

When I'm finished, I gather up the cloth, removing my sticky fingerprints from everywhere I've been. Then I rinse the cloth and set it back beside the sink, wrung out and neatly folded. Once, twice, third time lucky! Everything as it should be. Nothing out of place. Nothing missing... *except*...

Don't go there... I tell myself.

I flit through the living room, smoothing the crochet blanket that hangs over my gorgeous teal sofa. Straightening the pile of magazines on the coffee table; I sanded and painted that myself. Not that anyone is ever going to get to see this, but I always imagined having a cosy little sitting room, like this.

I glance up at my basement window, my sub-street view, all pale brickwork and black railings from down here. I watch people passing; a game of Misfits with the heads and shoulders gone. There's a pair of ankles, the hem of a pleated skirt. The owner striding merrily into her day, swinging a tote, a black-and-white scarf tied jauntily around the handle. I'm guessing brunch date with girlfriends at the French restaurant on the high street. What's it called... Bouchon, I think. She'll drink *real* champagne, not prosecco. Because she's planning her wedding, or maybe it's her hen. Maybe if I go there now, I'll discover she's an old school friend; I might even get an invite. They're going to... Paris. No... Venice! Oh, I'd love to go there. The Grand Canal.

Which reminds me, bike ride down at the canal. I mean, Coversham is not the Adriatic but still... places to be.

'Gotta go. Can't hang around here all day,' I say, waving to the woman who's already gone.

I sashay along my narrow hallway, painted red and covered with perfectly arranged postcards and paintings and pages from books I've framed and mounted. A bone china plate I stuck back together after it was broken in two pieces. A pencil sketch of a dragonfly Lauren drew at the canal when she was ten.

And then there are photographs, dozens of frozen forever moments. Mum, Dad and Lauren on the pontoon in France, that holiday when we were all so very happy. Mum in that dress that I loved with the iridescent sequins. Lauren with Dad smiling proudly the first time she rode her bike without stabilizers. And here she is at six and seven and ten and twelve and fourteen, and...

There is no fifteen.

That's why I don't talk to Dad anymore. And Mum? That's more complicated. We speak occasionally, cordial and spiky. Sometimes I just need to let the anger out. Because they never found her. They never brought her home.

But today is a day off. I've promised myself that much. Happy thoughts, lucky socks.

I trip along to my front door. Literally; I am often rather clumsy. I don't know when that started. Or why. Still, people say, 'That's just Rene.' I can almost hear the canned laughter.

Now I peer out the eyehole before opening it. Another little routine. I unfasten the locks in exactly the same order, before stepping out into the world that I control a lot less. The late-September chill rushes in around me, and the air has the sweet scent of autumn and dying leaves. Summer has passed, another year fading. A flutter of disappointment like a sycamore seed falling.

'I bet the trees will be beautiful today,' I say to myself. Because I read in a magazine that gratitude is a great way to stave off dark thoughts, and I have a lot of staving off to do.

I tug my bike out from the alcove of the porch, lugging it up the steps to the street. That's one part of basement living that I didn't think through properly. A bit like my view. Still, the extra effort keeps me strong and agile. That's gratitude. See, you'll find it everywhere if you look hard enough. Like most things.

I lift my leg to climb on my bike and then I'm hit with a bolt of fear. *Don't go there*, she says, *not today*. I look around as if she might be close. Something about the bike and the canal.

She doesn't want me to go back there.

'Don't be silly, Lauren. I'll be fine. What could possibly happen to me? Besides, lucky socks.'

I lift my leg, jumping on and pulling out into the traffic. I ignore a screech of tyres and the toot of a horn. Because today is *my* day off, and I'm going to do what my favourite T-shirt says.

I'm going to *own life.*

THREE

JANE

Today

Inside Jane's kitchen, the girl hesitates, a flicker of confusion. She looks around with what Jane will later describe to the police as something like recognition. Jane wonders if it was right to bring her inside.

She coaxes the girl to the chair; and at first she goes willingly. Then suddenly she turns back, hurries to the kitchen door. The girl twists the key in the lock and tugs it out, throwing it behind the picture as if she knows that's where it's kept.

Strange, Jane thinks.

One of the girl's filthy hands is pressed hard against the glass, the other holding tightly to the muddy, mildewed notebook that she seems to have dug up. The girl looks out at the garden with frantic shifts of her head. Is she searching for something, or someone...?

Jane shudders. She needs to call the police.

She eyes the girl, trying to categorize her injuries, thinking how best to describe her situation: *Alone. Scared. Bruised. Neglected.*

Jane shakes her head at the unspeakable horror that is in her beautiful kitchen. She guides the girl back to the chair where she can contain her, assess her, decide if she should call an ambulance first. She doesn't even know her name.

Her skin is as cold as ice to the touch. Jane drapes her coat around the girl's shoulders, as if that's why it was hanging on the chair all along. Is it a girl? Maybe a young woman. It's hard to tell beneath all the muck, or is it soot and dried blood? Jane is not at all sure, doesn't want to look too closely.

She returns to the counter, rummages in her handbag for her phone; times like this a landline would come in handy. At least she'd know where it was. A big old-fashioned thing sitting in the hall. Hadn't there been one there, years ago... when they moved in? She thinks of the last owners. Strange couple. Something awakening at the back of her mind. She's not sure why she thinks of them now.

'What did you say your name was?' Jane asks again. It's probably been long enough since she last asked her.

She doesn't reply. She gazes around, as if searching for something on a shelf, on the wall. Her brow rising and falling as if scanning braille. The girl pushes herself up from the chair and limps determinedly out into the hall. Jane watches as her bare feet leave dirty prints on the wood flooring, as she places a mucky hand on the curled white banister.

'Mum?' she calls cautiously as she peers up, her voice the hesitant bray of a distressed animal. The first word the girl – or possibly young woman – has spoken.

Jane hits call on her phone, hears the ringtone, then the answerphone message. 'Dan? Yes, hello, it's me...' she tells her husband. 'Not sure what to do really.' She pauses, eyes fixed on the girl. 'Bear with me. I've found a' – she lowers her voice – 'a lost girl. And she looks like she's been—' She pauses, not sure what to say.

'Daddy...?' The girl calls up the stairs again.

'Look, I'm quite worried,' Jane says. 'Quite' is an understatement. 'I'm fine. And I will call the police... but...' At those words, the girl's head whips round.

She understood that.

'Look, Dan, when you get this, just come home. OK? I need you.' Jane hangs up. She hopes he'll hear it soon and come straight home. These days she rarely says she needs him for anything. He'll get it. He'll hear the message and he'll come.

She slips her phone into her cardigan pocket and approaches the girl at the bottom of the stairs. 'She's not here. Your mother...' Jane clarifies, taking her arm and pulling it gently. She's afraid of breaking her.

But the girl doesn't relinquish her grip on the banister, and Jane is surprised at her strength. It reminds her of tugging limpets from a rock pool in Norfolk with her uncle, many moons ago. He'd spent hours with her, playing in the sea. She had a red and white bathing suit which she loved, she remembers now. Remembers she didn't see him again after that summer. Her mother said it made her uncomfortable. She'd always assumed it was the tides she was afraid of.

'Why do you think your mother is here?' Jane asks.

The girl searches Jane's face as if she's the one who doesn't belong. Jane breaks her gaze, glances at the girl's hands instead; her scratched fingers and broken nails. As if she's scraped her way out of somewhere.

The girl tucks her hand behind her back. The other still clutching the soiled notebook tight to her stomach. Is it what brought her to Jane's garden? How long has it been there?

'Come on,' Jane says as calmly as she can, guiding the girl back to the chair. 'You know, I have to call the police,' she says softly when she's settled. 'You know that, don't you?'

The girl looks at Jane, her eyes steely and defiant. She shakes her head, slowly, side to side, making her feelings clear.

Jane straightens, tuts to herself. 'Right, well.' Another

anxious smile. 'I suppose we could just take a moment to catch our breath, hey?' That disorientated feeling again, not sure what to do next. She's trying to remember how to be a patient mother; to play the persuasion game that she used to. Except then it was about eating broccoli or mushrooms, picking up socks from the bathroom floor, scraping their own plate and *actually* putting it in the dishwasher not leaving it on top for her to do later. Not convincing a young woman that the police will be able to help when she clearly needs it.

Unless... Jane glances back at the locked door. Unless there's some reason why she thinks she's in trouble. That she's the one who has done something wrong...

The kitchen is quiet. Too quiet. Jane's eyes creep back to the locked door, the key behind the frame. She's locked in with this girl.

'What did you say your name was?' Jane coaxes. 'Come on, you can tell me.'

The girl-woman looks at her, calculating something. She opens her mouth, forming a word. Then she closes it, drops her gaze to her feet. Bare feet, deep-under-the-nail dirt, scars at her ankles as if she's been bound.

Jane waits, aware of the knock, knock, knocking of her own heart, a pounding in her ears. She glances back to that family picture for comfort. Alice, her daughter, twenty and at uni. Maybe this girl is the same age. Who can say?

The girl looks around the room, her eyes drifting over the counter, the breadboard, the knife block. Her eyes narrow.

'Do you... know this place?' Jane asks quietly.

The girl doesn't reply.

Was she friends with Alice at school? Came here to play all those years ago, maybe buried the notebook as part of a game.

Then the girl turns to her and finally speaks.

'Home,' is what she says.

FOUR

RENE

Before

At the towpath by the canal, the sun is shining loosely. The bank is high with reeds and grasses that shimmer in the light. I take one hand off the handlebars of my bike and pedal slower, running my fingers through the long grass.

Freedom. I love the feel of sun on my skin.

It reminds me of that holiday in France when we were small, the dreamlike innocence of warm lazy days lying close to our mother on the beach; hearing the sea, counting the moles on her arm, the luminous colours of the sequins on her dress, worlds hidden within them. How I wanted that happiness to last forever. Except it couldn't. She would never let it.

Now I pedal along the path that snakes beside the canal. The water that looks calm but if you look closely, you'll see it drifts quickly. Flowing out to the estuaries where silt buries a great many things, never to be dug up or found.

For a second, I see frogmen diving in the canal's murky depths, bubbles under the surface tangled in the reeds. Searching for a body. Finding some of Lauren's things. Her second-favourite sweater, a spare T-shirt, a notebook of her writing spoiled by river water, a red panda keychain with her front door key still attached. Fragments of clues of where she was headed that they couldn't piece together. And in the dead of night, I whisper to myself: *Maybe no one cared enough to try.*

I get off my bike and it tumbles into the dirt, scuffing my shin. The light dips; the sun behind a cloud. A chill slips under the layers of my jumper and I wish then that I had worn a coat. I shiver and ask myself why I keep coming here.

Here. In the place that Dad used to bring us as children, to ride our bikes over rough ground, building our strength and agility that the cul-de-sac of Meadow Close could never give us. Throwing stones into the water, our childish laughter giddy as ripples.

Here. Where we would lie on our backs, watching the soft clouds lumbering across the sky like lazy animals. And afterwards, where we'd hide amongst the bracken as if we were forest nymphs. And when it was time to go, Dad would call: 'Come out, come out, wherever you are!' And we waited, trying to silence our pounding hearts, the anxiety rising in his voice. 'Come out, *please.* It's time to go. Mum will be worried.' Did we like that he sounded afraid?

Here. Where Lauren raced ahead of me into the world of a teenager. Sitting on the ground by the wall of the canal crying, talking of newly darkened things; *virginity, bullying, infatuation, divorce.* An entire vocabulary that I didn't understand. Her knees pressed to her first padded bra, her fingers through the frayed edges of one of Dad's old jumpers. Dark circles round her eyes where she'd rubbed at the mascara she'd borrowed from Mum.

Here. In the place where she left her bike that night. Her bike and a small patch of blood. Footprints on the icy wall as if she had thought about throwing herself in. A fourteen-year-old with everything to live for, who went out on a December night and simply never came home.

Now I step on drying coils of post-summer bracken that are turning yellow, seeing a half-submerged shopping trolley lapped by the canal's greyish water. Dad once said that it was the *Junkies* who left them there, and Lauren, bless her, had thought that Junkies were forest folk, the collectors of abandoned things, intending to make them into something new and wonderful one day. Just like the empty washing-up bottles and cereal packets in the box in the kitchen that we used to make into creatures and crowns.

Above me, the clouds have thickened. The threat of rain loiters in the smudges of grey cloud. Behind me there's a shushing sound; the soft wind in the grass like someone trying to calm a fractious baby.

Happy thoughts, think happy thoughts, Lauren tells me. *Please...*

'Look,' I say out loud. 'See how the grass shimmers in the sunlight.' But the clouds have blocked the sun. 'Look how the water flows so peacefully.' But the canal is agitated and has the palette of autumn and dead leaves.

I pick up a stone and throw it in.

'Look at the circles. Remember how we used to laugh as they grew bigger and bigger? Magic rings, mermaids' bubbles.' But there is no happy, magical laughter here. Not anymore.

'I'm sorry, Lauren,' I say. 'I thought it would be over by now.'

Shhhhh, the wind says, as if I am the one it is trying to silence.

There's a brick on the low brick wall, covered with lichen and moss. It's carved with the initials of kids who foolishly thought they'd be forever in love. I trace my finger slowly over the initials. *LF 4 PW*. Lauren Fisher for Pete Wise. Yes, she liked him, but she was fourteen and he should never have done

what he did. I blame him, amongst others. There's a list, but
don't worry, Pete, you're not the only one on it. And certainly
not number one, never that.

I trail the low wall that leads down to the bridge, remembering how we used to run under there and scream into the arch
until it felt like our lungs would bleed. The riverboats that occasionally passed, chasing them as they went. An obedient dog on
their prow, little curtained windows, flags and pot plants. Sometimes we waved at the owners, and sometimes they waved back.

'Wouldn't it be fun,' Lauren said once, 'to get on board and
just... drift away.'

'No, it wouldn't,' I told her in no uncertain terms. But
Lauren rarely listened to me.

A week before she went missing, I watched her climb up
onto this icy wall. Right here, in her school uniform and thick
winter coat. I told her to come down, but my voice was lost
amongst the barren branches. The tops of the new office blocks
visible through the leafless trees. Only then I saw what an
isolated and thankless place this had become. No longer the
forest of nymphs and laughter. Only the hum of a distant
motorway seeping through.

Lauren was placing one foot in front of the other, edging
her way along like a gymnast on a beam. Her slender arms
extended to give her balance. I thought of her slipping, the dark
water soaking into her heavy coat, the weight and the cold and
the blackness carrying her endlessly down.

'Be careful,' I called, but she didn't seem to hear.

She was peering out and down, into the dark water below,
as if to find her own reflection. And as she did, a small necklace
tumbled free from her scarf; a silver heart dangling at a right
angle to her chin.

And then her foot slipped. The heel of her school shoe that
she'd been told a *million* times she wasn't allowed to wear. A
flicker of fear striking her eyes and she was falling. Falling. Her

arms turning like windmills trying to grasp the air. My breath catching as I thought of the freezing water, her heavy coat, the black depths and the current you couldn't fight. How it carried things away...

I would never have been able to save her.

Then, sure as day, she straightened. Placed her foot perfectly, and her mouth twitched with a smile. Her grin spreading like a crack in the ice you could fall through. She was playing a game. A foolish one. She jumped down and stalked past me, back to her bike.

The years dissolve around me, and it's as if I can still hear the sound of her feet on the loose stones. As if I could still turn and see her walking away. Say something, anything, that might make things different.

A chill runs through me, colder than the September cold. I look around quickly. I need to go home. It's too isolated here, too alone. Shouldn't have come. My mistake. Summer is over. Again, and again. Another year. And another... something bad here.

'I won't come again,' I tell her. 'I... can't do this anymore.'

I lift my bike, and just then, a dragonfly skims over the water and lands on my fingers. Momentarily the sun shifts from behind the clouds, a shaft of light illuminating the hidden colours in the insect's beautiful wings. A glimmer of hope, a message not to give up. Then the dragonfly's abdomen dips and it flits away.

Off across the water, never to be seen again.

FIVE
RENE

Before

The wind has picked up, warning me not to stay too much longer. It's not the sunny place I had hoped to find, of warmth and happiness and freedom. Nor the place of epiphanies and answers. Portals through which Lauren might walk. There's only falling leaves whirling like dervishes. And memories that sting like hell.

I tug my bike upright and clamber on. I start to pedal, faster. I want to feel like I'm seven years old again – *that's it, you're doing it. Well done, good girl.* Dad's voice. Dad's encouragement. Making him proud. He loves me. Except, Dad was...

... *a liar.*

Just then a dog bounds out from the long grass and barks, and every part of my being soars up and out. My bike goes this way and that, and I'm grappling with the handlebars to regain control. My feet off the pedals, like I'm plummeting downhill in delight.

Except it isn't delight.

I've overreacted, I know it now. I grip the handlebars to try to regain control, my wheels steadying, my heart slowing. I twist my head backwards to see the dog bounding merrily away along the towpath; a brown-black boxer. Have I seen her before?

I turn forwards and—

boom.

My head hits something hard and my blood is all in the air around me; it lands before I do, like the first heavy spatters of rain on a hot day. And just like that.

Woof goes the dog.

Boom goes my head.

Spatter goes the blood-rain.

And the light in my eyes dances and spreads, a burning white-light brilliance. My head landing in the soft dirt with a thud beside a broken brick from the canal wall. Lucky to have missed it.

I lie still, very still, everything hurting. A thought uncoiling that maybe if I had been wearing yellow boots today everything would have been OK. My feet wouldn't have slipped off the pedals. I'd have been all right. Or maybe I should have just stayed home, eaten donuts, sipped Coke, watched half-life through my window. An old movie or sitcoms on TV, like we used to with Dad. All wrong decisions. Wrong, wrong, wrong.

Then I hear a car door slamming. Footsteps on the gravel. I lift my head, but I can't see anything. Only blackness. It's terrifying.

I hear Lauren's voice in my head. *Get up. Don't let him catch you.*

Footsteps. Close. A man's voice asking if I'm all right. His tongue thick as if he's been drinking. 'Here, little thing, you OK...?'

I would be relieved if I didn't think I recognized it. But I do, and I can't shut out the pain in my head. Or Lauren's voice – *Run! Just run!*

My mouth is full of the taste of dirt and blood. Grit between my teeth like pieces of shell from a boiled egg that hasn't been properly peeled. The footsteps, closer. Closer. 'Hey, little thing. Here, let me help you up...'

I force myself up to standing, dusting myself off, palms stinging against the fabric of my trousers. Horror flowing through my blood.

Is this how it happened to you? Do you remember, Lauren?

My eyes begin to clear. I twist, this way and that, searching. There's no one there. No car, no dog, no man. I'm alone. Only the distant rumble of the motorway.

But the front wheel of my bike is badly damaged, unrideable. I look around, confused. I take a step backwards. Just a silly accident. But I shouldn't be here. She tried to warn me. Not *here*, where it happened...

I back up, stumbling. Always clumsy, that's just me. Then I turn and run, abandoning my bike. I'll be too slow if I take it with its damaged front wheel. But the towpath is uneven, I almost trip – half-buried stones, rough tree roots – and my head hurts: *thump, thump*. I feel dizzy and sick. A bruise on my forehead, soft like a dropped peach.

I reach the edge of the woods and tumble out onto the pavement. A car thunders past, and I teeter. Too late to wave it down for help. Just lucky not to have been hit. I think of those stories, so many I've seen, where a girl escapes from one predator, only to be offered help by someone who... *Who tells you these stories? Who wants you to live in such fear?*

I walk quickly. Nobody passes, nobody appears and gradually, the trees fall away, the gated posh houses and entrances to pleasant cul-de-sacs giving way to townhouses which creep out in rows to crowd me. Denser as I get closer to town. Streetlights that are on, glittering with soft rain that has started falling in the deserted streets.

I reach the steps to my basement flat and cling to the handrail as I hurry down to my front door, feeling as if someone might be right behind me. My eyes finding the gold letter box and the cursive number eight. Eight was always meant to be lucky.

I unlock the door as I have a million times before. Going in and out to the shops, to the high street, to work, to see friends, to take dance classes, to put out the bin. I remember when I had a thing for writing in cafés. And once I even did a terrible open mic with my guitar, like I was Phoebe from *Friends*.

I see all those versions of me leaving, returning rushing through me. Heading off to gigs, reunions, outings with old school friends. Always a fresh pair of lucky socks. Occasionally I'd go and stand on my parents' driveway, feeling small and insignificant in that safe cul-de-sac of Meadow Close that led to nowhere. How I wished they'd come out and hug me, beg me to come inside. Tell me how much they loved me, even if I was mean and blamed them for everything.

I open my door now. My hands shaking as I close it, as I work my way up the four locks like fasteners on a bodice. Then the chain, locking myself in as a twenty-one-year-old enjoying her freedom still has to.

One last thing. I peer out the eyehole to check the world is still outside. To see that miniature view, round and contained and complete. The place where my bike no longer is, abandoned at the canal just like hers. Except, I made it back and she didn't. Ever. Maybe next time I wouldn't be so lucky.

I'm cold from the drizzle. The bruise on my head hurts when I touch it. *So don't touch it*, I tell myself. My hands are scraped, my ankles feel sore. I want to crawl under my bedcovers, sleep for an eternity, never to wake. I don't want to go outside ever again.

But Lauren whispers to me then:

How will you ever find me if you can't even step outside?

SIX

JANE

Today

Jane fills the kettle and flicks it on. She pours a tall glass of water for the girl. Ice? No, too cold for that today.

She looks back across the room, trying not to stare at the girl. Letting her eyes travel to other places, trying to ground herself in this space. Because what the girl said has shocked her.

Home.

Jane looks across the breakfast bar, the dining area, the sofa far off in the distant living room where Alice used to lie and watch *Gossip Girl*. The blanket rolled up in a basket now, so rarely used. She's trying to catalogue her home, her life. Because there's a ripple in it today, this girl has disrupted everything.

She sees the fine Indian rug that Aidan was sick on after his first time drinking too much; Dan was not amused even as they nursed him through his first hangover. The ornate wicker chair that Alice says she wants to inherit, and Jane says 'over my dead body', and they laugh. She hopes it's because neither of them actually wish her dead. The russet cushions Jane bought 'for a steal' at a pop-up store, embroidered with foxes, quite fancy for the price. She never admits where they're from, has conveniently forgotten when asked. The coffee table carefully curated with candles and books; she no longer needs to clear it of clutter twice a day. Her beautiful untroubled lifeless home, except...

She turns back.

This girl. Sitting there. Poor confused thing. Maybe it's a different house in the cul-de-sac that she remembers. She's made a mistake, it's not this one. This home is Jane's. Maybe after a while she'll up and wander back to where she belongs. Jane can just keep her here for a while until she recovers.

But she's not a dazed bird that has flown into Jane's window and will just up and away by herself. Jane knows she can't let that happen. She needs to call the police, no matter what the girl wants.

Yet Dan will be here soon, and he'll know what to do. He always steps up in these moments, like when the kids had a real problem. When Aidan accidentally broke another boy's leg, or Alice pranged Jane's car. Now she so desperately wants to hug her children or have them close to her. To know they are safe. This frightful uncertainty has her rattled. The house too silent, when it used to be so full of life. Alice at uni, Aidan working in Sheffield 'of all places'; that's what people say. Or is that just her that does?

She thinks back to the house when they moved in, remembering the neglect and old fittings, stripping the walls and repainting, trying to bring light to a house that was too gloomy and unloved. Aidan and Alice were mid-teens, vibrant, expansive with their lives and belongings, friends always traipsing in and out, shoes haphazardly abandoned by the door. Half-filled sports bags lying around to be miraculously laundered, piles of schoolbooks and junk food and *stuff*. Unmade beds with socks tangled in the sheets. Lights always left on. The fan in the bathroom constantly whirring. Nagging about chores that still needed doing, and then Friday night movies with pizza and popcorn and ice creams. The good, the bad and the ugly of it all. Missing it all so much now. Her wonderful absent family.

She tries to recall the past owners, had she thought of them earlier before the girl said this was home? Was that the reason she had done that? Something she's blocking out.

'Here,' Jane says, realizing she's still holding the glass of water, still standing in stunned stasis. She holds it out to the girl, who doesn't move, her hands clamped to the notebook in her lap. Jane lets her eyes dance down to the book's cover. She can't quite read what it says. *Nice Day*, or something like that.

'Where have you...?' But the girl averts her eyes, signalling she doesn't want to talk.

Jane nods.

Maybe she should offer her a towel to wipe her face, her muddy hands. Offer a shower or warm bath, that would be kind. But Jane's stomach tightens at the thought; *evidence*. The police will want to collect it.

'I'll just put it here, shall I?' she says, sing-songy and light like the world is just right. She sets the glass on the side.

Out in the hallway she calls the police. She tells them she's found a young woman, won't speak, filthy. A runaway or maybe even...

No, no injuries that look life threatening.

No immediate danger.

Yes, she's all right to wait with her. Yes, she can stay with her until they arrive.

They tell her it could take up to an hour. But someone is coming. *Soon*, they assure her.

Not soon enough, Jane thinks, but says thank you anyway. She can see her own hands shaking.

She heads back into the kitchen and finds the girl at the sink. Her head turned sideways, drinking from the tap like a cat, gulping it down, desperate and thirsty. Jane glances over and sees the full glass still sitting beside her chair.

The girl doesn't trust her, she thinks. But then, she asked Jane not to call the police and she did.

It is then that she spots the notebook sitting on the breakfast bar. She tries to be subtle, takes a small step forward, filled with a sudden overwhelming urge to look inside, see what answers it holds. But the girl is alert and fast. She follows Jane's eyes, lunges, grabbing the notebook, tugging it protectively into the hollow of her stomach.

They stand eyeing each other for what seems like forever. Then the girl sidles back to the chair, hobbling, clutching the notebook tighter to her belly. Never once taking her eyes off of Jane, even more wary now. Right not to have trusted her.

'I'm sorry,' Jane says. 'I'm just trying to understand...'

The girl sits silently, offering no explanation. Maybe, Jane thinks, she can't make sense of this either.

SEVEN

Before

Morning, and before I open my eyes, I make my list.

- *To be happy*
- *To write*
- *To save Lauren*

I open my eyes, no bright shafts of light at my bedroom curtains, the room basks only in gloom.

On my bedside table sits an unread *October* magazine, scissors on top, as if I'd planned to cut something out. I drop the scissors into the drawer; too much temptation in leaving them there.

Every muscle in my body screams as I move, and even though the bike-dog incident was already a few days back, I've not felt great since. A fever I can't shake. The cold, the damp, the fall, the fear. Too exhausted to do much, I've spent most of my time curled up on the sofa staring at reruns on TV.

Now I reach for my mobile. I *need* to get up, go to work. Or at least call David, apologize. For what? I ask myself.

For being sick...

Or for being the shadow sister...

'Hello?' A woman answers which I wasn't expecting.

I push the phone against my ear as I wander into the kitchen. 'Where's David?' I ask, confused. He's never not answered before.

'I'm sorry, David is not available,' the woman says curtly.

'So, where is he?' I ask.

'Can I ask who's calling?' She blocks my questions with questions. Who does she think she is?

I pull a can of Coke from the fridge and notice there are only two left. I thought there were more. Strange.

I take a swig from the can and bite into a donut. It tastes stale and the sugar is damp not powdery.

'I asked who's calling,' the woman says more assertively.

'It's Rene. I work with David. Or *for* him. I'm one of his... staff writers. Junior staff writer...' David always says I'm his most promising young writer, but she doesn't need to know that. I gaze down at the donut. It's coated in blue mould, and I grimace in disgust. I thought these things lasted forever.

'And who are you?' I ask, a dusting of that disgust tangled in my voice. I drop the donut into the bin, which needs taking out. Something smells terrible.

'I'm David's new *personal* assistant,' the woman says sounding absolutely delighted.

'Great,' I say, even though I don't think it's that great. 'So... can I speak to him then?'

'I'm sorry, but David's not here. And he's asked me to... *filter* his calls.'

Filter...? The audacity! I go over to my sofa and plomp myself down, tugging the crochet blanket over my legs for reassurance. *Filter?* I wind my fingers into the crochet holes. David has never not been there for me before. Never. 'But I need to talk to him,' I insist.

'Then you can leave a message. He'll probably call you back.'

Probably? Who does she think she is, this new *personal* assistant?

'Look,' I say, trying my best to be polite, not entirely succeeding, 'I understand that you're new. *Probably* don't know David as well as I do. Or know about our *special* friendship.' Oh, no, that sounds bad. That could get him into trouble. 'But I know he'll speak to me. Just put him on?'

'No,' she says bluntly. Then she uncoils a little. 'Like I say, you're welcome to leave a message...' I can hear her delighted personal assistant smile.

I growl in frustration and hang up.

Back in my bedroom, I sit on the edge of the bed, peering up at my walls for inspiration, some hint of what to do next. I gaze at the images, all never to be my life. Another growl of annoyance.

And that's when I spot her. A woman at a desk; grey pencil skirt, white blouse, big red lips, bigger red phone. The cord coiled provocatively around her finger. Is that what she looks like, this new *personal* assistant?

I jump up and try to peel her off my wall. She doesn't belong there, not in my room. Maybe I thought once that would be me. On my list to be so much more than I am now. *Smart, professional, important...* power job. Chief editor. Hotshot lawyer. Business mogul. C E *fucking* O.

And yet here I am, still wearing the same PJs I've had on since the bike-dog incident. With my arms up picking at the wall, I can smell my own armpits. I'm not in the best shape, that much is true, should probably at least shower, get dressed.

Maybe go to the office, confront this little Miss Red Lips. Is that what I'll do today?

Yes, that's it. David might come in mid-argument, ask what the *hell* is going on. His face growing steadily angrier as I tell him about her attitude and her *filtering*. Maybe he'll even sack her on the spot, tearing a strip off for being *so rude*. I'll watch her leave the office, her few pathetic belongings in a small card-board box, a plant and a thermo-cup, and her tail between her *probably* very shapely legs.

But wait, it's David I should be angry at. He's the one who told her to filter his calls.

Yes, I'll go to the office, storm in, slamming his office door before Miss Red Lips can stop me. I'll shout at him, thrusting a handful of paperwork onto the floor, shocked at my own audacity. Everyone gathering outside the glass wall, clutching their coffee as they watch excitedly. David and I throwing names at each other. 'You're an arsehole.' 'Well, you're insane.' A thud of adrenalin in my chest, more zeal than I've felt in months.

David will get up from behind his desk and come closer. I'll take a swing at him, miss, fall pitifully against his chest – oh, just like one of those midday matinees. My sobs offloading into his shirt, my small fists pummelling against him, desperate for the comfort that his arms might give me, if his hands weren't hesitating to touch me.

No. I shake my head, dislodging this childish fantasy. Because that's not what my relationship with David is about. He's *encouraging* me, giving my life purpose and direction. I'm his protégé, that's all. I am *not* in love with him, not at all. I feel the heat of embarrassment at my own imagination. How immature!

I remember the day I showed up at his office, told him my story, told him I wanted to write. At first, he was a little dismissive, suggested I come back when I was older. Then I told him about Lauren. That stopped him in his tracks. That I was the sister who didn't go missing. After that, we talked for a while. He listened. Then he said he'd give me a chance.

'Special projects,' he called it.

We quietly agreed.

After that, each time I went to the office, he'd hand me a folder, a picture and a name, a new person to interview. Inside I'd feel a flicker of curiosity. 'Everyone has a story to tell, you should know that better than anyone,' he'd say, tapping the folder. 'And *this* one is going to be even better than the last.'

And off I'd go to meet a perfect stranger in some new setting. In a library, a café, on a park bench by the pond. We'd throw bread to the ducks as they told me their heartbreaking and uplifting story. As I watched their mannerisms; as they dabbed at their tears, showed me photos or some precious trinket, unpacked their lives for me, gentle and raw. Survivors, all of them. Then I'd head back to the office to type it all up. *Tip-y-tip-y-tap*. A tale of hope and heroics. Then back to my basement apartment and its door with four locks; the only thing greeting me at the end of each day.

Now my mobile rings. I answer without checking the caller ID. It's a man's voice.

'David...' I say, relieved he's called back.

'Sorry, it's Dad.' He sounds surprised, or is it disappointed?

'Oh,' I say. 'And what do *you* want?'

'Nice,' he tries laughing, awkward and foolish. Then he waits for me to apologize. When I don't, he says, 'So, you're still talking to him then?'

'David? Of course. He's my boss. I work with him.'

'Right... still doing that.'

See how little he cares? He's not even interested in my aspirations, my efforts in life. 'Yes, "still doing that",' I say sarcastically. The silence uncoils.

Eventually Dad says, 'I found your bike down by the canal. It is yours, isn't it?'

He still goes there too? I hadn't thought of him doing that before.

'Front wheel's a bit banged up. But I brought it home. Thought I could fix it up, if you like...?' Another pause.

Nope. Not going to fall for it.

'So, what happened?' he asks.

What happened? What happened...? Lauren went missing and I can't stop going there in the hope something might be different. That she'll come back. And my whole life... won't be so... utterly horribly... shit.

'Love...?' he asks.

'Don't call me that!' I snap. 'You can't fix it. You can't fix anything. It's too late,' and I hang up.

OK, that was a bit excessive. But he had it coming. He's a liar. And I hate him. Either or both. Then a soft feeling of sadness uncoils inside me, feeling queasy like I've drunk bad milk.

'Donuts,' I say, jumping up from the sofa. That will cheer me up.

Only when I'm at the fridge do I remember there are none left. They were mouldy and I threw them out. I check the bin which is now empty. When did I do that? I think of the front door and the four locks. Don't remember opening them.

Memory is fragile.

And mine seems to be getting worse.

EIGHT

RENE

Before

In the back of a high kitchen cabinet is a packet of pills, what I call my 'pretty pinks'. Mum used to take them, so the habit started with her. A small act of kindness, or maybe she liked that I needed them too, just like her.

I pop a couple out. Two small circles of heaven. My mouth is dry as I pour a tall glass of water and let it quench my thirst as it carries the tablets away. *One. Two. Buckle my shoe...* I imagine them dissolving beautifully inside me. I gaze down at the packet. *Three. Four. Open the door...*

I push that thought aside.

Back on the sofa, I pull the crocheted blanket over me. I love this blanket, its neat flowered squares all stitched together. Its familiarity and comfort. A neighbour gave it to us when we were small and had measles. It was Easter and we couldn't eat a single chocolate egg. We used to snuggle up under it and Mum would read us stories. Dad would come in from work and he'd lean over to kiss us; first Mum and then me. 'Don't you look cosy,' he'd ruffle my hair. 'My princesses.'

'Right,' Mum would say, a flash of fake anger. 'And who is your queen then, hey?'

He'd lean over again, a handsome glint in his eyes. 'You. Always,' and he'd kiss Mum, this time on the lips. Then he'd pull back. 'What's for dinner?'

'I made you lasagne.'

'Oooh, our favourite,' and he'd look down at me. A nod and a wink, because it always was.

Now my stomach twists as if wrung out like a cloth. I'm hungry, but I'm not sure what I want. Maybe later...

I flick on the TV; it's daytime shows, all happy and sanitized. Women on a panel, laughing as they set the world to rights, safe topics that are on the fringe of important. There's a lot of lips and fake nails. One of them cries and the others say, 'Don't, you'll set me off.' Today they're discussing if your dishwasher can ruin your relationship, and coming up after the break, 'Is it OK to sleep naked with a friend?' Urgh. *Click*. Homes being renovated, quick and cheap and profit-making. 'Bodge-job,' Dad used to say. *Click*. Antiques and bargains, 'Who'd buy someone else's old junk?' Mum would say... *click*.

Junk. *Click*. Nothing. *Click*. Depressing news. *Click*.

I throw the remote at the cushion.

My phone is silent, David didn't call. But he will soon, just a case of waiting. Or maybe Dad will ring, trying to convince me he can fix everything, my bike included.

The room grows darker.

The pills dissolve.

I slide down the couch and my eyelids droop.

Lauren comes to me then in a dream. She's running, running frantically. Her arms thrashing in the dark against long, damp grass. Tiny drops that reflect the moon, like beads which she displaces and sends flying as she flees through the vast, dark fields.

As she's running, she's looking over her shoulder. She's

running away from something. Away from the canal. Faster and faster. Her voice gushing out behind her like a banshee, or a burst water pipe, gurgling as if strangled. Her hair flicking around as she turns back and forth, back and forth. Her eyes terrified. *Thrash, thrash, thrash* her arms and legs go against the long grass in the field. What is she running from, or to? Trying not to fall. As she becomes a blur before me. Supersonic. Frantic. Running on the treadmill of night terrors until eventually her screams dissolve into the dark pulse that comes out of me in sweat and fever.

I sit up.

The room is pitch-dark.

The pounding pounding *pounding*, like a fist on my door, wakes me with a start. But it's just my blood in my ears against the silence. It's late. Hours have passed. I grapple sightless for a switch, desperate to find it. When I do, I turn the lamp on quickly.

Light, such a relief. I hate the dark. Lauren is in there, whispering, sobbing. Begging for help.

My eyes adjust. My safe little basement flat coalesces into existence before my eyes. The books in neat rows on the shelves, the Russian dolls in an orderly line, the flamenco dancer beneath her cloche, poised to dance. The rows of scrapbooks, everything I salvaged or kept for inspiration. And there's no one else here, only me. So why can I hear someone breathing?

I click on the TV. It too has turned sinister in the small hours. As I flip the channels I'm bombarded by eerie banality—

...the chances of a storm tomorrow are a hundred per cent.

...their report shows damage to teenage brains held in solitary confinement...

...don't you understand I love you, I would never hurt you...

...those lies are the only thing keeping her alive...

Click. The screen goes black. I look at my phone. David hasn't called. Nor Dad. How easily he gives up.

I go into the kitchen and take two more pills. There's not many left, soon I'll need more. Maybe many more. Then I slip into my bed. No need to change. I'm in PJs already. Never did get that shower. My own smell, less fragrant than I'd like. Maybe tomorrow. *Tomorrow, maybe...*

I sink into the mattress, grateful for its softness. Still, I shiver, my body aching again. I focus on the pink glow of the room's nightlight like I did as a kid. Dad might, even now, be coming down the corridor to lean over and kiss me on the forehead. The weight of his body on the duvet. Wishing me sweet dreams. 'Night, love.'

Except no one comes, and the dreams are not sweet.

In the darkness, I can't shut out her voice.

What Lauren whispers is happening to her still.

NINE

LAUREN

Before

Alone. In the dark. Eyes closed. It was a game.

Try not to die, that was the game.

Try not to scream, that was also the game.

I could not see my hands resting in my lap, I could only feel them. I could not see the walls, but I didn't need to because I could reach out and touch them on all sides. And they were only concrete.

I could feel my heart pounding pounding. Counting out the seconds until I screamed or died and lost the game.

Left foot: a sound of metal. Tins and a tin opener shifting in the canvas bag. Right foot: a bucket. That would smell in a few days if I was still playing the game.

But then, it was my fault I was here. I *had to learn the hard way*, he'd said. He'd *told* me so. He'd warned me, *hadn't he?*

And yes, it's true, I'd spat at him at breakfast, and then I'd screamed, and he'd laughed, *Look who's gone a little mad today, Little L*, goading in his voice. He liked it when I went mad, because he could punish me. That's when the game started.

It happened quickly after that. A scuffle. Trying to fend him off, or lurch at him and scratch him – not sure which: towards or away. The dog retreating back into the corner, then barking, then retreating again. Her nails on the kitchen floor. And I knew that in the end I was out of control, unable to stop myself. Or him. As confused as that dog. He pulled me out to the back, out through that hidden cupboard in the kitchen, and I fought, even though fear had weakened me. Eventually I went stiff as a child having a tantrum.

This is for your own good, he said as he pushed me down the little steps. Into The Hole. The sound of the dog's bark fading. The blackness sliding over me as he closed the lid.

Confined.

And for the longest time, it was only blackness.

I cried. I sobbed. Snivelling. Snot from my nose dampening my mouth. And then the fear that I wouldn't be able to breathe. The panic. That all the precious air was used up. My hands pushing against the walls. Elbows locking, eyes so wide that any scrap of light would have found them, even swollen with tears. Except there wasn't any light to be had. Utter darkness.

And then, I was quiet.

I sat like a good girl, like we did in school, hands in my lap. Obedient. If I just did that for long enough, he might know and let me out.

But as I waited, it came to me. The lid had *already* been open. He never left it open. Kept the rug pulled over, in case someone came. So he knew what was coming for me this morning, before I even acted up. Before I swore and certainly before I spat. He'd prodded me just so I'd respond, like a trained monkey, maybe even for giggles and kicks. Was he laughing up there as I sat down here? *See, Little L, I know you better than you know yourself.*

I knew he wasn't punishing me for what happened this morning. Oh no. Not the spitting or the swearing. No, it would have been for some bad thing that I couldn't remember. Something from a while before that he'd kept in his head, and it had eaten him up that I should think I could get away with it. I wouldn't know what it was until I got out, and maybe long after that. When he was ready, that's when he'd tell me why he had punished me this time. And that would be the lesson. Something else to add to my list to NEVER EVER do again.

Go on, write it down.

Maybe it was a look I had given him a few days before, or the way I'd served up his food at dinner. Or something I'd written in one of my books and he didn't like the way it sounded. Or maybe not smiling as he stood in the bedroom doorway looking at me, or as he approached the bed. That he could see from the red of my wrist or ankle that I had tried too hard to slip the binders off.

'I don't need them, I won't run. You know that,' I pleaded.

Was he still mad about me losing the necklace? Throwing it in the bin. Under the eggshells and boxes where I knew he wouldn't bother to look. I told him I had no idea where it could have gone to, but he didn't like to think that it could have disappeared. That drove him crazy. Craziest. Because if the necklace could disappear, I might be next.

I saw his eyes dance across the carpet. Found him looking under the sideboard or lifting the mattress and peering under the bed, rifling through my old clothes in the drawer where I'd found that cherry lip gloss. *Where is it?* he insisted. *I can't protect you without it.*

Because he was protecting me, that's what he said. From the freaks that he told me would do terrible things to me. Said they would like to make a meal of me. And I saw it on TV, on those shows he showed me. Stupid girls who ran away, or went off on their own. No one to protect them. No one like him. Found in the woods, drowned in the river, murdered, raped. Barely even bodies. He cut those things out from the paper for me to read.

Just a little something to remind you of what's waiting out there for you if you do ever decide to run.

I stuck them on the wall as he told me to.

But he promised they would never find me like that. No, not me. He would always protect me, even if that meant making me spend time in the darkness. That was just to make me better when I got sick.

He was only ever doing all this for me, he said.

Then I was drowning back into the blackness of The Hole, the darkness of Missing, and into the idea that I was only the blackness. I lost myself into it then, and that meant I lost the game. I screamed his name. Screamed for him to come and get me out.

'Keele! Keeeeeeellllle!'

I wanted to be good, to get better. I had chosen to be here. And Keele was the one trying to protect me. From them. From Mum and Dad.

They were the ones that were bad, he said.

I saw myself running, in the night, hands out in front of me. Hands that were bloodied. Away from them. Towards the little white cottage lit by the moon. It *was* their fault. I couldn't quite remember why anymore. Too many pills. Too many knocks to the head. Too many years. Too many days in utter darkness. *Confinement*. Something about that word.

But I asked myself how much longer I had to keep playing this game.

Maybe this was the last time. Maybe when he lifts me out and he sees I've learned my lesson, he'll cook. A lasagne or a nice lemon pie, and he'll slide a new book across the table for me to read, one where the ending hasn't been torn out. Or a notebook to write in with lots of delicious blank pages, for one of my nicer stories, and he'll say, *Why don't you write one of your fairy tales, one with a happier ending?* A new pen with ink that isn't just empty. And a glossy new magazine full of people and places to dream of and be inspired. Glue so I can stick them up on my wall over all the missing girls who didn't have protectors.

I just want you to get better, he'd say.

He'll tell me how happy he is that I'm feeling better. Now I'm back to my old self. *Could we be happy again? Could we at least* fucking *try?* A twitch as he gently strokes my arm, tracing up to my shoulder, my collarbone.

Because you came to me, he'll say.

It was your choice, he'll say.

Was that what happened? I remember running, blood on my hands, in the night. The cold night. Away from them. To here.

All the things I have to do just so you can stay here. So I can keep you safe. So I can protect *you. Remember?*

I nod.

How they treated you. How they hurt you. And threatened you. To lock you up, like an animal. But you're safe here. So much safer.

'No,' I'll try to tell him, finding a tiny voice. 'It wasn't like that. I think I should go back.'

So were you lying to me? Louder, fingers tightening at my throat. *Were you always lying to me?*

'No, I wasn't,' I say. 'I told you the truth.'

So what am I trying to do?

'You are protecting me.'

What?

'You are the one taking care of me. I'm not well and I need to get better.'

That's right, Little L. But you know you can leave at any time. You know that? You've always known that. You're free to walk away...

One night he led me to the front door. I remember him opening it, wide and gaping. The cold and dark pouring in. The chill dancing over my skin. How sweet the air smelled. The scent of the outside.

But I hesitated, feeling my toes pressing against the worn carpet, feeling each one of them as if for the first time. Wondering if I still had the strength to run, to outrun him. To make it... to anywhere.

I wanted to launch myself out into the night air. But I turned my gaze down and forced myself to stand still. Because it was a test. And I knew the price of failing. I knew the price of running too slow. Of saying yes when I meant no. Of not believing he was the one trying to protect me. Of defying him. Of not trying to get better.

I stared at the carpet, didn't want to look out there, into the night that I couldn't reach. To let him think I still wanted that.

It took a long time for him to close the door. The longest time to shut the world away. Or maybe it just felt like that, to watch it leave me behind. To know I would only ever be here, inside.

That's right, Little L. Better the devil you know. Better to stay here with me.

TEN

JANE

Today

Jane hears Dan's key in the front door with a rush of relief.

She runs out to greet him, needing to intercept him, to explain her actions that she can't quite explain to herself.

'What's going on?' He launches into his own frustrations before she can even speak. 'I got your message and I came straight here. I had to leave a meeting...' Annoyance still in his voice despite the ten-minute drive. 'You know how things are at work right now—'

She holds up her hand and shushes him; that's enough to stop him in his tracks. She'd never normally do that.

'Look, I've called the police.' She lowers her voice. 'They're on their way... But...' Now she's got his attention she's not sure what to do with it. All the pacing and handwringing hasn't prepared her for this moment. 'I need your help. The girl I found, in the garden... She's in the kitchen, won't let go of something she dug up from our flowerbed – some kind of notebook. She thinks she's... *home.*'

Dan frowns, glances towards the kitchen. He wants to see

for himself now. Obviously wants to know what has got Jane so rattled. But she puts both hands onto his chest to stall him. 'Please, Dan... just take it very easy. She's scared.'

He takes this in, and then slips his way past her, into the kitchen.

'Hello,' he says, and Jane knows he's trying to sound confident, but his voice cracks the instant he sees the girl. When he sees what Jane was trying to warn him about.

The girl looks up at him; her huge eyes flashing fear and distrust, like a trapped and injured animal. She tries to retreat back into the chair, or into herself. Her wrists not much thicker than the wooden armrest of the chair. She turns her head.

'So, what's your name?' Dan asks. It's direct but he softens it with a smile in an attempt to show he's no threat. His voice is firmer than Jane's, and there's more certainty to it. Jane wanted this support but worries now that it's too strong.

Oddly, after a few moments, the girl looks up at him. Some mastery in his voice that possibly she feels the need to respond to. She searches his face but remains silent.

'She won't tell me,' Jane interrupts, and Dan flashes a look of annoyance because of it.

'You have a name, don't you, love?' he says as he lowers himself into the line of the girl's gaze. 'You can tell us.'

The girl tips her head. To Jane's surprise she opens her mouth and speaks. 'Rene,' she says and her eyes lift, brighten. She holds Dan's gaze for just a second before dropping hers away.

Dan turns to Jane, a moment of triumph. 'See. That's great, isn't it? *Rene*. That's just super.'

The girl offers them both a sliver of a smile.

And that's when Jane senses it, the girl's determination. Her defiance. A feeling that the smile isn't a smile because she did something right. Rather she'll do anything it takes to please.

Because that's the only way to survive.

ELEVEN

RENE

Before

I wake. Happy list.

- *Donuts. I'll buy donuts. Yes!*
- *I'll go outside. That's what I'll do.*
- *And I'll feel better.*
- *Maybe even write something.*
- *Maybe...*

OK, not much of a list, but it's a start.

I get up, tug on a jumper. It's colder today, I can feel it. I go to the front door, peering out the eyehole at my sub-porch; the empty spot where my bike used to sit. I unlock the four locks, then the chain and tug open the door. A frisson of excitement snakes in with the chill. I look to the steps, eight of them. One for each year that...

No. Something stops me. Not today. Not going out. Strike that from the list. Which means no donuts either. But I'll live.

Maybe tomorrow I'll feel better.

I turn to go back inside. My narrow hallway lengthens before me all the way back to the living room. Its deep red walls patterned with Lauren's objects and pictures, all perfectly arranged. I run my fingers over the postcards and paintings and pages from books, all cut out and framed. I stop at a photo of Lauren with Pete.

LF 4 PW. The brick at the canal. Pete Wise was her first love. Why has he started to return to my thoughts?

Pete who wrote songs for her on his guitar. Well, he said they were for her anyway. Probably said that to all the girls. He was cute, to look at at least. Shiny brown hair that slid over one eye. Cheekbones. Sharp and striking. A grin to swim in. Said he wanted to tour the world in a band. Maybe she'd come with him, or at least visit. *One day.*

I lift the picture down.

Lauren had liked him. Really liked him. Did he like her too? Except they'd broken up after a few months, some silly reason; another girl, was that it? Hard to remember the sequence of things from so long ago. But I will never forget that after Lauren went missing, he told his story. Or sold it. Even worse. I saw it in the paper. Someone showing it to me with a cruel grin. About them smoking drugs by the canal, about them making out under the bridge. Had Pete sold it in return for his fifteen minutes of fame? Why were people so desperate?

In this photo, they look so young, almost childish. Her fourteen, him barely sixteen. His arm around her waist, both laughing, her eyes sparkling with glee; is he tickling her or telling her a joke? Her fringe tumbling endlessly into her eyes. She'd wanted to grow it out, and she might have... if there'd been time. Why had he said she was troubled? Why had he told them those things?

This was the photo they had used in that article. This moment of excitement remade into something so haunting.

Maybe if he hadn't said those things about her, or even

broken up with her in the first place, this would have turned out differently. I put him on the blame list. Along with a few others I know. Like Mum and Dad and Shirl and all the other girls at school who isolated her... Then I hover over David's name. No, he's one of the good ones. On the Good List, which is a pretty lonely place. At least David wrote about her in a positive light; he wanted people to remember her... didn't he? Wanted to piece it all together, to find answers to what happened to her, didn't want people to forget...

'David,' I say out loud, almost stamping my foot. 'I need to speak to you.'

Yet why isn't he returning my calls?

I'm almost out of pills and I'm not feeling any better. I'm sweaty but cold. Hungry but nauseous. Exhausted but restless. What's wrong with me?

Nice hot bath. Add that to the list.

Take a bath, with candles and a book...

There. Done.

I head down the hallway to the bathroom and only then I realize I'm still holding the picture of Pete. I set it on the shelf between the mirror and the sink, then peer at my reflection. My skin has the palette of autumn and dead leaves. I'm not as pretty as I was, and never as pretty as her. Sickness doesn't suit me; I need to get well for both of us.

I turn on the water, feeling its warmth running between my fingers, seeing my small form in the distorted world inside the chrome tap. I imagine stepping through and living in that reflection. It couldn't be any stranger. Maybe that's where Lauren is hiding.

While the bath runs, I go back to the living room, past the shelves of books and pick one. Then I eye the Russian dolls that Lauren loved to nest inside each other. And here's Lauren's patchwork doll in pride of place; she called her Rebecca. Brown wool hair in little messy plaits, a blunt fringe that always refused to lie flat and would never be grown out. The embroidered apron over a flowery dress, boots with shiny blood-red buttons. How Lauren loved her, even if she was forever losing her, or forgetting where she'd left her.

Yet ironically Rebecca is here and Lauren is the one missing.

I pick up the doll and hug her. 'Sorry, Lauren,' I whisper into her cloth ear. I look her over and something about her... maybe the blood-red buttons, it triggers a memory. Or at least the hint of one. I carry her over to my writing desk and sit her on the corner beside a pile of notebooks, filled with scribbles and doodles and pressed flowers and ticket stubs.

Something is coming. A memory. Maybe it's one that matters. Really matters. Maybe if I catch it before it flits away, there might be a clue or a key inside. One that opens the door to solving all this. To freeing Lauren. And that's on the list.

So I lift the pen, and I write...

Lauren was barely five when she ran into the kitchen, a pattern of butterflies at the hem of her dress, an orange sash around her waist. Her face was upset. 'I've lost her,' she cried, clearly distressed.

It was spring, Easter had just passed. There were joyful daffodils on the kitchen counter and the cards on the shelf. Half-eaten chocolate eggs in torn silver paper stuffed back in their boxes and set out of reach. 'That's enough for today. You'll make yourself sick.' Outside the sun was finally shining, breaking through after a brief burst of afternoon rain.

'What's the matter?' Mum asked. She was stirring tomato sauce on the hob. She didn't even bother to look at Lauren.

'It's Rebecca. I can't find her anywhere!' Childlike consternation

in Lauren's young voice. The end of the world. 'I can't find her!'
She reached up and tugged at Mum's dress. 'Mummy! What if
the nasty man took her?'

'Oh, Lauren,' Mum said, noting Lauren's concern. 'Don't be
silly. There is no nasty man here.' She laughed to waft it away.
'No, she'll just be sleeping until you find her. Like the princess in
our story, remember. Waiting for love's first kiss.'

Then Mum turned and kissed Lauren on the forehead, and
Lauren nuzzled against her leg. 'I love you, Mummy,' Lauren
said.

'Yes, yes,' Mum said, patting her hair. Was she even aware that
she hadn't said it back? 'Or maybe she's just playing a game to
remind you to take better care of her,' she went on. 'Why don't
you go and check your bedroom one last time, and if she's not
there I'll come and help you look.'

Then Mum turned back to the sauce that had started to bubble,
spitting red juice up against the cream splash back. And she was
smiling again, a picture of domestic bliss. Rebecca would be
found, and Lauren would be happy, and Dad would come home
and set his briefcase in the hall, and Mum would ask him, 'How
was your day, dear?' And he'd kiss her on the cheek or the lips
depending on how the day had been. Then he'd ask her what was
for dinner, and she'd say pasta. Then we'd eat dinner, together.
The happiest little family. Almost. Almost...

'Mummy...?' Lauren said, her voice suddenly different from
before. That's when it started to change from what it ought to be
to what it became. 'Mummy, there's blood.'

And slowly Mum was turning, peering down towards the floor.

She stepped back to reveal the cream tiles beneath her. Three small red circles of blood, like little red buttons on Rebecca's shoe. And she must have known – even as she thought about the tomato sauce that had been spitting up from the pot – that it was too smooth and rich and bright to be anything other than blood.

Mum's eyes pinched closed, as if she wanted to unsee it.

She put her hand out to steady herself – a small gesture that was out of kilter with what had gone before. Her fingers touching the hot ring of the hob, but she didn't wince or even notice.

'Jim,' Mum called, her tone urgent. Not gentle or soft like before, though Daddy was not even home yet.

Later we heard Mum in the bedroom saying, 'Oh God... I'm losing my baby...' And until then we hadn't even known she was pregnant again.

Lauren loitered in the hallway, her hand on the white banister, hearing them whispering. Something that worked its way into Lauren's head. Dad saying, 'Not again. Not after what happened with Lauren.'

And Mum saying, 'I had to try. I thought this time it would be different... better...'

Lauren heard. She heard them talking. Had something been wrong with her? That she was bad and the next baby would be better? Her own mother who couldn't say that she loved her.

Mum's words danced through Lauren's head. 'She's probably just hiding. Maybe playing a little game. To remind you to take better care of her...'

Those words buried themselves deep inside her.

And nine years later, Lauren went missing.

'Oh my god. The bath!'

I jump up and run in to find it slopping over the side, onto the tiles. No apartment below is a blessing, no neighbour to accuse me of damage to their ceilings, their wallpaper, their precious priceless paintings.

I grab a towel and try to soak up the worst of it. Then I wring it out and hang it up to dry, taking off my clothes, folding them neatly over the rail before lowering myself into the hot, overfilled tub. It feels glorious, heat swimming up my arms and my shoulders as I lean back, washing away nearly all those upsetting thoughts.

What had they thought was wrong with Lauren?

Or had Lauren thought she could teach them a lesson?

It hurts to think of it. But something is hiding in there, an itch I can't quite scratch.

I lie for a while as if trying to dissolve, sinking lower. Lower. I could just slip into the warmth and silence. Close my eyes and drift under, forever. Another world below the bubbles that crackle in my ears. Only then I notice a noise along the corridor. There it is again. A knock. Then a thud. Is it the front door?

'Hello...?' a voice calls. 'Hello?' Louder each time. A man's voice. 'Rene, are you in there?' Must be Dad. Has he come about the stupid bike? 'Rene...!' Did he kick the door?

I get out, slushing more water over the floor in frustration, throwing a towel around me.

'Dad?' I say, heading down the corridor and tugging the front door open, my annoyance escaping with the steam off my skin. 'What do you want?'

But it's not Dad. It's David.

Stupid slip. I should have checked the eyehole. Mental

note. Always check. It could have been anyone. Except this time it's just David and he won't harm me. So that's OK.

'What are you doing here?' I ask, still gripping the towel a little tighter. But my voice softens.

'I've been worried about you. You've been missing in action for days, weeks. Thought I'd check in on my most promising young writer.' Maybe his personal assistant really has been filtering. Now there's a glint in his eye. 'So, how are you feeling?'

I think carefully. 'Um... Like shit.' I smile.

The heat of the bath has left me, and he shifts awkwardly, like he's expecting something.

'Did you want to come in?' I ask.

'Sure. Why not?' He peers in.

I hesitate. It's the first time I've ever let anyone inside.

But it's just David, so it'll be fine.

I step aside, feeling his closeness as he brushes past.

TWELVE

RENE

Before

We sit side-by-side on the sofa; awkward first-daters with no romance at all. I've thrown on fresh pyjamas which cling to my still wet skin. They're covered in strawberry-shaped pandas. Rather girly, if I'm honest. More like something they might wear in a children's hospital.

'Coffee?' I say, heading into the kitchen even before David nods.

'Sure. Thanks.' His soft voice, kind and reassuring,

I sniff the milk. It's off, and the coffee clings to itself in the jar like clumps of dried soil. 'Sorry, I haven't made it to the shops in a while...' I apologize vaguely. 'Can I offer you a Coke?'

I hand him the last one and sit opposite.

'Oh, a glass,' I say, jumping up again. 'Ice?' Even though I don't think I have any.

He shakes his head. 'This'll be just fine.' He lifts it in a hesitant 'cheers'.

I sit. 'Look, I'm sorry...' I say.

'For what, the coffee?' He sounds amused but he knows that's not what I meant.

'I just feel so stupid... this illness... I can't seem to shake it.'

'That's OK,' he says. 'I understand.' He always says he does.

'But I thought I was stronger than this.'

'You *are* strong,' he says. 'Stronger than you'll ever know. Than anyone will. You're a fighter. You'll get through this. You always have before.'

Before... Something in that word.

A light blush reddens my cheeks at his acknowledgement; I hope the flush of the bath hides it. I let my eyes creep back up to his face, his familiar blond curls that tumble over his dark-rimmed glasses.

I look away quickly.

Because David is married. A pretty blonde wife and a prettier blonder daughter. They stand as a happy trio in the frame on his desk. Together on a beach at sunset. And I'm not in love with him. I'm not. He's far too old. Probably even late thirties. I'm just a bit *jealous*. Some people get to live the picture-perfect life.

Yet sometimes, I see him watching me like I'm a different kind of animal. I know he likes me, cares about me. Wants something for me. Or is it *from* me? Those late meetings in his office when he reads over my work. 'This is good,' he says as he nods his head.

I stand close, not too close, watching his hands held prayer-like under his chin. Something curious in his eyes. He leans closer to my writing, picks up a pencil and toys with it between his long, slender fingers as if he might make an edit or two. But he doesn't write a word. He reads. And he listens. He just gets me.

'I'm worried,' I say and his brow furrows for me. 'I can't risk this.'

'Risk what?' He tries to laugh it away again.

'My job. This apartment. My life.' I hesitate. 'You...'

A more quizzical expression crosses his face. Or is it concern. He's never wanted to give me the wrong impression.

'I just feel like it's all... slipping away. Like I can't keep doing this. I'm... giving up.'

'No!' He stands. 'You can't do that. You'll fight this,' he says. 'You always have.'

... *Always*

He scans the room then, eyes settling on my desk. 'Did you write something today?' He shifts towards the notebook as if sniffing it out.

'Maybe...'

'About Lauren?'

I don't answer.

'Tell me.'

'Why?' I ask back, a little defensively.

He approaches the desk, Rebecca doll still sitting there. He looks at her and then down at the pile of notebooks. Is he wondering what I have written?

When he realizes he can't see without opening a notebook and prying, his eyes travel around the room, then up to the framed picture of Nanna on the wall above the desk; a postcard she sent to Mum years ago. He reaches up with his slim fingers and touches it. Why has it drawn his attention?

Then he turns, walks over to my shelves, runs his finger along the row of Russian dolls, lifting the middle one gingerly; the one Lauren used to call 'Mum'. When he puts it back it's out of place. I shift at the unintended micro-chaos he's creating.

Then he lifts a book from the shelf – this month I've arranged them by date. When I'm bored, I arrange them a lot. By title, by author name, by main character's name, by colour. Once it was by how much I loved them, which was hard. Each of these books means so much to me.

But David is still exploring the shelves. Then his eyes come to rest on the bell jar at the top, out of reach, furthest from danger. A glass cloche over a little Spanish dancer. He reaches up and lifts the glass, the mechanical music starts – *plink, plink, plink* – slow and off-kilter. The dancer beginning to twirl. She's not fully wound and sounds wrong. David raises his hand, and I suddenly panic that he will drop the glass cover. It will slip, shatter, the whole thing destroyed.

'Please!' I say, moving towards him, grabbing his hands, careful not to knock the glass from his grip. A strange feeling courses through me as I actually touch his skin. 'You can't just come in here and touch my things.' I feel exposed, vulnerable. My voice sounds raw. 'Who do you think you are?'

He steadies my hand. 'Someone who cares,' he says. 'About you. And the truth. I don't want you to give up on that either.'

Why? I want to ask him. Why does he care so damned much?

But I know the answer.

Lauren.

He wants to know the truth about her. Of course he does.

He met her briefly, the May of the year she disappeared. He was on the panel at the school Careers Fair, and she approached him about her writing. He showed interest. Afterwards she sent him some of her work, and he wrote back to her, encouraging her, telling her she was a promising young writer. She sent a few more. He told her he saw her potential, and that had meant a lot to her. An awful lot.

Maybe *too* much.

She called him, a few times. Then a few more. Was she hurt when he told her she should come back when she was older? By the end of summer, he told her to just leave him alone! He was trying to do what was right for them both, wasn't he?

But Lauren hadn't seen it that way. She was angry...

Angry enough that later she would be convinced to do something stupid or just wrong.

So, how had he felt when he heard a few months later that she had disappeared? Had he felt upset, disappointed, guilty, or even a little afraid? After all, she had just been a teen looking for someone to give her attention, to tell her she was special when no one else did. Couldn't he see that? Couldn't he have just tried? No. He had turned her away.

And where had she gone next?

I feel a knot of my own cloying guilt. Always have. That David was somehow implicated in all this. He shouldn't have been. I've tried to tell him it was a mistake.

Still, he wrote about her. Those articles. Was he hoping that she would see his words too, know he still cared, wanted her to be safe? A message to her to come home. That he knew she hadn't meant to do what she did.

Or was it that he felt he needed to clear his own name.

I cover the Spanish dancer, shocked at the thoughts and feelings that David's presence in my flat amongst Lauren's things has provoked.

'I'm just trying to protect things,' I say quietly.

'Why?' he asks.

'Because... I don't want them to get broken. They *mean* something.'

'But don't you see?' He moves closer, looks like he wants to take my hand but doesn't. 'I'm doing the same. I'm trying to protect you for the same reason.'

I round, our eyes searching each other's. His shift from green to grey in this light. Beautiful, intense, maybe a little calculating.

'Why?' I ask.

'The truth. You know what happened to her.'

'No, I don't,' I insist. Then I lower my voice. 'It was someone else's job to piece it all together. To find her, to bring her back. I was a child then and I can't do it alone now.'

'But you're not alone,' he says. 'You have me.' Then he puts his hand in his pocket and takes something out. 'I'll help you, in any way I can.'

As his hand opens, I see a silver chain snaking free between his fingers. *Lauren's necklace!* The one that slipped out from under her scarf as she stood on the wall that day. Now cupped in his hand like an injured bug he's saved from being trampled.

'Where did you find that?'

'The canal.'

'When did you go there? Why didn't you take it to the police?' I extend a finger to touch it.

'The police?' David recoils his hand, closing his palm.

'There might be fingerprints.'

'Only mine.' He narrows his eyes. 'You want them to question me again?'

Again...

'That was a mistake. They never really suspected you.' I look back at him but his eyes have darkened.

'I nearly lost everything. You know that.' His voice is tight, a flash of something in his face, close to the surface. Hurt, or maybe anger.

'I'm sorry,' I whisper quietly. 'Lauren wouldn't have wanted that.'

His face softens again. His eyes shift back from green to grey. Calmer. 'Anyway, it's not for the police. It's for you.' He lifts my chin to face him. 'It means that what is lost can still be found.' He pauses. 'Like the truth.'

'Don't ask me that. I can't remember.' I shrug him off. 'It's been too long, too many things... My memory is too fragile.'

'Then write it down, the story.'

'No,' I say more forcefully.

Is that what he's after, my story? *Her* story.

'Look,' he pauses, 'I can't hold your job open indefinitely. But if you take this "assignment" for me... for us... then... well, we wouldn't have to call it sick leave. You don't even need to leave home. Better just to stay here, safe. Work on this "special project", for us. How does that sound?'

'And it won't see the light of day until I'm ready,' I ask, and he nods.

I cross to the window, and I gaze out, or rather up. Street level. Needing light. A woman in sparkly red heels walks along in a flurry of leaves. Beside her a skeleton, white bones on black fabric. Are they going to a party, could it be Halloween already? October ending. Is she Dorothy from *The Wizard of Oz*? 'There's no place like home.'

'Please,' David says. 'I'm trying to help you. I just want to know something, anything.'

My shoulders drop, my eyes glaze. 'I only know that... it was *their* fault.'

'Whose?'

'My parents. They... *threatened* her, that night at the house. That's why she ran away.'

The street is empty. No sparkly shoes, no leaves, no skeleton bones. So quiet, I can hear my own heartbeat.

'It was *their* fault.'

David crosses to me. I feel his closeness behind me. 'You know that's not true.'

I can feel his warmth behind me, but he doesn't touch me. Doesn't lay his hand on my arm, even if I wish for the comfort of his touch.

'When was the last time you spoke to your mother?' he asks gently.

I shrug. I call her occasionally, we're polite and brief and shallow and mean. Though she'd say it's me that starts it.

'Tell her to come,' he says. 'Listen to her, what she has to say.'

Then he turns me back from the window towards him. He searches my eyes, then takes my hand, lowers the necklace into my palm, closing my fingers over it.

'Find what's lost. The truth. The real story.' He lifts my chin again with gentle fingers. 'You can free us all.'

I feel his face right in front of mine. I close my eyes briefly, pinching them tight. I don't want him to kiss me, never did.

'I have to go,' he says, suddenly awkward, and I feel the cold as he shifts away.

When the front door is locked behind him, I turn my back, feeling its solidity against my spine. Feeling the certainty that I couldn't follow him even if I wanted to.

Stay put. Stay safe.

Only then I glance down at the necklace resting in my palm. The one Lauren was wearing just before she disappeared. The silver is worn, the engraving almost too scratched to read.

Almost, but not quite. It says:

I Will Never Let You Go

THIRTEEN

JANE

Today

Jane watches as Dan bends, brings himself to the girl's eye level, hands on his knees, to make himself less intimidating. 'And why are you here... Rene?' he asks, trying out her name.

He leaves a space for her answer, but she doesn't say a word.

He waits, then asks again. 'Why are you here? And...' he stammers, 'where have you been?' His questions come in pairs now, and Jane can tell there are others queuing up to get out. She feels his impatience, but maybe the girl has told him all she's willing to.

The silence rules the kitchen. Its clean surfaces that the girl keeps running her eyes over. The faint whir of the heating that has come on.

Then the girl speaks. 'This is my home,' she says. She tips her head curiously as if Dan is the one who doesn't belong. 'Why are you here?' she says.

Dan nods as if he doesn't know how to respond. He crosses the kitchen, scooping up Jane with him and brings them to stand by the sink. He pours himself a glass of water and gulps it down before coughing to clear his throat. He kneads his thumb and finger deep into his forehead as if massaging away his own headache. Several times he opens his mouth to speak but nothing comes. Jane simply watches him.

'Look, I've got some papers in my study, maybe the sellers' details are there. A phone number. We could try calling them.'

'The sellers...?' Jane asks, but he's already gone off towards his study.

She thinks of the people she met briefly when they were buying this place, how it was reduced for a quick sale. Curtains drawn. The wife pale and sick. The husband who barely looked up from the carpet. The agent who continued his jubilant praise: 'look at the fantastic layout', 'the windows', 'the garden'. 'A lovely *family* home.' Had he winced when he'd said that before hurrying them upstairs to the master bedroom?

'Not my daughter's room.' Jane has a vague memory of the wife calling up the stairs after them. 'We keep that door locked, I'm afraid.'

Jane had assumed at the time that they were divorcing. But now she tries to recall if there wasn't talk that they had a daughter who ran away. Some inclination that the father was under the shadow of doubt. The daughter troubled, into drugs. But that was so many years ago.

Dan emerges from his study and bounds up the stairs without a word, more sprightly than Jane has seen him in years. 'Must be in the files I put in the loft,' his words trail after him.

'And what should I do?' Jane calls up to Dan on the landing. He is already tugging down the ladder from the hatch, and he climbs up without answering.

Jane turns, no clearer.

She steps into the alcove in the hallway, to be sure she's out of the girl's line of sight from the kitchen. This place where a phone table might once have stood. A big old-fashioned red phone, the type with a handset and cord. Jane seems to vaguely remember it there. Remembering that she liked the location and dimensions of the house, the garden was pretty, but feeling there was something oppressive about it; or about them, a desire to leave. Already thinking how she wanted to refresh all the rooms. Now she opens her mobile, and without thinking searches *Runaway Meadow Close*.

Sure enough, a row of stories appears. She feels a rush of disquiet seeing the headlines that lead a path back to her home. She's never searched for her own home before. Why would she?

Runaway Lauren Fisher. Still missing Lauren Fisher. Suspicion hangs over father of missing daughter. Local man David Pritchard taken in for questioning.

Jane feels deeply uncomfortable – a sense of horror even – seeing these articles, a photo of a teen girl in all of them. The same image, over and over. She looks familiar, similar to this girl sitting in her kitchen, though not the same. The one in the photos is younger, prettier. But also, her face seems different: the shape, her forehead, it's smaller. There's an interview with the mother, saying how much she misses her. Yet she looks glamorous, barely a hint of the faded, pensive woman Jane remembers meeting in this very spot.

We keep that bedroom door locked.

'Got it,' Dan shouts down with a breathless voice from where he's been hefting boxes.

Jane's eyes creep back to her phone. The horror there now too, as well as sitting in her kitchen chair. There's an interview with some lad, Pete Wise. A photo of a young man with his arm halfway around a girl. They're laughing, frozen in motion. The article says that Pete had been Lauren's on-off boyfriend in the months before she disappeared. They'd made out, smoked drugs, some trouble at school. Yet she was barely fourteen.

The whole thing unsettles Jane. A girl had gone missing from this house, her home, eight years ago. Was that the coldness in the walls that Jane had felt? Painstakingly ripped out and painted over. Decorated it back to being a lovely family home, for her and Dan and Alice and Aidan. But a question remains.

Jane goes into the kitchen and crosses to the girl, crouches beside her, one hand on the arm of the chair to steady herself. The girl thinks she wants the notebook, tugs it tighter against her.

Instead, Jane asks, 'Who is Lauren?' She dares to gaze into Rene's eyes. Soft, almost affectionate, willing her to trust her. She shifts her hand onto Rene's arm, intended as kindness.

A tear rolls slowly down Rene's face; a small clean trail left where it has fallen.

'She was my sister,' Rene whispers, her voice almost nothing. 'I was trying to keep her alive.'

FOURTEEN

LAUREN

Before

Back in The Hole. I thought I was doing better. Thought the last few weeks I'd been really good. Maybe it was true what he said, that it was my fault. *I'd* brought this all on myself.

The hours passed and the tears dried. Nothing to do but wait. The panic slid down to the quiet place where it throbbed at the back of my skull, and I started to feel other sensations, like the hunger in my stomach, the rawness in the back of my throat, the pain in my shoulder from where he'd shoved me down. And fear.

One day I might put you in there and just forget where you are...

I reached down into the canvas bag, scrabbling around for something to eat. It wasn't big in The Hole but things still got lost in that utter darkness, like a lip gloss or key in the bottom of a torn pocket falling through into its lining. Or something important I'd wanted to say to Mum but there was never the right moment to say it.

In the bag at my feet, I found two tins and a blunt tin

opener. Oh, and a small bottle of water. Maybe I wouldn't be in for long this time, just a few hours. He just needed to go somewhere or do something, *OK?* Like it was a discussion, and we'd agreed. Dragging me in and shoving me down, hurting my shoulder on the way. Bolting the hatch and then coming back just after. Throwing in the backpack with the tins and the tin opener and a small bottle.

You know you made this happen. All of this.

And yes, he was right. I had.

I'd told Keele I was getting sick again, what with all the time in The Hole and locked in the upstairs room with the shutters down and never allowed outside. So he'd started to let me sit in that room at the back with the tiny window while I worked polishing parts. The ones he lined up along the floor for me on old newspaper. *Money doesn't grow on trees,* he'd say. *And I can't go out to work because I've got to stay home and look after you. So now you can work too. It's either this or some other kind of work.* That grin I hated. Whatever kind of work was he suggesting?

He sold car parts and got 'good enough' money. He'd take pictures and worked away at putting them onto the computer in the living room. The one that I was forbidden to touch unless he wanted to show me something. Some news story about a poor girl found dead or a disaster that had happened: a disease outbreak, a terrorist attack, war. Or that there'd still been no reply to my last email to Mum and Dad. *Well, that's their choice too, isn't it? They know where you are and could come fetch you any time. But it seems they don't even want to write back.*

So, I sat polishing the car parts and I was always too slow, and Keele would come in and lean against the door and count the pieces laid on the newspaper and he'd tut. *You'll have to sing for your supper tonight,* and he'd smile. It wasn't a handsome smile. And singing wasn't singing at all.

I hated cleaning those parts, my fingers covered in sludge

and oil and the paint thinner I used for cleaning. When I held my hand over my mouth at night to stop me *singing* too loudly, I could always smell it on my skin.

So maybe being alone in The Hole was OK for a while, I told myself. I sipped the water, cautious at first. You never know. Once, he'd filled it with turps and it stank the little hole up, and every breath of air was filled with fumes. I was afraid of going up in flames.

That was a mistake, he said when I got out. *You didn't think I did it on purpose, did you, Little L?*

And what was I supposed to say?

'No.' I shook my head. 'It was a mistake,' I repeated. Because he was looking at me in that way that meant he was testing me to see what I'd say.

I had to pack up in a hurry. And whose fault was that? I'm the one making sure you've got what you need down there, while you're "getting better". He'd grin. *I'm not mean, am I?*

'No, Keele. You're never mean.'

But he was. He was really mean. No matter how many times he had me tell him that he wasn't. I'd seen how cruel he was to that dog and he claimed to love her too. The pitiful look in her eyes which followed me around the room, as if I could do something to help her. As if I could protect her when I couldn't even protect myself. I'd watched her take a beating, and in those moments I just thanked God it was her and not me. Only afterwards, I'd lift her ear and whisper, 'I'm sorry for thinking that. That I was glad that it was you. I wish it didn't have to be either of us.' Then he'd shout and the dog would snarl and I'd jump. That always made him laugh, pitting us against each other.

I wound the tin opener round and prized up the lid, and I ate my food from the tin sightlessly. It was sweetcorn, creamed. Not kernels, no crunch. I rooted around to pick out the juiciest bits, savouring them one by one, just in case it was going to be

longer than I thought. I hated the slimy juice, but later I would
be happy to drink it. To have something to fill me up.

I knew how it felt to go hungry, to crumble in on myself like
one of those tower blocks being reduced to rubble.

I reassured myself that there were two tins, so maybe that
meant it would only be a short time, even if it could also mean I
would go hungry. There was no telling what was in the other tin
until I opened it. Keele once gave me dog food. He said the label
had come off. *Just a mistake*, he'd said. 'Just a mistake,' I'd
repeated.

As I ate, my fingers felt wet and sticky, and I thought about
washing them. About being able to run them under a tap,
endless flowing water. Of letting it gush into my mouth and
over my face. I imagined a bath. What I wouldn't give for one of
those. The hot sweet water swilling all around me. Bubbles
crackling in my ears as I slid back into them, spooning their
warm loveliness onto my arms and chest. Not like the short,
cold showers Keele let me have occasionally.

You paying the bills, Little L? Keele would say. *Well, when
you do, you can have all the long hot showers you like. Until then,
count yourself lucky. Count yourself lucky to twenty, and then,
Get Out!*

I imagined lying in a bath, and when I was done, stepping
out, steam rising from my skin, wrapping myself in a fluffy
white towel, and when I was dry, I would put on a pretty dress,
something that floated when I twirled. I'd brush my hair and go
out and off to work, or meet friends for lunch.

I lowered the lid of the tin and as I did a thought crept into
me. The lid slicing down through skin. Me bleeding silently
into the darkness. Keele's face when he opened the hatch and
found me lying there; eyes wide. Really gone.

But it was a stupid idea. I couldn't, even if I wanted to. He'd
already made sure of that. The lids only made dull scratches. I'd
sharpened one on the concrete for hours, and still the cuts only

stung, never really bled, and I couldn't let him see the scratches again. He'd remind me, *This is why I have to protect you from yourself,* and his eyes would stare deep into me.

Then he'd smile, and I knew what he was going to say.

You asked me to look after you, didn't you? And that's what I'm trying to do. But maybe your parents were right, maybe you're beyond helping. Maybe that's why they were happy that you came to me...

His smile fading. His voice lowering. His eyes shining.

Remember what you told me about your mother? How she tried to get rid of you when you were a baby. How difficult she always thought you were. And you know what my uncle Ray used to tell me...?

His eyes darken. *Some kids are just born bad.*

Darker. No blue left at all. *And those kids... they'll never get better. No matter what we do.*

FIFTEEN

RENE

Before

Evening. I sit on the sofa and eat beans on toast for my tea. The bread is that white stuff that could survive a nuclear holocaust. And baked beans... absolute comfort food. Total favourite. Right up there with Ready Brek and golden syrup. I'm lucky because this was pretty much all I had in the cupboard. Shopping, *tomorrow*. On the list. Check.

Oh, and maybe call Mum.

Maybe...

I'm watching a sitcom, an episode I've seen a hundred times before; there's something comforting in its canned laughter and safe predictability. The heartbeat of voices going up and down in a way people don't really do. I recite the lines along with the actors, imagining I hear laughter at my words too.

Mum never liked this show, it was Dad who sat with us and watched it; Thursday evenings, homework all finished. Lauren would glance at Dad, and he'd glance back at her, just missing each other's gaze, like ships that pass in the night. Something sad in the distance growing between them. As she turned thirteen then fourteen. Him more awkward with his hugs, less frequent at entering her bedroom. No tuck in at night. Missed dinner times. Arriving late, later. Problems at work, meetings, traffic, excuses to be somewhere else. The TV screen the only thing that occasionally brought them together.

But there wasn't hate. Not yet.

Only boredom. And maybe that was more dangerous, in the end.

The show ends. I hum along with the theme tune. Then the silence is audible. My flat immediately too quiet.

I glance at my notebook, somewhat guiltily. Thinking of David's visit. My promise. His 'special project'.

Not tonight. Too tired.

In the kitchen I pop the two last pills from the packet that Mum gave me. I fill a long glass of water and stand briefly looking into it as the small maelstrom within settles.

Talk to her, David had said.

But it's not that simple. Our relationship has never been *easy*. Most days I blame her for giving up so readily on Lauren. I know I'm supposed to always love her, but I can't. Had she ever really loved Lauren? Isn't that why as a teen she went looking for it in other places?

The pills are slow. My head hurts. And thinking about Mum makes it hurt more.

Write. The truth.

I cross to the desk and sit. A flicker of memory, as if the television is still on. I pick up my pen, and the words flow.

Lauren has just turned seven. She runs into the kitchen full of excitement. Dad is close behind her, and both their faces are glowing from an afternoon of fun and fresh air.

Dad had been teaching her to ride her bike without stabilizers. They've got gloves on and they smell of the cold. There's a dried leaf in Lauren's hair. They've been down by the towpath. I imagined her little feet pedalling frantically to avoid falling. Dad telling her to stay focused, not to get distracted by a playful dog.

'The towpath?' Mum says as she set out the plates. 'Why did you need to go there?'

I could almost taste the lasagne baking in the oven. My stomach rumbling with anticipation.

'Only junkies and perverts go there,' Mum said.

'Rubbish, it's a lovely spot. We like it, don't we, love?' and Dad turned to Lauren and she nodded enthusiastically, because that was what he wanted her to say and she was always eager to please him. Something special in their bond. Such a daddy's girl. Besides, she did like it there. It was mysterious and magical. A place of dragonflies and fairy trees. Who knew what could happen there?

'What's a junkie?' Lauren asked instead, and a look passed between Mum and Dad.

'Your daddy will tell you.' Mum smiled as she handed that ball to him.

But Dad said, 'Tell Mummy what we saw today, Lauren.'

So Lauren began, 'We saw a... what's that big bird-thing called?' She turned back to Dad, but he didn't answer for her. Not like Mum; he waited for her to remember for herself, his eyes encouraging her. 'A heron, that's it, isn't it, Daddy? Big as a ter-o-dack-til,' and she made a caw, waving her arms above her.

I remember the shadow they made, the swing of the light that hung over the kitchen table as she accidentally hit it. The orb like the moon on a string, swaying, swaying, back and forth and the whole room shifting. Mum's hand shot up instinctively and steadied the light because she liked things under control, not reeling back and forth and back and forth.

'My grandpa used to shoot herons for eating the fish in his pond,' Mum said sharply. She was setting the knives out, perfectly straight.

'He had a gun?' Lauren asked, impressed and terrified.

Mum swatted it away like an annoying fruit fly. 'Oh, just an old air rifle for scaring things away,' she said, making sure the glasses were evenly spaced and the right distance from the placemats.

'And for getting your father up the aisle,' Dad said, and they both laughed, though Mum stopped sooner. A joke that maybe stung just a little.

When Mum had finished dishing out the lasagne in crisp well-cooked squares she said, 'Help yourself to salad.'

And when she was seated, Dad said to Lauren, 'I was proud of you today.' I saw his face and eyes illuminated by the steady kitchen light, glowing like they had when he had come in from the cold.

Mum looked up at Lauren, reaching out her hand to take Lauren's fingers as if about to say grace. 'Me too. I'm proud of you. I always will be,' and she leaned over and pulled Lauren to her, kissed her gently on the forehead.

Lauren tipped her face down to hide the red flush of her cheeks. This scene of perfect family happiness. Yet seven years later, Lauren went missing.

Except that wasn't true. Mum wasn't proud of Lauren. Or certainly not in the end.

So, what changed? How had they grown to hate poor Lauren? To abandon her in the terrifying darkness of Missing.

I hear her whispering, *whispering*. That's why I'm afraid to close my eyes, to fall asleep. Because in the darkness, I hear what she tells me he does to her.

SIXTEEN

RENE

Before

Before I open my eyes, I make my list. Today's is simple.

- *Call Mum*

Just that.

'Why aren't you at work?' she asks, her voice already accusatory.

'I'm sick,' I reply.

'Again?'

'Yes "again",' I mimic. I can tell how this is going to go. *Thanks, David* – see, gratitude.

I head into the living room and coil my legs up on the sofa under the crochet blanket for reassurance. Wishing her to be that Mum she once was. Her soft voice, reading stories cuddled up. 'Thanks for the sympathy,' I say.

'Oh, you know what I mean,' she lightens. 'It's just that—'

'Believe me, I like it less than you do,' I cut her off, otherwise she'll head off into some long speech about how all this affects her worse than anybody else. *Poor Mummy*. How she's suffered.

'Did you tell your dad?'

I'm caught off guard by this question. 'Dad? Why would I tell him...?'

'You know, you two always seemed so close. Too close, I thought at times. Almost conspiratorial.'

'And what's that supposed to mean?' The first rise of my voice.

'Oh, he could do no wrong in your eyes. And you *always* took his side.'

'No, I didn't!' I protest now. 'That was Lauren, not me. They were the ones that were close. Or used to be. You've no reason to be jealous of *me*.'

'"Jealous"?' An explosion of her laughter. 'Don't be ridiculous.' She waits for her comment to sink in. 'All I'm saying is, it's a shame if you're not speaking. There's no point bearing a grudge as I say. Especially towards your own parent.'

Bearing a grudge...? My hackles are already up around my ears. The hypocrisy of this woman. My mouth falls open, incredulous. So much to unpack.

'"No point bearing a grudge",' I retort. 'When did you ever say that? And what about you and Nanna?' My voice escalates.

There's nothing to be gained from this conversation. I should stop now before it implodes.

'Nanna?' Her turn to sound shocked. 'What's any of this got to do with *her*?'

A thought creeps into my head. Maybe this has everything to do with her. I think of David touching the framed postcard. Then I hear Mum turning her forced breaths into sarcastic laughs.

'That's what you called to do, to upset me?'

'Upset you? No, of course not!'

See? All about her. I'm sick and now I've upset *her*. Zero to hero in sixty seconds. She's faster than a Porsche.

I take a deep breath. This isn't how today should go. 'I... didn't mean to upset you.' Calming. God, I hate her. I really do *hate* her. Her little tactics to keep us from talking about what we really should. About Lauren, amongst other things. 'I think we need to talk!'

'I thought we were. We are,' a shallow trill. 'Look at us, talking.'

'No. Not on the phone. I...' I swallow, not quite believing that I'm doing this. 'I need to see you.'

Need, not want.

Her turn to be unsure. 'Right, well, you're always welcome here at...' She doesn't say home. She wouldn't call Meadow Close that, not anymore. She lets the word flutter to the ground.

Still, I picture the faux-Elizabethan red-brick in that cul-de-sac. The rockery, the pretty shrubs at the front, daffodils that pop up each spring, the yellow rose bush growing in the back garden. Inside the cloying, familiar flock wallpaper, the blush-coloured carpets, the dust made warm by the radiators. The stairs that are too narrow and creak, the white handrail curled at the end and marked from years of hands running up and down. I remember how I would sit at the bottom, waiting for Dad to come home. Waiting to see him put his briefcase in the hall and stoop to kiss me. 'Hello, love.' And later, where I would sit and listen to them whispering in the kitchen about Lauren, and trouble, and arguing, stabbing each other with quiet words as their marriage tore under the strain.

That's not the house where I want to go to talk.

Ever.

Mum picks up on my silence. 'I suppose, we *could* meet somewhere else... Maybe in town... for a coffee.' She's warming to the idea. Because it's her idea. She always liked those best. 'Yes, there's a lovely new place just opened on the high street.

Fresh pastries and Italian coffee. The best sugared donuts. I know you like those—'

'Here,' I say tersely, not about to be tempted. 'I need you to come here.' *Need*, not want. 'I think it's time. And David said—'

'David?' A mock smile creeping into her voice again now, a little piece of rediscovered power. 'And what's any of this got to do with him?'

'He's trying to help me.'

'Is he now?' She sounds sceptical. 'Grown man like him wanting to help young girls. What's in it for him?'

I can feel my frustration building. 'He's here for me.'

'Like he was for Lauren?'

She lets the silence sit, as if a dish she's just served cold.

'Because you know what she said about him, don't you? What she said before she—'

'That was a lie,' I snap.

'Lauren was adamant at the time.'

I feel a sickening pulse of guilt. 'She retracted it, didn't mean it. You know that; she told you she was sorry. It wasn't meant to... she was just—'

'*Confused?*' Mum offers. '*Vulnerable?*' She's trying to put words in my mouth. 'Yes, that's true. She needed protecting, like you do. But she wouldn't let us. Like you won't. And in the end, she—'

'Stop it. STOP it!' I shout. A sting in my throat. 'David just wants to help. He wants her to come back. Safe. Not like you!'

I'm shocked by my own audacity. I want her to say that's not true. That she wants nothing more than to see Lauren again.

Instead, she lets out a tired sigh. 'Lauren isn't coming back.' Her voice is still. 'She's... where she chose to be.'

'*Chose?* How can you say that?' My voice erupts in horror. 'She didn't choose *any* of this. She's suffering. Always. I should never have called you. Never!'

'Wait,' Mum says, as if realizing just in time. 'Please.' Softening, knowing she's pushed me too far this time. 'I think maybe David is right. We do need to talk. And... that means you need to listen.'

Listen to her, he'd said.

'All right,' I say, and we hang up.

Neither of us saying goodbye.

SEVENTEEN

RENE

Before

I pace. I go to the door as if attached to it by a piece of elastic. I peer out the eyehole thinking of Mum's imminent arrival. She'll be here any moment. But then I won't be able to control her in the way that I can from the end of the phone; to cut her off if I want to. She'll be here, in my home. No escape.

The porch is empty. Whether I like it or not.

I return to the living room, rearranging things, as if somehow that matters. The order of the books, the exact angle of the framed pictures, the spacing between the Russian dolls. I straighten the glass cloche on the Spanish dancer and wind it again. How good I am at nurturing this little menagerie of belongings. As David said, protecting things that don't matter because I can't protect what does.

I could sleep, but dreams of Lauren are always loitering in there. Her cries, her screams.

I water my plants; they perk up a little. I stand them all together. 'There's safety in numbers,' at least that's what Dad used to say. One of his lame expressions. Yeah, because he always liked to escape into a spreadsheet, rather than talking to us.

I go to the coffee table and pick up the necklace, thinking of David. Maybe I should call him, tell him Mum is coming. He'll be pleased with me. *Gold star. Employee of the month.*

Or call Mum, tell her to come more quickly. It feels like I have more time than I know what to do with, and also as if it is running out.

Tick, Tock.

I sit at the desk, looking up at the picture of Nanna, the one that David touched. *What does any of this have to do with her?*

I take the picture down and examine it more closely. It's black and white and faded. Of Nanna on the prow of a ship, an unknown man at her side. Yet written across it in cheerful yellow print, the words *Happily Ever After*. Had she married this stranger? Was this their honeymoon? Was he the one that Great-Grandpa chased up the aisle with a gun? Why had I kept this? Why did I think it mattered?

Even this desk; it used to be in my parents' guest room, a little oval mirror on top making it a dressing table. Although I'm not sure where that part went. I see Nanna, on the rare occasion she came to stay, laying out her earrings and trinkets on the top as if on display in an antique shop. A poorly clasped tortoise-shell case, loose pink powder spilling out. Beside it a tissue with a blot of coral-coloured lipstick, lying like an abandoned kiss.

Then the sound of Nanna singing drifts into my head. *I love you, a bushel and a peck...*

Behind me the Spanish dancer plinks to life. Probably because I overwound it. I'm overwhelmed by the faint scent of Nanna's perfume, a hint of cloying floral sweetness and must, like second-hand dresses or things taken down from the loft.

'She always left a trail,' Mum used to say.

'A trail of misery,' Dad would joke.

And Mum would half-laugh, but not really. Like it hurt, and

she was the only one who had a right to disparage her own mother.

The dancer plinks once more. Its trapped song. Something... *hovering*... just there, waiting in the wings.

Write, David said. *The truth.*

I pick up my pen, open the notebook, and a sentence spills out of me.

My grandmother, though I never really knew her, for reasons that made sense to others and not to me, might have called this 'confinement'.

I sit back and push the pen away. That ugly word. Why would I write that? A prison of letters, trapped against the page. I look up at the window, the street railings like bars. People passing busily as their day continues.

Confinement.

No, it was something Nanna had said about Mum. About Mum needing to go somewhere. To get help before she *hurt* someone. Or someone else. Had she hurt someone before? Had she hurt Lauren? Some fragment of memory so fragile I have forgotten to cut it out and glue down. Maybe because it's too ugly to keep.

I hear Nanna's voice. Something meant to be a secret, something whispered, overheard. No... told to Lauren. Intended to be unkind, tangled in Nanna's perfume and her must, the sweet dryness of her pink face powder like sugar on donuts, a coral-coloured kiss on Lauren's cheek. The lilt of Nanna's voice that sang about love. Another plink of the Spanish dancer as if warning me.

Mum hurting someone.

Needing help.

Nanna coming and Mum sending her away.

Something... unlocking...

I lift the pen again, and the words demand to come out.

*My grandmother, though I never really knew her – for reasons
that made sense to others and not to me – might have called this
'confinement', which would have made it sound at once glamorous and frightening. Because she was like that, Nanna. Glamorous and frightening. She told stories that excited and upset me.
Yet I loved her.*

*When Lauren was eight, she came to stay. Nanna sat with her
arm around Lauren, and she sang about loving her 'a bushel and
a peck'. My mother heard. She stormed into the room and slapped
her mother hard across the face before yelling, 'GET OUT!'*

*That slap, like the sound of ice cracking. I couldn't explain it.
Not then. Not now. And nobody tried.*

*Nanna's hand rose to her cheek. She stood quickly; the bone
china plate with the biscuits falling from her lap and hitting the
floor where it broke in two. Nanna's fingers on the spot where her
daughter had struck her. Her coral-coloured lips opening and
closing, forming an oh! with the shock of it.*

*Nanna packed her bag, all her trinkets and dresses so carefully
unpacked now hastily thrown back in like jumble, and she
muttered of 'confinement'. Something about a baby, and Mum
needing to go away. To get help. She shouldn't keep trying. It
wasn't safe. They couldn't let it happen again. Not after what
happened with Lauren. Because this time she might really hurt
someone. This time things could be so much worse.*

Then Nanna was gone.

Forever.

Almost.

When Lauren was ten, we found this picture of Nanna. A photo made into a postcard and sent to Mum. In it Nanna looked like something from the 1920s, even though she was born long after the war. But she had the look of a Vogue *model, or at least a showgirl dressed up in* Vogue. *A nice hat with a pin through it. She was on the deck of a ship called* Eternal Voyager, *her arm linked through that of a man we'd never met. But he wasn't escorting her; she seemed to be the one catching him.*

We found that postcard amongst all Mum's things, in a box at the back of her wardrobe. I remember staring into it, imagining I could still hear Nanna singing. I wanted to see if I could find something that might make me think 'ta-da!' Like pulling a magic flower from my sleeve. Joining the dots backwards; the unanswerable questions of why Lauren would one day go missing. But I couldn't see anything other than that Nanna was catching this man, and he seemed to be rather enjoying it.

We shouldn't have been rummaging through Mum's stuff, and when we heard her coming up the stairs, Lauren hid the postcard under the pillow. But of course, Mum found it. And she was angry. Angrier than usual. SHOUTED. Even when Lauren said I had done it.

'Don't be ridiculous,' she snapped. 'You can't blame Rene for everything.'

Would she slap Lauren too?

'I don't want you to have anything to do with that woman! She's a witch. Do you hear me?'

But that woman was her mother. How could a daughter hate her own mother so much?

Then Mum put the picture back into the box and pushed the box back onto the shelf. Not before I glimpsed the image of a black and white cyclone. A baby in the womb: eight weeks, five days. Was that what Nanna had meant? Another baby? I thought of the red spots on the floor years before.

Then Mum cried. Even more when Dad came into the room and tried to comfort her. He looked at Lauren with a soft accusation, and Lauren turned away. But I couldn't take my eyes off the place where the box was hidden. How many other things had Mum kept up there? Was it right to hide so much?

'She knew it would upset me,' Mum said quietly to Dad.

'It's not her fault,' Dad said.

'It never is,' Mum said, teeth gritted, annoyed at him now too. I didn't know if she meant Lauren or Nanna. But I should have seen it, right there in front of me.

Nanna,

Mum,

Lauren.

Like Russian dolls in a row. Or a timeline you could follow: C follows B follows A, discuss.

And four years later, Lauren went missing.

My hand aches as I set the pen down. There are no answers here, but certainly some questions for Mum. Why did she strike Nanna? Why did she send her away? What had Nanna meant about something bad happening with Lauren?

I go back to the sofa and curl up under the blanket, fingers worming into the holes, fighting not to close my eyes. On TV, Madonna is dancing away, enjoying a holiday, or needing one more likely. She looks pale and scruffy. I think of Mum liking this song when it came on the radio in the kitchen. Singing about a holiday and looking happy.

Everything hurts. I've checked the packet, but there are no more pretty pinks. Maybe Mum will bring me some, along with all the answers to all my questions. The most important one being: *How do we bring Lauren home?*

I eventually go to bed, the glow of the bedside light mildly comforting as I stretch myself out and gaze up at my inspiration wall. I imagine that Dad will come soon, lumbering down the corridor. How he'll sit on the duvet and lean over and kiss me, wishing me sweet dreams. 'Night, love...' he'll say.

Except he never comes.

Because he made us think he loved us most.

But in the end, he lied too.

EIGHTEEN

JANE

Today

Jane watches as Dan copies the numbers from the A4 paper into his phone. Then he hits call and pushes the phone against his ear.

'Hello, yes. Hi. I'm Dan Hallman. Is this' – Dan flips the paper again – 'Jim Fisher?'

Jane watches Dan as he listens.

'Right, well, I'm... as I said, Dan Hallman of Meadow Close.' Dan nods. 'Uh huh. Yep. That's right.' A flicker of a smile, then it falters. 'Well... this is going to sound' – he grapples for a word – '*weird*. But there's a girl here, a young woman. She says that... do you, *did* you... have a daughter?'

Jane is anxious now. Should they be calling this man before the police get here, telling him where she is? Of course, what father wouldn't want to know where their missing daughter is? But that cloud of suspicion... Jane hears noises on the other end of the line.

'Right, no. No, I promise I'm not prank calling,' Dan continues. 'She's here. Yes. Says her name's... Rene.'

There's a sound. A gasp.

'OK, OK. Right, look.' Dan pauses, clearly there's some sort of activity, of emotion, on the other end of the line. She thinks she hears the man's voice saying, 'Oh my God! Thank you.' Then she hears what sounds like sobbing.

After a while Dan speaks again. 'Yes. Yes. That's right. Meadow Close. Number eight.' Dan lowers his voice into the phone, telling the man. Telling Jim Fisher, 'Yes, the police are on their way.'

Jane holds her breath to try to hear the other end of the call. She wishes Dan would put it on speaker but realizes why that would be selfish. She glances over at the girl through the kitchen door. She is still gazing at the ground, as if only now becoming aware of her filthy feet.

Jane turns back to Dan. He nods, says, 'Uh huh,' several more times before saying, 'We will.' Then Dan ends the call and lowers the phone.

'What did he say?' Jane asks.

'Hard to tell. He was obviously upset, in shock. Angry at first. Thought I was... anyway, hope he's all right to drive. He reckons less than twenty minutes. Maybe he'll get here before the police.'

Jane feels that wave of anxiety again. Wants the police here first. Surely that's only right. Now it seems so obvious. What if the father is somehow...?

She goes over to the girl. 'Your father is coming.' She watches the young woman's body language as she mentions him. Is she afraid? She noticeably shifts, then a faint hint of a smile. Good. That's good, isn't it? 'He'll be here in about twenty minutes or so.' She glances back at the clock.

'Look, your tea is cold. You don't like it? Can I get you something else?' Jane asks, standing straight, lifting the mug.

'Do you,' the girl's voice is raspy, as if she has smoked too many cigarettes. 'Do you have a can of Coke?'

Jane is not sure. 'Let me just check,' she says.

She opens the fridge and can't find one. 'Wait a sec,' she says, heading through to the utility. Inside an upper cupboard is a half-empty box of Cokes from a party Aidan had before leaving last year. They're warm but they'll be fine. She can add ice. Jane goes back into the kitchen and pours one into a glass, the thud and crack as the ice machine on the fridge crunches out blocks.

'You want a slice of lemon?' Jane asks as if the girl is a regular guest now.

Rene shakes her head.

'Here.' Jane holds out the glass and is pleased when Rene loosens her grip on the book, letting it sit against her stomach. More relaxed, more trusting. The girl reaches out to take the drink with both hands. Jane's not sure if she can hold the weight of it in her tiny, thin arms.

But she does and she sips, a look of sheer pleasure creeping across her face at the sweetness of it.

'Mmmm,' she says, making a sound into the otherwise still and silent kitchen. Then she licks her lips.

NINETEEN

LAUREN

Before

A thought went round and round and round in my head, and the thought was:

Keele is evil. Keele's not kind.
Keele is really fucking with my mind.

A ditty. A little earworm, burrowing its way in. Nothing to stop it going deep into me, eating my brain. Like a song I might have heard on the radio as I was getting ready for school back at home in Meadow Close all those years ago. The mirror steamed up from where I'd had my morning shower, applying my mascara in the circle I'd wiped clear, my mouth hanging open, so I didn't poke myself in the eye. Rubbing away the little black smudges with the ends of my fingers, and I could hear Mum's voice calling up the stairs.

'We're going to be late, *again*,' she'd lie.

'I'm *already* ready!' I'd lie back.

Her thumping up the stairs, Dad coming out of the bedroom, them meeting on the landing with their half-whispered spat as they passed, thinking I couldn't hear them. 'Let her be,' Dad saying. 'You always take her side,' Mum saying.

Turning up the radio to block it all out.

And that's when I heard it. A song. Some banal pop song that I almost liked, a lame hit of the moment. And it would creep in, and I wouldn't be able to shift it all day. It would replay in my head as I sat in the back of the car on the way to school, as I sat at my desk through the boredom of class. As I loitered in the playground waiting for my sometimes friend Shirl to come back from Spanish. I would let my mind wander back to that song and lose myself in it.

An *earworm*. That's what Pete called it.

'Stupid pop song,' I'd say, walking home along the canal with him after school.

'You love it really, such a pop chick,' he'd mock, his lopsided grin as he leaned over and shunted me. Some form of affection. 'Or you want me to play you some real music?' and I'd blush and turn my eyes to his T-shirt. *Kill Your Heroines*, it said. One of his favourites. A hole on the sleeve and a dark smudge where the strap of his guitar rubbed.

'How you doing, Pete?' I asked now, sitting in The Hole.

'Better than you,' I could hear him joke. He always smoked and joked. Never serious, not for a moment.

Truth was, I couldn't remember what he looked like anymore. Only occasionally in dreams when I saw him, I knew it was him. When I called, he turned and there was something that made me know it was him, some essence, even when his face was somebody else's. Sometimes someone I'd seen on TV long ago, or someone I'd cut out from a magazine before the scissors were taken away. Sometimes even Keele's. Occasionally, I woke with a fleeting joyous sense that I had gone back in time and was free. I was fourteen again and waiting to meet Pete. This had all just been a dream. Or the nightmare it had become.

When I got the chance, when I was in the little room with the shutters and the car parts, I'd pull up the loose floorboard and I'd take out my small collection of things, looking at the faded newspaper article that Keele had given me. The one I'd hidden but told him I'd thrown down the toilet because it'd made me too upset. Instead, I hid it in the place with the stories about all the survivors, the ones I'd found in magazines or the local paper, and the ones that David had written, before Keele stopped everything coming.

But this article, with the photo of Pete and I, the one of us at that party when we were young. Me barely fourteen, Pete almost sixteen. A joint between his fingers and his head turned away. Me with that stupid fringe that I had wanted to grow out. Us frozen in a moment of laughter. Forever happy. Keele had said he wasn't sure if he should give it to me. Said he didn't want to upset me too much, but from the section he'd cut out, it was clear that Pete still couldn't keep his mouth shut. Always looking for his fifteen minutes of fame. Why had he said we'd smoked drugs at the canal, or made out? *Why had he said I was troubled?*

David had written a few pieces that Keele had given me fragments of, and they were nicer, kinder. Said I was talented, could write, had a great future ahead of me. And Keele would laugh as he snatched them away.

'What did the rest say?' I'd ask, and Keele would just shrug, as if it meant nothing. As if it didn't matter what David had said. I imagined he was trying to tell me something, if I'd only been able to see the rest. I might have been able to fathom it. A message. A code.

David always said, 'There's a reason we write a story. Something we want to get across. A message we're trying to get through to the reader, a thought we want to leave behind when the reading is done.'

He'd told me that, and he'd also said he'd seen something in me. Yet he'd also told me to go away and come back when I was older. And I might have, if things hadn't gotten so messy. If I hadn't said those stupid things about him. A sense of drowning in guilt that made me panic. Why had I muddied the waters...? Would things have been different if I hadn't?

Keele said they were better off dead. Both of them. The things they said and did. *No friends of yours, Little L. No friends of mine.* And yet when he gave me those scraps from the paper, or I found them, I questioned everything. Maybe Pete and David still cared. So I kept those papers in that special hidden place. And the hours stretched, and my thoughts wriggled and the ditty tormented me like an earworm.

Keele is evil,
Keele is kind.
Keele is really fucking with my mind.

TWENTY

RENE

Before

'I didn't know doctors did house calls anymore,' Mum says from the kitchen.

She's taken off her coat and is wearing a summery dress and strappy shoes, strangely out of season for October. Her hair bounces as she moves, and her fingers and toenails look perfectly painted to match.

'Well, she came as soon as I called her,' I say, a little dig I can't resist, even if it doesn't register.

Mum drifts around the kitchen, putting away packets and tins from her shopping bags. I watch her as intently as I might a wasp I don't want to lose sight of.

'I'm just glad they're taking good care of you,' Mum trills merrily as she busies herself. When she's done, she starts making tea.

Inside me, there's a glimmer of anger, a hint of furious hurt that I'm keeping tucked inside. A deep pocket. For now. It's been a while since I've seen her. Sure, there've been snippets of conversation by phone, but not a full-blown sit down and chat.

Not like this, not for a long time. Possibly years, but who's counting.

Mum turns and smiles as if she knows I'm watching her; she's always liked being centre of attention. She seems relaxed, nothing different about her at all. Maybe a few more grey hairs, her skin a bit more lined. And she's still beautiful and self-absorbed. No sense of inner turmoil; how?

'She was very kind,' I say.

'Hm?' Mum asks, clearly not listening.

'The doctor.'

The doctor I made up. Because in truth, I'm good at that. I should stop before I dig a hole that's too deep to climb out of. I haven't seen a doctor. Who knows what they might have said? Maybe I should send Mum away and see a doctor first, come back armed with terrible diagnoses to make her feel guilty. Like those people in magazines that no one believes until they are proved right. *Chronic, Terminal, Fatal!*

'And what exactly *did* he say was wrong?' She stirs a mug of tea by the sink rather knowingly.

'*She* said...' I try to think what she might have actually said. '"Let's see how the blood tests come back."'

Oh God... where did that come from?

Mum stops stirring for a moment, an uncertain hesitation. 'Blood tests? Well, that's *good*, isn't it? I mean, if they do *real* tests they'll get *real* answers.'

She flicks a smile over her shoulder before turning back and putting her foot on the pedal of the bin. She dangles the teabag like a dead mouse before dropping it in.

'And did they say what they were testing for?' she asks as she crosses from the kitchen and sets the mugs down. She sits opposite, crossing her ankles, and as she does her wrap dress slips open just above the knee.

I want to tell her to leave. We are not this, this mother and daughter. We don't belong like this, being almost 'nice'. Ever since what happened to Lauren, I hate her. I can't ever forgive her for what she did, or didn't do.

'I don't know,' I say vaguely, wishing I'd never started this conversation about the doctor. 'Glandular stuff,' I say. It's all I can come up with.

'Really?' Mum lets out a short laugh. 'Funny,' she says. I cock my head quizzically. 'You always did like to copy Lauren. Remember, she had glandular fever just after her fourteenth birthday? She was in bed for weeks, not well enough to leave the house for ages.' Mum says it almost wistfully. 'She couldn't eat. Had fever and hallucinations. Said even the TV ads made her feel queasy. She thought I was the devil himself...' Mum laughs at the irony. 'Can you imagine?'

She sips her tea, doesn't seem to mind that it's scorching hot. Well, a devil wouldn't.

Then she lowers the mug, her focus suddenly further away. 'Yet for those few weeks, she let me care for her. Too sick to fight me, I suppose.'

Her gaze seems to cloud, a hint of happiness.

'Then she got over it and went back to school. Everything back to normal. All better.' Then she lowers her voice almost conspiratorially. 'Although her moods were definitely worse. All that thundering up the stairs and slamming of doors. If you can call that better.' Another amused laugh.

Doesn't Mum realize what a terrible time Lauren was having when she went back to school? Pete had lost interest, the cliques in the classroom had all shifted. Her best friend Shirl no longer was interested in being her BFF. Lauren was miserable and alone, wasn't that plain to see? Those horrible rumours. Mean. Untrue. Didn't Mum remember that? Lauren had tried to tell her. Wanted to...

Then I think of something Nanna said all those years ago as she scrunched up dresses and thrust them back into her suitcase. After Mum sent her packing just for singing to Lauren.

'She was always cold, always heartless. Didn't know how to show love to anyone...'

Nanna was right.

'Lauren was ill,' I say. '*Really* ill. And when she went back to school things... were *bad*. Not better! They made fun of her.'

The Kissing Disease... that's what they said. *Slutty Lauren got the kissing disease,* they taunted. Even 'Cuckoo Kirsten' who *everyone* made fun of, and Lauren had always tried to be nice to. When Lauren told Mum how unhappy she was, Mum dismissed it, said it would 'all blow over'. Even spun off into talking about how popular she'd been at school. Of course she was. Of course.

But the worst thing was that it seemed to be Pete who was the source of the rumours, as if he'd got what he came for and had moved on. Lauren heard the girls laughing at her in corridors, in the changing rooms after netball, in the loos as they wafted smoke away. *Slutty Lauren...* No one defended her, not even Cuckoo Kirsten. Maybe she sang loudest of all, glad to be out from under the glare of the mean girls.

And then there was Shirl. Lauren noticed that she'd started writing Pete's name in her exercise book. *SW 4 PW.* Mrs Shirley Wise... Had she had something to do with it all? Because she'd always said Pete was such a loser; but sometimes after school she told Lauren she couldn't hang out, somewhere else she needed to be.

Lauren spent a lot of time alone after that, heading to the canal, even bunking off school when it all got too much, claiming she was feeling unwell. Smearing tears from her eyes when she thought someone might see her, throwing stones into the water as if smashing in the faces that she imagined on the surface. Everything had changed and nobody cared. Dad was never around anymore, never asked. And Mum was Mum was Mum.

Then suddenly everything changed. The day of the Careers Fair. The day she met David...

'So when will you get the results?' Mum asks, snapping me back from my thoughts. 'Did he tell you?'

'*She*. And no. I forgot to ask.'

Mum tuts under her breath. 'I should have been here,' she says as if reminding herself. 'You still need help with these things. I mean, look at these poor plants. You need me around. I've practically got green thumbs.'

It almost sounds concerned, then she flips her hand disinterestedly, looking at her perfect nails.

'Look,' I say, reinstating myself, because none of this matters. 'I want to talk.'

Mum opens her mouth to speak, to declare we are speaking, but I raise my hand and cut her off.

'I'm writing something, about Lauren. And I want to ask you... about Nanna.'

'Nanna?' It's Mum's turn to be off-guarded. 'Oh, let's not talk about that old *witch*.'

She sets her tea down quickly, and instead begins rummaging in her bag, pulling something out. It looks like a notebook, and immediately I know she's going to try to distract me. Off on some other topic that she can control. But I won't let her. Not today. I won't. Then I see what she's holding.

'Your dad found this in the garden,' she says, the corners of her mouth twitching as she sets it in her lap. 'He dug it up down by the rose bush.' She picks up her mug, not sure whether she's going to give me the notebook or not.

'The rose bush...?' I ask. I picture him kneeling there.

'Oh, he still goes there sometimes to tend that old thing. You know he planted it for Lauren when she was born?'

Of course I do, how could I forget?

'It's hardly got any roses left these days, but he tries to keep it alive. Knows what it means if it finally dies...'

I don't want to talk about Dad. Or roses, or even this note-book. I want to know about Nanna, why Mum sent her away. Why Nanna said something about Mum hurting someone. What happened with Lauren. Why Mum never loved her.

But she continues, 'He doesn't like it when anyone goes near it. Wouldn't let anyone else dig around there. Very secre-tive, if you ask me.'

Mum looks at me then, raising her eyebrows as if I'm in on that secret. 'You know what's he's like; who knows what he gets up to when no one's watching?' She lets out a clipped laugh as if it's funny, but I can see that she's turning her wedding band.

'How... is he?' I venture. Not what I want to talk about, but I'm still curious. A slight detour won't hurt. 'How are things between you two?'

'Us? Oh, couldn't be better.' She's dismissive again, that flap of her hand. 'Better than before anyway.'

Does she mean before Lauren went...? Slamming doors, arguing. No, she means after Lauren disappeared, surely.

A question starts rising. I can't help it. All this talk of how happy they are now, the idea of Dad down by the rose bush, the notebook. So many buried things.

'Do you think you did enough to find her? Do you think you both really tried?'

Mum's face shows a stab of dismay, but it settles into a vague confusion as if I'm not understanding something that everyone else knows.

My voice strengthens as I ask again. 'Did you do enough to look, to tell the police all that you knew? Did you show them everything, no stone unturned? Did it matter to you to make them keep looking, to join all the dots?'

Mum's face bursts into an expression of anger, disgust, hurt at the accusation.

'Because really, she couldn't have *just* disappeared. There had to be an answer. Somewhere, someone had to have known *something*. People don't just vanish! They can't. You had to know more.'

My voice rises, my anger building.

'Because something happened to her. Something terrible. You know that. You've *always* known it, haven't you...? Did you tell them everything you knew?'

Mum shakes her head, her eyes clouding, as if seeing another place. Tears building. I'd expected her to be angry, but instead she says: 'You've got this all wrong. You're... wrong about me.'

I stand. I don't want to hear it. Poor her, poor Mum. I know she'll tell some sob story about herself.

But David's voice in my head. *Listen to her...*

'Lauren was *special*,' she says quietly, her words cutting through, and I turn back. 'She had a mind that could be wonderful and frightening. An imagination that meant she was in her own world most of the time. She didn't see the truth about people. Didn't trust the ones who loved her and trusted people she probably shouldn't. She was naïve. And young. Still so young. Didn't understand what playing with fire could do.'

Mum sets the mug on the table. Pushes one nail under the polish on her thumb. 'I tried to warn her, but she didn't want to hear. Disliked me more for it. Thought she knew better. It was me she didn't trust most. I suppose... that's understandable. I suppose, that's my fault because...'

I search her face. Is she admitting some wrongdoing that affected Lauren? No, I need to steel myself, to stay strong. I can't soften and feel sorry for her now. This is about helping Lauren.

'They never found her body,' I say. 'There was blood on her bike. It was damaged, paint from something she'd hit, like a car. An accident, down at the canal. How do you explain all of that?'

But somewhere inside I am thinking, maybe I should have

asked why she thought it was her fault. Why Lauren didn't trust her.

Listen to her...

'There were footprints on the wall,' she says quietly. 'Her things in the water... an old jumper, a book, her keys...'

'But not her,' I say. 'Did you tell them to keep looking? Did you keep asking questions?'

'You think we didn't?' she asks, her eyes looking up at me.

'Tell me about Nanna,' I say, trying to hold her gaze. To return to the original thought; the whole reason she's meant to be here.

She pulls her eyes away. 'I thought you might like this.' She holds out the notebook. She absolutely does not want to talk about Nanna, her own mother. She doesn't care that I have questions, that I want to try to understand. 'It is yours, isn't it?' she asks.

If I say it isn't, she'll take it away. But Lauren would have wanted someone to read it, and that someone to be me.

'Of course it's mine,' I answer with a light smile, reaching out and taking it.

I flip it open, seeing Lauren's girlish handwriting. Surely Mum has already noticed that. Hearts and scribbles. A doodle, flowers. A stick man stabbed cartoonishly through the heart. Initials. *LF 4 PW*. The PW had been crossed out and KC added.

KC

How long since I have seen this book with its *Nice Day* cover? I turn the page.

Once upon a time... it says.

Something crashes into me. I close the notebook quickly. A shudder. Was this why David said I should call Mum? First the necklace, now this? Something he knew, something leading me... where? Somewhere. A scavenger hunt that weaves its way to finding Lauren.

A strange pungent scent from the book steals the breath from my lungs. Lauren's perfume mingled with earthy mildew. I force a smile, enfolding the book tightly in my arms like the girls used to do with their books by the lockers, protective and confrontational.

'Have you read it?' I ask tightly.

'Me?' Mum looks at her nails as if barely interested. 'I assumed it was private. I will if you like.' She extends her hand.

Does she expect me to believe that? That she didn't pry. After all, she read Lauren's diary once; Lauren left her a note inside. *If you're reading this, then you're a fucking bitch.* I know Mum had fumed but couldn't confront Lauren. It was sheer perfection.

Mum definitely read this.

'Look, you said you wanted to talk. Was it really about Nanna?' She's the one to sound impatient now.

I *did* want to talk, yes. But things have changed. 'David said I should see you... and now I have.'

I stand abruptly, clinging to the notebook.

Mum's smile drops. 'That's it?' Her eyes search mine. 'I came all this way for...'

'Yes. Sorry. I'm really rather tired suddenly.' Because I'm desperate to read the notebook.

LF 4 KC

'It's this glandular thing,' I say, making my excuses. 'It affects my energy levels. Comes and goes, you understand. And the nice *lady* doctor said I should avoid stress. But let's wait for the real results, hey?' A false smile. I can't help but dig at her with her own words.

Mum stands uncertainly, glancing around as if to find out what she's missed. For a second she seems lost. Then she lifts the bag that has been sitting at her feet. She tips it out, pouring the contents across the coffee table. I can feel her pulling herself back together, like a monster not ready to be defeated just yet.

'I put food in your fridge. I tidied your kitchen. I got you a new magazine. I even stopped off for fresh donuts because I know you love them. And *this* is how you treat me?'

I'm barely listening. Because on the table I see a packet of pills.

'I have feelings,' Mum is saying, wanting me to look at her.

But my eyes are on those pills. Her pills. The ones she always gave me.

'You want to blame me for what happened to Lauren? For her illness and her behaviour and her mistakes and her loss. Fine. Do it. I'll accept my part.'

What part?

But my eyes are fixed on those pills. And the scent of the book. The words. *Once upon a time...*

Mum starts grabbing at her purse, her lipstick, her keys, all the things that have fallen out. She shoves them back in her bag, like Nanna with the dresses into her suitcase that day. Mum skirts the pills, doesn't appear to notice them. Then suddenly she stands abruptly and asks, 'Why do you hate me?'

The air in the room goes cold, as if a door has suddenly been thrown open.

Because you let Lauren go. You never brought her back. You didn't make them look hard enough. You gave up on her. Even before she went. You wanted a better life, an easier one. To be happy. You left her to suffer, forever and endlessly. You told yourself it was her choice. But it wasn't, it was yours! You wanted this. All of this. Because you never loved her.

That's what I want to say, but I don't.

'I don't hate you,' I say.

Because that is also the truth.

TWENTY-ONE

RENE

Before

I find myself alone on the sofa holding the notebook.

There's something about it, the smell from the earth that has tried to reclaim it, and also some happier scent of Lauren at fourteen: sweet dewberry perfume, vanilla soap, coconut body lotion, cherry lip gloss, and Mum's borrowed Elnett hairspray. Each smell tethered to a memory.

The book has a white cover, decorated with flowers and butterflies. Or did, before it was *married* to the soil, before the filth of years claimed it. Embossed stitches of turquoise, pink and yellow, all sewn through with a silver thread that catches the light. The cover appears to swirl and shift. Or maybe that's the pills, two of which are dissolving in my stomach. Possibly three. Not that anyone's counting.

I feel bad that I called Mum and then sent her away. An aching guilt that I didn't listen. But seeing Mum had upset me more than I had expected. I tell myself it's the book's fault, not mine, or even hers. It just *distracted* me. Convinced me that that was all I needed right now.

I shunt down on the sofa, stretched out under the crochet blanket, enjoying the growing pleasure of the pills. Maybe I'll take one or two more after reading this. Nothing to stop me. I have plenty now. More than enough to do whatever I want...

Yet holding this book, I see fourteen-year-old Lauren sitting by the rose bush at the bottom of our garden. The dappled sunlight dancing over her face as she's reading to me one of her fanciful stories. Our laughter drifting around us like poplar seeds.

Lauren is no longer a girl, not yet a woman. Her face has lengthened, she has small breasts, her new body makes her sit more self-aware. Her hair has darkened, her fringe backcombed. In the past Mum would have brushed her hair until it shone, and then banded it into two obedient bunches, each adorned with a pretty hairband or bow to match her dress. Yet that was long before. Or maybe never. Was Mum ever really that kind of mother? Certainly, by this stage Lauren rejected any attempt to tame her hair – or anything else, for that matter.

But Lauren is excited again. I can hear it in her voice. It's May and she has just met someone. His name is David. She met him at the school Careers Fair, and it's made her happy again. Hopeful. After Pete and the glandular fever and the rumour and the girls. Now she doesn't care because her dream of becoming a writer feels like it's one step closer.

I look down at the notebook, examining it as if to find answers. This book with the *Nice Day* cover embroidered on it. The butterflies poised to flit away. Mum had bought this for Lauren for her fourteenth birthday, and Lauren had dismissed it as too childish, a disappointed look on Mum's face. But secretly, Lauren had liked it.

Read it, Lauren urges me now.

I open it, and immediately I feel an unsettling twist in my stomach, like looking in that box in Mum's wardrobe. Hidden things we weren't meant to find.

Once upon a time...

The smell is replaced by the scent of roses; the ones that Dad planted when Lauren was born. As we sit beside them, I am listening to her voice, her story, even as I see the first brown-tinged edges on the yellow roses. The scent swirls and the brown spreads as Lauren reads me her fairy tale. Words that are beautiful and captivating, and something far more ominous in between.

Once upon a time, there was a Princess. She loved to sit beneath the rose bush at the bottom of the palace gardens. Her father had planted it for her when she was born, intended as a constant reminder of how her parents loved her.

Every summer the roses blossomed, and the smell was sweeter than warm cherries and richer than jasmine at sunset. The roses were yellow. Yellow as the sun or the yolk of an egg.

But evil was at work in the kingdom. A curse that had been waiting in the rocks of distant mountains. A curse that had been cast out by an ancient and vitriolic witch who had released it from her bitter lungs, it flowed down into the kingdom on the wind, and there it waited.

The Princess was happy and growing ever more beautiful, even if the Queen was often sullen and the King was increasingly distant. Still, she believed they loved her. Even if they never said it, she had the roses to reminder her.

For thirteen years.

Then on her fourteenth birthday the curse found her. The curse from the witch. She pricked her finger on a thorn, and seeing the blood, she found she questioned if they loved her. It filled her. And that year, no roses grew to reassure her.

The happiness in the palace faded quickly, and the bushes were nothing more than bare branches and thorns. Passing princes all turned out to be shallow and unkind, and she wondered who, if anyone, would ever really love her.

One evening, with winter approaching, dusk had begun to settle, and the Princess sat in the garden. It was then that she heard a sound at the gate. It sounded like a chorus of people celebrating, which tempted her to look. She lifted the latch on the palace gate and opened it. What harm was there in leaving the garden for just the briefest of moments?

Immediately she was drawn into a raucous crowd. They pushed and jostled, jabbed and tussled, they danced and fought, mingled and wrestled. They trod on her dress, spilled drink on her shawl, tried to manhandle her and touch her, and then they departed, leaving her thrown to the ground, barely recognizable as a princess at all.

She tried to run back to the palace, but the gate was locked from the inside, and it was only then that she felt truly afraid. Locked out. Alone. She fell down and wept.

Then she heard a voice.

'Are you alone?' a man asked, and she raised her face to see a handsome reveller.

'Yes,' she replied, for his voice seemed kind.

'Why are you so sad?' the Handsome Reveller asked, and she

realized only then that that was exactly what she felt. No one else had ever asked her why.

'They don't want me,' she said. 'They never did. And now I can't get back inside.'

But the Reveller just laughed, warm and throaty and inviting. 'Inside? Why would you want to go back in there? The world is far more exciting than any palace. Come with me, and I will show you.' He reached out his hand.

And so it was that the Princess took it, feeling its strange exciting energy, his warmth and protection. They rode through the night on the wind of excitement, but when she reached his home, a small white cottage lit by moonlight, he threw her in a tiny cell, made her his servant, and was brutal and cruel. Sometimes there was a place he put her with no light at all. Deep and dark. Soon she forgot that she had ever been a princess. Or had ever thought she was loved.

But as the wind grew colder and the nights grew darker, the Princess realized that the loss of the yellow roses had only been the beginning of the curse. Deeper and darker. She regretted the day she had ever stepped outside the gate or met the Handsome Reveller or agreed to go with him. She knew that things could still get much worse... that this wasn't the end of the story.

TWENTY-TWO

JANE

Today

Jane waits in her kitchen, which has taken on a slightly earthy smell. It's the girl and the notebook. And the thought of what might have happened.

She stands in the steady low January light that will soon start to be hugged by early darkness. She's already switched on the lights under the units, grateful for the soft glow. She realizes she hasn't really known what waiting feels like until this. She's waited for pregnancy tests, and blood test results for herself and Alice; she's waited on university entrance results and exams and to hear that Aidan has changed his mind and will go to uni after all. He hadn't. She's waited to hear if she got a job or a house, this house.

But now she is waiting for someone she barely knows. Jim Fisher. A man she met briefly many years ago. Who owned this house with his wife before they had. And that wait is killing her.

Jane busies herself in the kitchen, washing the cups in the sink – she usually puts them straight in the dishwasher – but this gives her cause to stand looking out the window at the leafless rose bush with its mound of damp, almost-frozen mud heaped in front of it. And a hole.

She came back for the notebook, Jane thinks.

She glances back at Rene who has barely moved, other than to sip her Coke and, once or twice, open the book and peer inside it.

Have they done the right thing to call her father? Has she made the police realize how urgent this is? Jane feels protective of Rene, has a sense that she doesn't trust anyone near her, so vulnerable and damaged, childlike in her manners. And dirty. A fleeting thought: *It's as if she's dug herself up from this very back garden.*

The police will find out where she's been, what happened to her. All the questioning, that in itself will be quite an ordeal.

She starts boiling the kettle again, for her and for Dan. Dan has made himself scarce elsewhere in the house, he's good at that. And Jim. Will Jim take tea when he arrives? She checks the time. Seven more minutes, give or take. And what will they say to each other? The return of one of his daughters, and the frightening news about the other.

Because Lauren is still missing.

Jane comes out from behind the kitchen counter and approaches the chair where Rene is sitting. Should she offer her some socks for her feet, a blanket for her knees? The kitchen is warm, but the girl is shivering.

'I'm making more tea if you like,' she says softly. 'Or is there anything else I can get you; maybe you're hungry?'

The girl looks at her and her gaunt face and tiny wrists suggests she must often have been hungry, but she shifts her head and shakes it just a little to say she is not.

'Right.' Jane straightens, turns, then turns back and looks at the book clutched in Rene's hands. This is why the girl is here. Or part of the reason. Rene thinks this is her home. Time has stood still for her wherever she has been and she doesn't know that another life has gone on here. If Jane had been at her doctor's appointment just a little later or decided to go shopping or gone back to work, what then? Would Rene have stayed, waiting to be let into the house. She might have hunkered down next to the garage, waiting for them to return. Or tried to break in, or even just wandered off. Jane might have been none the wiser.

Still she feels the question on her tongue. 'What's in your book?' She tries to sound casual, not riddled with intrigue as if all the answers might be written inside it.

Rene tugs it into her. Into her belly that is all jumper and shirt and no fat at all. She's not letting it out of her grasp.

'Did you write something in it, or did someone else?'

The girl nods, maybe not aware that she has given one answer to two questions. Jane waits, but she doesn't say more.

So, she stands, letting her eyes stray towards the front door. She wonders if Jim will be here any minute. 'A watched pot never boils,' she thinks, hearing her mother's voice say those words.

She goes back to the counter and the cupboards and starts getting the teapot out, filling it with two Yorkshire teabags and setting out three mugs. One for each of them: her and Dan and Jim. It feels like the wrong thing to be doing but she can't think of anything better. She's not sure she's prepared for such a situation as this.

A family reunion, of sorts.

TWENTY-THREE

RENE

Before

I throw the notebook away. It isn't a fairy tale, it's horrible and frightening. It hits the pot plants, and one of them tumbles off the sill. The pot shatters.

My phone buzzes and I jump at the sound.

'Hello?' I say, picking it up quickly, expecting to hear Mum fishing for an apology. She's home and she's found the courage to start shouting at me, to say all the things she didn't when she was here.

'It's me,' he says instead.

'David?' My relief palpable.

'Are you OK?'

'Yes,' I say, even if it's a lie. *I just read something horrible, about a girl that gets taken away by this Handsome Reveller and how he locks her up forever.*

'Rene?' he asks, leaving space for me to reply. When I don't, he says, 'Tell me, how's the story coming?'

'Story?'

I find myself scooping up soil and I cut my finger on the

broken pot. Instinctively, I suck it and it tastes of soil and metallic blood. Like that day at the canal. The bike-dog incident, when all this started to slide.

'I mean the assignment...' David tries to clarify into my silence. 'The one you're writing for us.' His tone drops, more hushed. 'More importantly, for Lauren.'

Is that what he's after, her story? Like juice from some exotic fruit. Because really, what does any of this have to do with him? Why is he so concerned about her? Maybe Mum is right. I am nothing more than another hopeful young writer. Being naïve.

'I know that you're starting to see the truth,' he says.

How could he know that? How could he know what the truth is? Maybe I *should* be wary of him. But then he's the one who has kept me going. His kind words, his encouragement. He believed in Lauren, like he believes in me. He just wants to keep me going. And I owe him. Because...

'You're remembering,' he says.

'Yes,' I reply. 'I'm remembering things...' As if letting out an inch on a rope. 'Things I thought I'd lost. Or haven't allowed myself to remember.'

'That's good. Because deep down you know why she went. And more importantly,' he pauses, his tone lowering further, 'you know what's stopping her from coming back?'

It takes me a second to realize what he just said.

Outside, despite the darkness, there's a flash of lightning. Or is it just the force with which I blink?

'Stopping her? What do you mean "stopping her"?' My mind reels. 'She can't come home, or she would.'

'You believe that?' he says.

'Of course I believe that. Someone has her, someone cruel.' I struggle to find the words. 'They took her, and they won't let her go. She can't escape.'

'Why? How are they keeping her? How are they doing that?'

I look up at the picture of Nanna then down at the notebook still on the floor. *A curse passed down through generations.*

'I... don't know,' I falter, tears welling. Some feeling inside so huge and jagged that it will tear me apart if it tries to come out.

I look up at the window. The threat of a hard storm. Shadow and leaves dance across the pavement, another flash of lightning, unseen branches bending and twisting in a mounting wind.

'You spoke to your mother,' David says. It's not a question, it's a statement.

'How do you know?'

A vision of her dress sliding open. Her strappy heels, her painted nails, that bounce in her hair.

'You need to listen to her. Ask her about Nanna. Ask her why she was hurt and angry that day. Why Lauren didn't trust her. If you want to get Lauren back, ask her for the truth.'

I open my mouth to say something. *It's her fault.* I've told myself that a million times. Or have I been told that a million times...? And by whom?

I look up, seeing someone moving out of view. The hem of a grey coat hurrying to the right, in the direction of the steps down to my porch. A dog running ahead off its lead; a brown-black boxer, just like the one from the canal, the day of the bike-dog incident. A taste of blood and dirt in my mouth. I shudder.

'Look, I have to go,' David says.

'No, David, please. Don't—'

I'm scared to be alone. I need him to stay and talk to me. My mind is scattering, maybe the pills or the need for more of them. Or the storm that has suddenly started. Heavy fat rain. Another crack of thunder. Maybe the man in the grey coat is approaching my door even as we speak.

'Tell me something,' I say. 'Tell me about some argument you had with the people in accounts. Or the stupid advertorial that marketing wants you to run. Tell me about how useless the boy in the coffee shop was this morning, who gave you semi and not full. Or that new writer you took on who can't even spell their own name. Or maybe her, Red Lips. Your new personal assistant. Is she still filtering? Tell me, David, tell me anything... David? *David!*'

Maybe it's the storm, but the line has gone dead.

TWENTY-FOUR

RENE

Before

At the eyehole, I can't see anyone, despite looking repeatedly.

I've cleaned up the broken plant. I've found my luckiest non-pair of socks: space cats and rainbow hearts. Now I wait on the sofa in the low light, grateful for the lamp on the desk. It seems to brighten things just a little, but barely enough.

Outside, the rain pours, occasional flashes of lightning. Water runs along the street in rivulets, and even the brickwork has turned blotchy with damp. I listen for a sound at the door, think I hear something and then think I hear nothing. Who would be out in this? Only a madman.

I lift Lauren's fairy tale again, running my fingers over its cover. The smell has lessened, more perfume than earth now. I get up and sleepwalk over to the window. Something in that dim storm-light, I see the rain drumming, then gradually lessening, then drips like last tears, something therapeutic in it finally stopping. *Drip drop.* The light begins to clear.

I feel quietened, released. My thoughts calmer. I take the notebook over to the desk and set it there.

Write... David's voice in my head.

But I can't. Not now.

Or maybe because... I didn't listen to her. Next time I will. If there is a next time.

Out in the corridor at the door I peer out the eyehole again, this time bothered to see what I see. The view is empty, but not entirely. There's no man in a grey coat or a black-brown dog. But my bike sits back in place, the wheel perfectly workable. Was it Dad I heard during the storm? Was he knocking, trying to get my attention?

I fetch my mobile and reluctantly call him.

'Hello, love,' he says, a gush of enthusiasm at the sound of my voice.

'Was it you?' I ask tightly.

'"Was it me" what?' For a moment he sounds confused.

'The bike. You fixed it? Did you put it out there?'

'Well, I promised I would, didn't I?'

I stare out the eyehole then turn and look at the corridor, the red walls, all the pictures and objects carefully arranged. Lauren on her bike with stabilizers, Dad grinning beside her. Mum, Dad and Lauren on the pontoon in France. That badly drawn dragonfly sketch, not good enough to take pride of place on anyone else's wall. None of these things would be here if it wasn't for him. What he did... making her absent from our lives.

'You can't fix things,' I say angrily. Seeing Lauren at six and seven and eleven and fourteen... 'It's too late. And you're the one that broke them.'

'I'm sorry.' His voice sounds smaller, more uncertain. 'Please don't be angry at me. I didn't mean to—'

I think of what I asked Mum: 'Do you think you two did enough to try to find her?'

He draws in breath. 'We did everything. Everything we could,' he says. 'And I'd have done anything,' his voice cracking. 'Anything. I mean, people said Lauren was troubled, but they also said she was special. Pretty and clever, curious and smart, and determined. They said she could have been anything, and yes, all of that was true. But there was more, so much more. Things no one else knew.' He paused, suddenly overwhelmed. 'Because she was *my* Lauren, my *amazing* daughter—' his voice shatters. A sob escapes. 'It hurt so much to lose her like that. That they took her. It broke my heart.'

There's a pinching breathlessness in my chest. An ache so deep. I want to hold him, hug him.

But I can't. I can't let him fool me. It's a lie. My defences, my self-preservation. 'This is your fault. You know it's all your fault. Yours more than Mum's. You're a liar.'

'I didn't mean to... I never—'

'Stop it!' I shout. 'I should never have called you. Ever. I can't speak to you. You make me so *angry*. David said I should try to look and listen in a new way, but I can't. I don't hear anything different.'

'How can you talk to him and not me?' He sounds so rejected. 'Why will you listen to what he says and not me? Your own father, who loves you?' The question swirls, hanging there in the corridor like some magician's trick levitating above me. Any moment now it will come crashing down to the floor.

'Because... because...'

He's right. Why do I turn to David for support and hate Dad? Dad who used to love us so much, be there for us. So much more than Mum.

'Because... Lauren did something to hurt David. And I'm... trying to make up for it. But you, you hurt her, and then you gave up looking.'

'No,' Dad pleads. 'I'd have done anything to bring her home. Anything. It wasn't me that brought danger into our home. It was—'

'Liar,' I shout, and I cut the call.

· · ·

Back in the living room, I'm agitated from speaking to him. I pace, restless, my thoughts racing. I swallow two more pills. Maybe too many.

On the desk is the fairy tale. It doesn't change anything. None of it does. Lauren is still there in the darkness of Missing. I think I'm solving things with these clues, but I'm just unravelling. I'm not stronger, I'm weaker. And Lauren is still endlessly suffering. No one to rescue her. Only people who claim she was special but didn't bring her home. Mum, Dad, David. Even Pete. All guilty.

Then I think of what Dad said: *It wasn't me that brought that danger into our home.*

So who was it?

I put pen on paper, watching as it comes. His name. That first moment we met him.

July. Hot. Ice-cream weather.

Chalk dust dancing in sunlight beams, coloured by the stained glass of school windows. The whole day passing reluctantly. Time dripping as if melting in the heat. School almost finished for the year, the summer term crawling to an end. The Careers Fair displays dismantled, projects sent home, artwork unpinned from the walls, leaving marks and odd clumps of Blu Tack. Everyone tired of school by then, even the teachers were done.

One. More. Week.

It limped towards summer vacation.

Outside the street was already deserted. No mothers left standing, not in that heat. Not a car on the road, or a bird in the sky. Yet there we were, and so was he.

Mr Colson.

He was chatting with Mum, and she laughed in that way she sometimes did, with her head tipped back. 'Flirty,' that's what Dad would have called it. And fourteen-year-old Lauren hadn't liked it. She hadn't liked it one bit.

She didn't want to be there in that heat any more than that brown-black dog did. It was pacing in slow, anxious circles, foaming as it panted. Maybe that was why Lauren had thought of stroking the poor beast.

At that exact moment, Mr Colson put his hand on Mum's arm, his fingers on her bare flesh in that strappy dress. Lauren reached to stroke the dog, and Mum laughed. Maybe that was why the dog barked, lurched, bared its teeth.

Lauren pulled away, her fingers wrapping around her wrist. Chewed fingernails with chipped purple polish that she had been told for 'the last time' not to wear to school. How many times had she been sent to the science labs to remove it with acetone? But today it was even too hot for that. They'd let it slide. The nails looked like four small puncture wounds. Like teeth marks. As if the dog had actually bitten.

'Jesus!?' Mum said. 'What kind of bloody dog is that?'

And Mr Colson had smiled as he said, 'She's a boxer-rottie cross.' He said it proudly, and yet it made Mum draw in breath as if blowing up a balloon in reverse. 'She's normally very placid,' he reassured. Then he moved towards Lauren and whispered low, so only she could hear. 'She's probably just a little jealous.'

A chill breeze flashed through the air, and in the heat it felt delicious.

Lauren had already noticed Mr Colson standing at the school gates a few times before, had once thought she'd seen him smile at her. She lowered her head and looked at her wrist where she was pretending the dog had bitten her. Maybe she even blushed.

'Are you all right, Lauren?' Mum demanded. 'I mean, he didn't actually bite you, did he? Would he?' She had already turned her attention back to Mr Colson. Lauren was annoyed at how little she cared, but not entirely surprised.

'Actually,' Mr Colson said, looking to Lauren, his delicious smile again, 'it's a she. She's a bitch.' He meant the dog, or maybe not.

Lauren turned, her smile only half-choked behind her hand, and she let her eyes creep back to look at him. She knew he knew what he had said. And that was when we saw it, his boyish, forgivable charm. His rough-at-the-edges appeal. Even though he was older than Lauren, and younger than Mum. A look that made them both vie for his attention. The whole reason they were standing in the blazing hot street. His dark curls, his swimming-pool eyes, the flex of his cheek as he smiled, all illuminated by the intense summer light. A lick of sweat on his forehead.

I didn't like it. But I could see it. Could see why.

There was no air, no shade, no breeze. Only the red-brick school minus its four hundred pupils. A silent language lab full of head-sets hung on hooks, a lobby full of portraits and prizes. A few teachers shuffling papers, drinking a last bad coffee in an old, familiar mug, longing to light a forbidden cigarette after a long,

*weary afternoon. But we stood together in the heat in the road
outside for what felt like forever.*

'I think this was a bad idea,' Mum said, breaking the silence.

'All your ideas are bad ideas,' Lauren snarled.

*Mr Colson settled the dispute. 'I thought you needed help with
your car.' He put his hands in his jeans pocket, casually. 'Like I
said, I can come back to yours and give this old thing a once-
over.' He tapped the bonnet of Mum's car and smiled at her.*

*'I'm not getting in the car with that dog,' Lauren said. The dog
that was now slumped on the pavement, melted into a puddle of
panting fur, almost even cute.*

'Oh, for God's sake,' Mum said, a line of sweat on her top lip too.

'But I don't want—'

*'Lauren, nobody cares anymore what you want. Would it be too
much for you to put someone else's needs first? It's you I have to
ferry around in this old thing. He's just trying to help me, which
is more than I can say for your dad. He heads off each morning in
his company car and returns late from... wherever, while I have
to use this old heap.'*

'Mum, it bit me!' Lauren protested.

'No, it didn't. It's just another of your made-up stories.'

Mr Colson looked between mother and daughter.

Then Mum proceeded to walk to the driver's door and get in, reaching down into the well next to the gear stick and pulling out her sunglasses. Something was bringing on one of her headaches, you could tell.

'I really can fix it,' Mr Colson insisted. 'I'm good with these old beauties.' He leaned towards the open door. 'The one thing I know how to handle is cars.'

He had his hand on the roof, revealing a damp circle under the armpits of his shirt. Then he said something else, something only Mum could hear. She nodded her head, her smile uncoiling, and she laughed, head tipped back. Flirty...

'I'm NOT getting in with that dog,' Lauren reiterated. 'And if you fuck *him, I'll tell Dad.' It was calm and hard and sure, splitting the heat in two.*

Mum stared at her with a look of pure fury. 'See?' she asked the audience on the other side of the windscreen. 'Lyrical enough for you? Is that what you teach her in school?' She peered up at Mr Colson.

'He doesn't teach me. He's a sub.'

He shifted awkwardly, a little of his confidence dented. 'For now,' he said, gently lowering his hand from the roof, a flicker of disappointment. 'But if I was your teacher, I'd say you have a wonderful imagination, an interesting turn of phrase and a healthy awareness of risk.' His eyes fixed on Lauren. 'Take it as a compliment.'

She smelled him then, his mix of sweat and aftershave, his proximity and his energy, too close and too wrong. His hand resting on her arm. She hadn't seen him do that. She didn't pull away.

'Me, I'm a book lover and a classic car enthusiast in my free time.' He leaned in closer to Lauren and said quietly, 'And I don't fuck mothers.'

'Where's your car?' Lauren asked. 'Why don't you go in that?'

'Sure, you want a ride with me?' He picked up his toolbox and started walking back towards a polished classic convertible Jaguar, the colour of Sunday-roast mustard.

'No,' Mum snapped, a protective uncertainty creeping into her voice. 'Lauren comes with me.'

So, Mr Colson tailed us like one of those old cop shows on TV. Mum didn't speak to Lauren the whole way home. Colson parked up on the drive and set to work under the bonnet of Mum's car, and Mum offered him a beer, stepping over the dog in her skimpy sundress. Lauren heard her asking about his job. Heard Colson saying he taught English when he could. Had once thought he would be a writer. An embarrassed shrug and a slug of beer before lowering his head back under the hood.

'Lie Down in Darkness,' Mum said, as if from nowhere. Mr Colson reappeared from under the bonnet. 'It was my favourite book,' she said. A piece of knowledge that no one knew, or maybe had never bothered to ask.

Mr Colson reached into his shirt pocket and pulled out a white packet of cigarettes. He offered one to Mum, and she accepted. He lit it for her with a little yellow lighter, and she exhaled naturally, right there in Meadow Close, where anyone could see.

'What's your first name, Mr Colson?' Mum asked, tucking a strand of hair behind her ear, not bothering to hide her coyness.

'William,' he said quietly, 'As in Styron.'

Mum smiled, and seemed to like that he knew who had written her favourite book.

They smoked.

In silence.

There was a smear of something black across William's cheek, and Mum's hand kept reaching up and falling away as if she wanted to wipe it but was afraid to. Then he put out the cigarette and grinned, before lowering his head back under the hood, and Mum returned inside.

Later, Lauren wandered over and asked about the dog. Colson told her he walked her down by the canal some days. He asked if she'd ever been there. She told him that it used to be one of her favourite places. 'Magical,' she said. He nodded. She still liked to go there sometimes.

'Maybe I'll see you,' he said.

'Maybe,' she said vaguely.

A short while later, he came to the kitchen door, called out to Mum that he was finished. Mum called back that she was 'up here', and I watched as he crossed the kitchen, putting his hand on the white curl of the banister and slowly climbed the stairs. As if he knew Lauren was watching. A conflict of jealousy and rage rising with each step he took.

He never returned to school in September. He was forgotten by Mum and the rest of the teachers. By everyone. But not Lauren.

And then three months later, Lauren went missing.

I run to the bathroom, waves of nausea flowing through me, vomiting into the bowl. Eventually I smear a hand over the back of my mouth, rinsing it with water. Spitting out bile.

Too many pills, or this illness, or maybe just the horror of realizing Mum knew about Mr Colson. She was the one who invited danger into our home. So why hadn't anyone mentioned him to the police? Demanded to speak to him, to go there, see for themselves. To check if Lauren was there. *Always in the last place you look.* Dad's voice. Dad's stupid expressions. *Hindsight is a powerful thing.* Isn't it just, Dad? Isn't it just.

I peer into the mirror, and it's almost as if I see her face peering back. Bruised, hollow-eyed, terrified. A palette of autumn and dead leaves.

Mum should have told them about that day, her little secret with their coy cigarette, talking of books and her hand rising and falling. Him climbing our stairs like a slow determined invader. Or was she too embarrassed to admit it? That she brought him in.

Just one more thing she preferred to keep hidden. Pushed to the back of memory like a box in the wardrobe. Secret things she didn't want anyone to know about.

And what was the price of that?

TWENTY-FIVE

LAUREN

Before

It was dark in here. A black hell. I've cried, I've died. I was back to trying to keep a grip on sanity. Not to scream and lose the game. Or starve.

I reached up and untangled my hair, because that's where I'd hidden the pen. Or at least the twisted plastic inner ink tube from the Biro; nothing more than a thin blue vein with a nib. I held it firmly in my hand so I wouldn't drop it, lose it into the darkness, and then I let my fingers slide between my legs and into my pants where the sheet of folded notepaper was tucked like a sanitary pad.

Stupid? Maybe not, Keele. Let's just see where this leads us.

Because this was the only place I could write this note and him not see. So, I held the paper down on the concrete. Felt where the corners were. And on the top right I put *November. Wednesday*. No date. No year. It didn't matter, and I didn't know anyway. It could be October still, and any day of the week. There's nothing to tell me. Time is fluid, slipping and sliding. No sell-by dates or newspapers or magazines. Even the dates on the long-life milk cartons were no longer any use. Nothing fresh. But the weather seemed like November, and I liked Wednesdays. That's the day we used to have English Language, creative writing with Mrs Holmes. It didn't matter, not when they read what I had to write. The date would be the last thing on their mind.

And the lad who I had seen yesterday was going to help me. Even if he didn't know it yet, he was going to be my hero. I even thought I recognized him. He was going to take my letter. Because if a postman could bring a letter, he could take one away. Sometimes Keele sent letters back. Like the one I had seen last week in the drawer. A woman's name scored through. Jacqueline French. NOT KNOWN AT THIS ADDRESS.

I wondered if she was an ex-girlfriend. Even his ex-wife. It made me think of the dusting of pink blusher powder I'd found in the bathroom drawer. And that cherry lip gloss, although that seemed more childish. Which made me think of the children's book amongst those on the shelf in the back bedroom. Had there been a mother and child here before?

This morning, at breakfast I had knocked the pen off the counter, stood on it, heard the plastic crunch as it snapped. And Keele came over and gripped me by the chin; hard, tight, brutal. Breathing onto my face.

'I'm so clumsy,' I said and I started to cry, and he started to laugh and he let me go. He knew I loved my pens, my writing, would never damage one of those. Even if these days he checked everything I wrote. Could only write freely in my head these days. Strange distorted things, becoming worse than dreams.

I put the broken pen in the bin, and could barely breathe as I stuffed the blue vein of ink up into my sleeve. Only later I hid it in the tangled knot of my hair. Because I had to write something soon and not in full view, not where Keele could see what I was up to. The note that would escape just like the necklace had. He'd started strip-searching me again. The paranoia had returned. More binders, more time in The Hole. More pills. More sleep. Occasionally I hid them. One or two. Here and there.

I'd seen the postman when I was sitting in the little room with the frosted window and the wire inside that looked like hair trapped in ice. I was polishing car parts when suddenly there was a commotion. The dog had barked first. Then a lad's voice had started shouting 'Oi, get your FUCKING dog away from me!'

Barking, barking. Shouting.

I shuffled over and looked down and there was someone just on the other side of the glass, squeezed between the side passage and the outside wall of the shed. What was he doing there? I imagined I saw a plume of smoke. His padded jacket with the orange strip distorted as it brushed against the white pebbledash.

I thought of shouting, hammering on the glass, making him look up and see me at the window. But Keele would have got to me or maybe hurt this lad before he could get away. Really hurt him.

So my mind went back and forth. *Shout. Don't shout. Shout. Don't shout.* Still the scream was already in my throat, trying to find its way out, but fear held it in.

'Hel-lo... hell-o!' I whisper-shouted.

But the postman had already run off. 'Fucking kick your dog in the face if it COMES NEAR me again...' I heard him holler as he fled.

I looked at the car part I had been cleaning, thought about throwing it at the glass, wondering whether it would be enough to break it or at least get the lad's attention. But it would probably only attract Keele's. And I didn't want his attention. Besides, the pieces he gave me were only small and light. Nothing I could hurt him with or break things with, like I had before.

What the hell are you doing here? Keele's voice. *Get the fuck away.*

'I was just—' the lad shouted back, voices fading.

But the voice of the lad was drowned out by the relentless barking of the dog.

Get out of here, you freak. I'll kill you if you ever come back.

'And I'll call the police on you!'

And then silence.

Was there something familiar about his voice too?

Had he looked and sounded like Pete?

Maybe Pete had regretted something after all. Maybe he'd come looking for me... had seen me up there beyond the glass. Even now, as I sat in the blackness of The Hole thinking about it, knowing he might be telling them. 'Yes, I saw her. It was definitely her. By the window. It was Lauren. We have to go back for her.'

Could I wait for that?

No.

I had to write this letter.

I wrote each word in the dark, not knowing if one word was on top of the other. I thought of someone actually receiving it, and who that might be. What if it found its way to Mum? How would she react, seeing the ugly truth that was escaping from me as I wrote.

When I got out, I was going to slide my letter inside the one with the address scored out, seal it shut again with the last of my precious glue, all used up from sticking those horrible stories and pictures up. Then my letter would go, out into the world, maybe with that postman, the one that might be Pete, and someone would open it. My little cry for help, black on white, written in this hole. Written on concrete in utter darkness. And on the front of that envelope would be this address with a blood-red scrawl across it in Keele's *own* handwriting. And the name of a woman I didn't know. Jacqueline French.

Genius. Not so stupid Little L after all.

Because that's how they will find me.

TWENTY-SIX

RENE

Before

I wake from another nightmare, shivering and cold. Maybe the heating has gone off, unpaid bills. That's all. I'll take a hot shower, after that I'll feel OK. Maybe I'll make an effort to get dressed, put on some make-up. Try to go out, meet friends or go back to work. Back on track.

I close my eyes, because I've yet to make a list today. And this one is a bit different. More of a plea.

- *I want a normal life.*
- *One that isn't splintered with nightmares.*
- *One that doesn't cling to every thread of hope.*
- *One where this stops now.*

Because those other lists, they're just interferences. And I'm done with that.

I wander along the red corridor, gazing at the front door, my bike visible, right there on the other side. I could carry on like before. Before the bike-dog incident. I could make myself go back to that life when I questioned less and enjoyed more. Skipping merrily between donuts and distractions. Instead, this is eating me alive. But... I can't. Things have... shifted. And something is coming for me.

The truth.

I go into the bathroom, turn on the shower. The water is warm, or at least warmer than I feel. I stand under it until I've stopped shivering, and feel cleaner and fresher and almost ready for a new day. Getting out, I see Pete and Lauren's picture still sitting on the ledge. I should hang that back up; I should, but I don't.

I wrap myself in a soft fluffy towel and drift back along the corridor to the front door. I stand on tiptoes to peer out the eyehole. Yes, bike still there. Ready for my day. Tempting me to come out, get on. Off to work. See how easy it could be. I could go and see David, or a bike ride, down at the... *No!*

But as I step back, I see a letter lying on the carpet.

I pick it up and examine the envelope. It doesn't have my address on it, only words sprawled across it: NOT KNOWN AT THIS ADDRESS. And a name. Someone's that I don't recognize: *Jacqueline French.* Who is that?

My head begins to pound, my hands to tremble. Already I sense I don't want to open it and even less to read it. Because it isn't a bill or a reminder, and it isn't a postcode lottery offer.

I slide my finger along the edge, careful not to cut myself. I draw out the little folded sheet of paper, grubby and crumpled. The handwriting is girlish, like the words in the fairy tale. Except this is messy, overlapped. A desperate message with horror scrawled through it.

Lauren's words on the page.

November.

Wednesday. I think.

He's going to kill me.

I'm going to die in here.

His name is Keele. He's keeping me locked up in total darkness and don't think I haven't thought about trying to escape. I've nowhere to go and he'd catch me before I got anywhere, and bad things wait out there too. I know. He says I'm just confused. That he is the one protecting me, making me better. That's what I asked him to do.

I don't remember.

Take this letter to the police. Tell them to bring a gun. Because he's big. Much bigger than me. And he's got a dog. I'm out past the old white cottage along the lane on Prestleigh Hill. We're all alone here. When you come, I'll say my name is Cathy and I'll blink three times. Then you'll know it's me. <u>Cathy</u>. *Because that's what he's told me to say. Not Lauren. Never Lauren. He says I can't trust anyone. So we have to use this signal. OK? Cathy. Three blinks.*

If you can't see me, I'm under the garage. Under and to the left, below the hatch. Beneath the rug. Behind the kitchen cupboard. It's made of concrete. God knows I've scraped at it enough. So I know.

If he sees this letter, he'll kill me for sure. DO NOT SHOW IT TO HIM.

Maybe I have written this all on top of itself. Maybe it is hard to read. I'm writing this in utter utter darkness, on concrete. But I have no choice. This is the only place, because he sees ALL.

You probably don't believe me but tell the police to come. Don't come yourself. He'll convince you that everything is A OK. Because he's a psychopath. DO NOT IGNORE. DO NOT!! THIS IS <u>NOT</u> A JOKE. You have to <u>BELIEVE</u> me before it's too late. Promise.

Oh, my real name is Lauren Fisher. Did I tell you that already? I don't know how old I am, but I've been here a long time. My parents know, but they don't care. They've never replied to my emails or come to see me. Even though they know I'm here. The truth is Mum tried to kill me first. That's what Nanna told me. And maybe Keele's right that I was born bad. He's just trying to make me better. But it has to stop. Or he'll kill me.

Please
Lauren.

TWENTY-SEVEN

RENE

Before

Mum lifts her mug and sips her tea, keeping her eyes on me. Doesn't seem to see the letter I'm holding. Or is she trying to ignore it? I can't believe I called and asked her to come. Or how fast she came this time. Yet now she's here, uncertainty swills in my stomach.

'They say it is going to snow tomorrow.' She looks towards the window, as if I have asked her about the weather. 'That's early, isn't it?'

On the table, a magazine she's brought me. *November: Short Days, Darker Nights.*

Didn't she hear the urgency in my voice? As I told her I had something I needed to show her.

Soon we'll call the police, side-by-side, holding hands for courage. She'll barely be able to contain her tears. Shouting at them – *come now!* Finally, we can save her.

'Mum,' I say, needing to pull her back from talk of imminent snow. 'I have something you need to—'

But she interrupts me, as if some part of her can sense

what's coming and doesn't want it. 'I know how hard this has all been on you. All these years... living this life... I feel so terrible for you. It's taken its toll, hasn't it?' Her gaze is wistful. 'But hopefully soon you'll start to feel better again. To feel strong enough to carry on as you were before.'

'No!' I snap. I need to show her the letter. We can't get distracted. Not today. I have proof of what is happening. In black and white.

But she isn't listening. 'Because we don't want this to get hold of you again,' her voice suppressing mine. 'Lauren wouldn't want this for you.' Soft pleading in her voice. 'She'd have wanted you to live the life she couldn't. You could be anything. And yet, here you are doing' – she gazes around my small flat – 'this.'

'As if you'd *care* what Lauren really wants.' The comment bursts from me. *You never loved her!* The letter scrumpled in my furious grip. *You even tried to—*

No, show her the letter first.

But Mum closes her eyes as if a reset before saying quietly, 'This *illness* of yours. These strange ideas. These... things you imagine. It's dangerous.' I open my mouth to say something, but she says, 'And I should know.'

My fingers tighten on the letter, thinking of Nanna's voice. What Lauren has written here. 'She thought you wanted to harm her, didn't she?'

Mum gazes up at the framed postcard of Nanna, before her eyes return to her own hands.

'She did,' she says quietly.

Mum closes her eyes and they remain shut for a long time, as if searching for something inside her. When she opens them they glisten, trapped tears. I can see she's resolved to tell me something.

'When Lauren was born, I became... unwell.' She fumbles

over the words. 'My mind played tricks on me. I didn't know what the truth was anymore.'

She opens her hands as if showing me something, but there's nothing, they are empty. Then she reaches down into the bag at her feet and rummages before pulling out a white packet. It takes a moment for me to realize it's cigarettes, like the ones she smoked with Colson that day, loitering by the car. She opens the lid and slides one out.

'I didn't know you...' but she waves my words away with the unlit cigarette between her fingers as if they are smoke.

She takes out a little yellow lighter and lights the cigarette. She takes a long breath in, holding it, before releasing something of herself on the whitened breath. Her shoulders fall.

'After Lauren was born, I heard things,' she says. 'I heard Lauren crying in the sound of running water when I took a shower. I heard it in the ringing of the phone. In the whir of the washing machine, in the wind through the leaves of the trees. In the kettle boiling or even in the silence. Everything carried the sound of her crying. It never stopped, and yet... it wasn't her.'

Mum takes another draw on the cigarette, delicate against her red lips; she's painted her mouth just like her nails. I can imagine Mr Colson watching them, that day, fascinating and beautiful as she is. I burn with a certain type of rage as her cigarette burns down.

She toys with the yellow lighter. 'I was always afraid I might harm her.'

'But you never would have,' I insist. I want her to reassure me. My eyes on her. 'Would you...?'

'When Lauren was about six months old, I went for a walk by the canal. I had been cooped up, afraid to leave the house, confined and overwhelmed. Everyone else seemed to gush over their new babies, how well they were feeding, how well they slept, their milestones and developments. Everyone, that was, except me. I was exhausted, knew something was wrong. Even as she lay there quietly, I heard her endlessly crying.'

Another draw on the cigarette. Another release of smoke.

'Your dad said it would do me good to get out. A bit of sun on my face, wouldn't do me any harm.' She smiles, but it is derisive. 'I couldn't stop the sound of her crying. As if she was suffering, and I couldn't do anything to help her.'

Another plume of white smoke uncoils into the air like an unworldly confession.

'That day at the canal, the sky was grey and huge. The water was agitated as if it knew something. I pushed her along the path in her pram, asking myself what I was doing there. Even if I knew...'

She drags on the cigarette more urgently. Something is unravelling within her. Something Nanna had said, that is written in Lauren's letter. What was Mum going to do?

'They say babies can sense tension, but Lauren was silent. She just lay there, contented, eyes wide, watching the clouds lumbering across the sky. But I could hear her still. Crying. Always crying.'

I think of the sound I hear late at night, of Lauren whispering to me. Of her sobbing. Pleading. Terrible things. I hear it in the leaves at the canal, in the running of water. I can't shut her out either. Was that how it was for Mum? That inescapable, endless sound of pain.

'I sat on a bench beside the canal, wondering why I had taken Lauren there. I was afraid for her and for me. I sat with my hands in my lap, staring at them, clinging to my own hands as if I could control them. Yet I watched myself reaching into her pram, saw myself lifting her up, tugging her free of her blanket—'

Without warning Mum drops the cigarette into the glass. It hisses angrily against a drop of water. Extinguished.

'Not long after, I went away for a while. I was diagnosed

with Postpartum Psychosis. There wasn't much known about it back then, and there wasn't a great deal of support. Your dad took care of Lauren, and I went... somewhere to recuperate. A nice place by the sea, that's what my mother called it.' She glances towards the window again, as if she still might see it, or hear the sound of gulls. An uncertain smile. 'She called it my confinement.'

'You told Lauren all this?' I ask, but she doesn't seem to hear me. She's gazing at the window. Is she thinking of the sea view, hearing the gulls?

'Your dad was wonderful with Lauren, and she was happy with him. They seemed to bond instantly. I had always wanted a perfect little family, something to repair what I never had. And there it was, right in front of me. Except I wasn't part of it.'

'Nanna said something to Lauren, didn't she? She told her you tried to—'

'That witch. She told Lauren about me not wanting her, about me not loving her. Being cold, which was rich coming from her. So, I had no choice. I told Lauren the truth, but she was too young to really understand...'

I think of Lauren hearing those words. How tormented she must have been to know her own mother had thought about harming her. Even if Mum had only meant it to explain. Lauren felt unwanted. Worse still, worried that something was wrong with her. Or she was something bad.

'Mum,' I lean in, tempted to touch her leg but not wanting to break this spell. 'Maybe Lauren didn't understand what you told her. That you were ill. She was so young. It wasn't her fault, any more than it was yours.'

'She felt I'd rejected her. She wanted to...' she falters.

To what?

'To *punish* me.'

I pull back, shocked. 'That's not what happened. She wasn't

doing this to you.' I hold out the letter. Suddenly it all comes crashing down. Selfish woman. All about her.

'What's this?' she asks sharply.

'A letter. From Lauren.'

'Don't be absurd.' Her long fingers tipped with perfect red nails hesitating to reach for the envelope.

Yet a sense of relief floods me as she takes it. The idea that someone is finally seeing it, that this will end soon. She holds it and the address where Lauren can be found is caged beneath her fingers.

She examines it, reads it, barely moves. Her breath locked in her lungs. Then she folds it and slips it back into the envelope, sliding it onto the table as if casting a secret ballot. It sits there beside the glass with the dead cigarette with her red lipstick on.

Then she gets up, walks across the room, to my desk. On the corner is the notebook and I can feel the heat rising inside me as she reaches for it.

'Have you always thought I was stupid?' she says, and its harshness surprises me. Her fingers lifting the cover and my throat tightens. 'Was it meant to be a joke?' She almost laughs. 'You didn't really expect me to believe it, did you?'

Eyes on me. Then back to the book. I swallow.

'I mean,' she continues, 'how could something like this have even got here? It hasn't even got your address on it. Or your name.' Her eyes narrow. 'What game are you playing?'

I'm shocked by her words, her tone. This isn't how it was meant to be. The holding of hands, the calling of the police.

'No, Mum, you don't understand. She—'

But Mum raises her hand, cutting me off.

'How could Lauren,' she rounds, 'being held by this crazed *psychopath*, make it all the way to your door, all the way here and then decide at the last minute not to ring the doorbell? Not to knock. Not to speak to you.'

'It wasn't like that,' I stammer, thinking fast. 'Someone must have helped her. Someone brought it. Maybe the postman.'

'The *postman?*' she laughs. 'Who knew *you* live here?' Her voice incredulous. 'But didn't just *call* the police?'

'I... don't know.' I shake my head, crumbling inside my own answers. She's tying me in knots. She always has. 'But Lauren's alive and she needs our help. She's fighting and we can help her.'

I can see the fragments in her eyes, as if she's breaking apart too.

'Why did you never care enough?' I say. 'You could have told them about Colson.' Her face changes. 'Yes, that's right. Mr Colson. Your little *dalliance*. Because that's where she is. You know she's there, alive, don't you? You *wanted* this.' The words rush out without me able to stop them.

'How *could* you!' she retorts.

'Yes, this was the perfect solution. This way you didn't have to get any blood on your own hands.'

Mum gasps. 'What are you saying?' Tears in her eyes. 'Stop it. Stop saying these things. You're... not well, I want to help you. Make you better. Did David put you up to this?'

'David? He doesn't even know about the letter.'

'You told him everything else. Is that what he's after, more sordid little secrets?'

The helplessness is rising. Sitting together, holding hands. No chance of that now.

'Because it was David who started all of this. He was the one who filled her head with ideas. Told her to use that little imagination of hers, to write her crazy stories, things about us, about me. She was innocent before him.'

I shake my head. She's confusing things. This isn't about David or stories. She's just ashamed of what she did with Colson. Can't admit she brought him to our home. That *she* brought this on us.

Mum turns. Her wrap dress fans out behind her, her hair dancing out in an arc. 'I can't listen to this anymore. I can't be the villain forever.' She scoops up her bag, heads out into the hall.

'But Mum, she's alive and she needs us. The police—'

The door slams before I can reach it. I pummel on it in frustration until my fists are hurt and bruised.

'I hate you,' I scream. 'I hate you! This is all your fault...'

But now I'm alone again. Even more afraid, because something Mum said was frighteningly true. Someone brought this letter to me.

TWENTY-EIGHT

JANE

Today

'Bathroom,' Rene says to Jane.

'What's that, dear?' she asks, turning from the sink at which she's been dithering, toying with the idea of calling Alice. She wants to talk to her, know she's safe. That's the reason she's holding her phone. Or the reason she tells herself.

'Did you say bathroom? Yes, of course.' Jane hurries over and offers Rene a hand as she tries to stand. Although Jane herself feels jittery and upset, not sure she's much of a support.

Because the truth is that for the last few minutes she's been searching, reading up about the missing sister: Lauren. Conflicting stories that seemed to lead nowhere. A local man had been taken in for questioning, an editor she'd met at a Careers Fair, but he was released without charge, asked to be left alone. Privacy for his family, for his wife and their newborn baby. An ex-boyfriend who said he'd slept with Lauren. Later said they only made out. She was only fourteen after all and was probably afraid of getting into more trouble himself. Had Alice slept with anyone at fourteen? Such a sordid tale that seemed unnecessary for him to share even if it was true; why had he said such things? And the parents – Jim and Sue Fisher – pictured at the canal standing together, distress etched on their faces after another fruitless search. Not holding hands. Jane doesn't want to see guilt in their faces, but is it there?

In none of this is there any reference to a sister. There is no mention of Rene.

Jane guides the girl to the downstairs toilet, thinking of asking, of saying something. She opens the door and lets go of Rene's arm. The girl seems to hesitate as she steps inside, glances at the William Morris wallpaper, then back at the door, not sure whether to lock it or not. She leaves it a little ajar.

She's afraid of being trapped, Jane thinks and wishes she hadn't.

Jane steps back a little, stands outside, just across the hall, near the alcove where the phone stand might have been. She doesn't want Rene to think she's listening, but she wants to be sure Rene's OK, that she doesn't fall, hit her head.

'I'm right here if you need me,' she calls out lightly, trying to sound reassuring as she loiters there.

When the front door knocks it makes her jump.

'Dan...' she calls up the stairs. Then more softly to the girl beyond the door. 'Are you all right in there?' Wondering if Rene heard it as well.

Is it the police, or Rene's father?

Jane hears the sound of running water. The sound of hands being washed, splashing as if water onto a face. She's worried about the evidence. Should she say something, not to wash it all away? But the water keeps running, even as Dan stays upstairs and the door knocks for a second time. It doesn't surprise Jane that the girl is scrubbing her face, as no doubt the girl has looked at herself in the mirror and seen how filthy she is. And Jane is annoyed at herself. Rene's not a body, she can tell the police what happened. Who did this to her, and why. She can tell them her story and where she has been.

The door knocks for a third time. More urgency. A man's voice. 'Hello...?'

'Right,' Jane says, turning to the door with whoever is waiting on the other side. She wishes she had an eyehole, so she could peer out. Her heart pounds because she has a sneaking suspicion that she knows. She twists the lock, and it opens.

'Hi there,' she says with false joviality.

There's a man standing there. He looks anxious, haggard. Probably older than Dan but not much, less well-groomed and less well kept. He's wearing a grey suit that seems to hang off his bony shoulders as if the hanger is still in it, making him look even more gaunt. He's alone.

'Can I help you?' Jane asks, that polite shop-assistant voice has returned.

'Is she... here?' he asks, eager but also uncertain, as if he's made a mistake. Or is afraid he has come to the wrong house. Hopes this is a bad joke. He has a half-hidden smile, but not a happy one. She can't quite read it.

'Yes... could I ask your name?' Jane says, still prim.

He tells her it's Jim, and she asks – sorry for being formal – if he has any ID. He fumbles in three of his jacket pockets before pulling out a tatty black wallet, tugs free a driving licence. He hands it to Jane, and she reads that his name is Jeremy Fisher. He explains that Jim is... he hesitates, searching for the word... a nickname. 'My wife preferred it.'

'Can I ask you to wait,' she says and shuts the door, twisting the lock just to be on the safe side. She wonders where the wife is; why he hasn't brought her too.

Jane goes across to the toilet door, knocks lightly. 'Rene dear. Your father is here. He's outside.'

She listens; the water stops abruptly. She hears the circular holder rattling as Rene uses the towel, and Jane can't help thinking that it will need changing, washing, no matter how much water Rene has used. She dislikes herself for thinking it, but her thoughts are not her own today.

The girl steps out looking cleaner and a little steadier. Her face is uncertain. Jane wonders how she feels about the fact that beyond this door is her father.

'Do you want to stay here, or go and sit? I can bring him into the kitchen if you like?'

Where should this reunion take place? Jane is thinking, and is Rene just wondering why Jane hasn't already let him in? Is she desperate to throw her arms around his neck?

'Dan...!' Jane calls upstairs impatiently, startling the girl. Jane's voice is so different from the quiet one she has used with her. It reminds her of when she would shock the kids if she was ever riled up enough to shout.

'I think I'd like to go and sit,' Rene says, pointing back to the kitchen.

Jane nods, follows, watching as Rene resumes her spot in the chair, tugging the coat back around her shoulders; taking a moment to arrange herself almost regally. Jane suddenly feels the urge to cry. The girl's face. This moment. This... everything.

How would she feel if this was her Alice? If this was her about to see what Jim will see. She can't comprehend it. She hurries back to the front door and opens it with an apologetic look, just as Dan appears from the study. He wasn't upstairs at all.

'Sorry to keep you waiting,' she says cordially to Jim, and she moves aside to let him in.

The man – *Jim* as his wife prefers to call him – lifts his foot and takes a step inside.

TWENTY-NINE

LAUREN

Before

It wasn't the postman who came back. But still I heard someone.
I should have known, been more scared.

But I was in the little room upstairs, the one where I spent
time when I wasn't good and I wasn't bad and I wasn't busy
with the house or cooking or working on the car parts. I spent
hours there. The room had bare floorboards and a chair with a
rickety leg. Shutters over the window. Nothing to see, no
window. The only thing...

My loose floorboard, the one I'd spent hours, days, weeks
jimmying free, getting splinters under my nails. The place I
kept my secret things. It had taken months to bring them
together from their little hiding places. One one week, one the
next. The inspiring magazine pictures, the news clippings, the
cherry lip gloss, and a tissue with a smear of blusher from the
bathroom drawer. Slowly but surely curated, united.

Now I had some of them out and had been looking at them
one by one, nothing more than scraps and silly mementoes and
images, but all things that Keele didn't know I had, which felt

good. My things, simple as they were. My secrets. But I had also been thinking about my letter, what was happening to it. How far it had travelled. Who had got it now. Whether Mum and Dad would see it.

My ears listened for a single step on the carpet of the stairs. To hear if Keele was coming, which gave me just enough time to put everything back and close the floorboard and cross to the corner so he wouldn't suspect anything. Keele must never know I was hiding things.

Not again.

Not after last time. What he did to me.

Then I heard a car out on the lane, distant at first. I expected it to pass, but then I heard the metal gate screech open and tyres on gravel. Then it pulled up, came to a stop. Car doors slamming, two of them. Thud. Thud. Voices talking faintly as they walked along the path to the door, voices that echoed across the wide, open fields.

The dog barked and Keele yelled, *Keep it down*. Then he stopped. *Oh my*, I thought I heard him say, *this is going to be fun*.

I strained to hear more over the buzz of silence. Then the doorbell, that made me jump, and then the door opening and voices, muffled. A man. A woman. Keele closing the door and standing in the hallway. The voices becoming quieter, lost, no longer drifting up the stairs but filtering through the floorboards from the living room below.

Someone come to buy car parts, perhaps. But Keele never allowed them near the house.

I toyed with the idea of screaming, thought about it so viciously that my head felt as if it might explode. It rose inside me like bubbles spilling over the side of a boiling saucepan. But something warned me to hold it. Not to do it. I knew what happened if I got it wrong, if it was a test. The threat of failing.

Guess again, Little L.

As I listened, everything became vivid. Every grain of the floorboards, each chip of the painted skirting, every word on the page, every colour in the pictures. I gathered my secret things together and shoved them quickly back under the floorboard.

It was just the television, I told myself – Keele had told me it didn't work, though sometimes I heard it when I was lying awake in bed at night.

Or maybe it was something on the computer, which I was forbidden to touch and he never used when I was around, unless he wanted to show me something. It sat on the desk in the living room tormenting me with its promise of a way out. Another route through which my screams could escape. But who would I contact? My emails to Mum and Dad had gone unanswered for years.

The dog barked. Keele shouted, then laughed. The sounds from below, the low rumble of more talking, like the distant threat of thunder.

I shuffled across the room, the plastic binder at my ankle meant I couldn't stand properly; he was using them more and more because *I can't trust you these days, can I?* True, not true. Said he could see it in my eyes that the madness was creeping back in.

I pushed my ear close to the space at the bottom of the door, smelling the dust buried in the gap of the doorframe. Threads of old carpet. Someone was down there, two someones, and they were talking to him.

Uncertainty rushed around in my head like children playing musical chairs. My throat tightened and lightheadedness taunted me. *Scream – Don't scream? Scream – Don't scream? Get it right – Get it wrong. Pass the test. Fail. Good night. The end. No one ever goes home.*

I waited and couldn't hear anything more.

So I did it. No, not a scream, but something else. My body

rebelling against my warning. Survival instinct. I kicked the chair with the wonky leg, and it rocked back and forth. It could have been an accident, but I scuttled back and huddled tight in the corner.

Were they looking up, asking what that noise was?

'Someone up there?' they might say.

I held my breath, waiting to hear. Rushing, shouting, thumping, demanding. The wave of years finally crashing down. Something. Anything.

Nothing.

There was nothing.

Seconds spooled out like a cotton reel rolling away under the bed.

Nothing.

So I crept back, and this time I knocked the chair clean over. A sound that a house couldn't make by itself. The excuse already forming in my head, *It tipped as I was sitting on it. I didn't realize there was anyone downstairs...*

A feeling of dread, knowing Keele would have heard it. Knowing he would know I was lying.

And, what next?

He would hurt me. He would ask me, *Haven't I knocked that trouble out of you yet?*

I crouched in the corner as if he was already towering over me, and I listened over the rush of blood in my ears. Could I still hear them talking?

No. Only a long, raw silence.

Then the door slowly opened.

Well, well, well, Keele said, entering the room. I could see the tension in his arms by the way he flexed his fingers. Opening then closed, closed then opening. His knuckles white against stretched skin. *Something going on up here I should know about?*

I saw the way he glanced towards the door. The way he checked to see if anyone had come up behind him. Fire in his eyes like he was livid, but his voice was only calm.

You trying to get my attention?

He tipped his head towards the door.

You know I have guests. What, you want to meet them, is that it?

Why was he smiling? A sneer distorting his mouth. Something in his face that I hadn't seen before. Tight lips, flaring nostrils. Was he... excited?

Let's make it a party. I think you'll enjoy it.

I shook my head, crouching further into the corner. It couldn't be good if he was going to let me meet them. What he'd said the other day: *unless you want to make money another way.*

'Who... are they?' I stammered.

Friends, he said. *You want to speak to them?*

I shook my head.

Why, have you got something to hide?

I could see his eyes wide and black and illuminated by the bulb in the centre of the room. I could see that he was busy planning. That strange energy.

'I didn't...' I struggled to explain, sweat rising on my palms.

But he shook his head. *So I just imagined it then? That I heard you up here busting the place up. Like a lunatic who needs proper treatment in order to get better.*

'The chair fell...' I whimpered. 'I sat on it and it... tipped.'

He lurched at me then, gripping my chin, clamping it in his hands. Staring deep into my eyes. So deep, as if down into hell.

Little L, he breathed. *You have no idea, do you? No clue what is about to happen.* He held my gaze and in his eyes, I could see very bad things running like a movie. *Or... you can try to show me what a good girl you can be. That would be better.*

He pushed me away, walked over and straightened the chair.

Let's talk about this 'after'. When they've gone. Assuming you're still here. He paused, just long enough. *First, come downstairs and show your pretty little face. Tell them in your own words what you've been up to. Tell them who you* really *are. You remember your name?*

Cathy. Three blinks.

And that made me think, what if it's someone who got my letter?

Still, he peered around the room as if sensing something else, as if a dog sniffing it out, and my eyes went to the floorboard which only I knew could be lifted.

Would he see?

Good, he said, his eyes coming back to mine, as if he was almost satisfied.

He came over and crouched down, pulled out the knife to slit open the binders at my ankles, glancing up at me as he squatted by my knees. Any second could be the second, except it never was. Could I kick him in the face? Grab the blade. Was I strong enough that his hands couldn't get to my mouth before I screamed? Could I do it at just the moment that he untied me so that I could bolt down the stairs fast, so fast before he grabbed me? Could I create enough commotion that they would hear, or see...?

No. I couldn't. And these were his friends.

He looked up and smiled, and something in my weakness and his strength made me weaker and him stronger. He pulled my socks up over the cuts where the binders rubbed. I kept thinking that it was a trick. He would never let me meet anyone. Not anyone good.

Out of the room, almost falling with giddiness.

Of course, he said, turning back to me, *I think they might be the police. But how can you tell?* He paused to let it sink in. *I mean, what if they are those, those... like those ones we saw on TV, remember? Those freaks who go around* pretending *to be the police and then taking vulnerable girls from their home. Out into the woods and...*

He let the thought soak through.

I didn't check their ID. But I'm guessing they are who they say they are. Right, Cathy...?

He would never let me meet the police.

I shifted back, two steps up.

But don't worry, if they try to take you, I won't let them. He leaned in close. *Because I wouldn't trust them. I'd be* afraid *of what they would do to you.* He flashed the knife, still in his pocket.

We got to the hall. The door to the room was just in front of me. I saw myself rushing in, into the arms of those people. Screaming for them to save me, keep him away from me. Another version of me already in the room and spilling it all out. But I walked in slowly, feeling my fingers clenched, my toes against the carpet, the pit of my stomach rising into my throat. My hair hanging down into my eyes. The thread of my jumper over my thumbs.

Well, here she is. My girl. Never likes to miss a get-together, do you, Cathy?

Keele laughed. Would he have been so amused if they really were the police? Why wasn't he nervous, when it was all I could do just to breathe?

The woman, no uniform – her shiny hair swept back into a smooth, high ponytail like a plain-clothed policewoman from the TV like I might have once watched with Dad – she said, 'And what did you say your name was?'

My mind flipped. Sheer panic. My chance to react, show something... or just to get it right.

Hey, Keele said. *Don't be shy.* Why was he smiling?

'Catherine,' the word came out, and everything swam. I blinked. I was the one they were looking for, *if* they had received my letter.

'Nice to meet you.'

'Cathy,' I said instead. Because I'd written Cathy, and I blinked again. One. Two. Three. But they didn't catch it. They were distracted, like I was an afterthought.

'Cathy,' I said again.

Blink. One. Two. Three.

Didn't she notice my clothes, my hair? I pushed my sleeve up, hoping they would see the backstory of scars, small scratches from the tin lids and binders, my bruises. But they didn't glance at it. The woman turned to the man and exchanged a look. Something, like I was crazy. *Cuckoo.* They nodded.

'Right,' she said and almost smiled.

If they were the police, wouldn't they be more concerned, more inquisitive? Wouldn't they notice the scrapes and bruises?

But they were turning away.

'Look,' the woman was saying, 'that dog's behaviour is not acceptable, not even on private land. And you threatened that lad.'

They were here about the dog?

The man seemed more interested. He glanced back at me once or twice. I could sense him watching me as the woman spoke. He was taller, tattoos on his forearm. Could a policeman have tattoos? He wasn't as big as Keele.

Nothing hasty. See if it's a test.

'The man who came here had the express purpose and job to deliver post.'

Post. Were they from the post company? If they'd not seen my letter, that meant no guns. And no police meant no backup.

'Take it as a warning. After this, we'll have no choice but to take action.'

They were moving towards the hall. Job done.

'That's it?' Keele asked, as if he wanted more.

'Why? Is there anything else?' The woman turned back, a

look of challenge on her face. She glanced at me then. She didn't like Keele, or maybe she liked him too much. His eyes alight, swimming pools on a summer day. He used his left hand to push up his right sleeve to the elbow. Strong arms. Muscular. Handsome once.

Then he turned and looked straight at me.

'Cathy,' I repeated, blinking.

The woman looked at me, no real kindness in her eyes. Where was the sympathy, or the suspicion?

'She's pretty "special",' Keele said.

The woman tried to stifle a smile.

Heat on my skin, my eyes unable to focus. I looked at the man's shoes, the leg of his trousers, up to his shirt, trying to follow a line. Where was his badge, his radio? Then I tried – just once – to look at his eyes and they met.

I wanted to lead his gaze back down to my ankle. Down to the place where the trouser leg was over my sock, over the skin that was raw from the binder. I thought if he was really a policeman he would follow my gaze, like that game with the metal wand, leading over a winding rod and every time you went wrong it buzzed. And that buzz jolted you even though you knew it was coming. Each time I started to lead his eyes, he didn't follow. Not to my ankle. Not to my scars.

And they were leaving, small gestures, saying unimportant things.

'All right, well just keep it under control in future.'

Inside my mind was hollering. *Now! Now!* I should shout out. Tell them I was Lauren and please, please, take me. I wasn't Jackie or Jacqueline at all. I wasn't special, in any sense of the word.

Outside the living room they were moving into the hallway. Didn't they see the locks, the shutters? Why wasn't I speaking up? Fear. Terrible, terrible fear. Years of programming. They were leaving and any second it would be too late.

Then the man stopped, looked back, down at the metal hoop on the wall just inside the living room door. Where the rope or the binder could hook to restrain me.

'What's that?' he asked.

I clenched my breath in tight, waiting for what Keele might say. They would catch him out, I wouldn't even need to scream. They wouldn't like his answer, they would see what they had suspected all along, and if it was a test maybe the test was for him. They were going to cuff him, arrest him, take *him* away. It would be over, and I would be free, and I would tell them everything about the rope and the binders and The Hole and the years that had disappeared in darkness when he was trying to make me *better* and only making me worse, and weaker, and confused, and I didn't really know how long it had been.

But Keele spoke. *Yeah, it's for the dog. She's a bit unruly, as you say.*

He smiled and the maybe-policeman smiled back.

'I...' I opened my mouth. Words like bubbles, starting to rise up.

They looked at me, just through the doorway. All eyes on me. The front door opening, the world outside revealing itself, cold and bright. I had no rope, no binders. Could I make it past all of them? Could I run for my life?

'If you must keep a dog like that,' the woman glanced at me, 'it's a good idea to keep it on a very tight lead. Even muzzle it.'

The feeling was like cold water swirling around me, rising with every second.

'W... W...' I said, wavering.

They were stepping over the threshold. Keele was closing the door. They were going. I had either passed his test or failed the last one of my life.

'W... Wait!' I shouted.

Nothing happened. Long, forever moments.

Then the man turned. He tipped his head, as if he hadn't really heard me. 'Sorry?' he said.

'He... punishes her... severely,' I said. Each word took so much effort.

'Well...' The man nodded, glancing towards the woman. 'He shouldn't do that.'

He was outside, a flicker of concern shifting through his eyes. A pinched brow, or maybe just the bright November day after the gloom of inside.

I spoke. 'Take her... with you.' Each of my words almost impossible to form.

The man seemed to laugh. 'Sorry. But if we take her, she's unlikely to find a good home.' Had he glanced at me? 'And you know what we'll do with her then, don't you? We'll be forced to put her to sleep. Better that she stays here. But try to take better care of her, OK?'

Then he was ambling up the pathway, the woman already at the car, getting into the driver's seat, showing that she was the one in charge. As if that was the point she was trying to make all along, an annoyance in an otherwise menial day.

'Wait,' I shouted. But it was too late. Keele had his hand over my mouth and had pushed the door closed, his mouth against my ear, the knife against my back.

Well, that went well, Keele said softly. *Don't you think?* He tugged me hard, as if trying to make me nod, my neck feeling as if it might snap. *And what did you say?*

He loosened his finger from my mouth.

I can't hear you.

Could I still scream? They were just outside. Then there was the sound of a car engine starting up.

What did you say? His question like that knife, sharper and harder.

I thrashed, his hands lowering over my eyes. Blackness already.

'*He punishes her severely.*' *Was that what you said?* And he was laughing, louder with each second, his confidence growing to fill everything as the sound of the car disappeared back across the gravel and along the lane and away, away, away through the empty fields.

THIRTY

RENE

Before

It's dark. My head hurts, and I wince as I turn. I'm not in bed, I'm on the sofa with the soft crochet blanket half over me.

My hand goes to my temple, exploring what feels like a soft spot, like damaged fruit. I quickly remove my hand, check for blood on my fingertips – there's none thankfully. What happened? A terrible dream. Nothing more.

Then I hear something in the hall.

I edge around the door, along the wall. The sound comes again. Someone is knocking at lucky number eight.

Through the eyehole I see a man and woman standing side-by-side on the doorstep. They're in uniform. *The police.* They've come about the letter. I can tell them everything. Finally, someone who will believe me.

The man seems more bothered by the cold. I watch him rubbing his hands together, blowing into them. The November chill has set in everywhere. And there's still the threat of snow Mum spoke about.

I edge the door open, and even the dull light makes my eyes hurt. I squint into it.

'You called for help?' the man says.

'I did...?' I say, sounding unsure.

'So, do you need assistance?' the woman says more assertively.

'I do. Please, come in.'

They nod, more to each other than to me, a glance that says they already know what they're dealing with. They follow me inside.

I offer them tea. Politely they decline. Blank emotionless expressions on their faces. We sit; me facing the window, them facing me. I take a deep breath and tell myself to stay focused on why they are here.

The letter. And saving Lauren.

'I need to show you something,' I say, wishing they could take their eyes off my forehead. I can't explain how I got that lump. Maybe I walked into a door. Maybe that's what I'll say if they ask.

Instead, I hand them the letter. It's the woman who takes it, not before putting on a plastic glove, unhurried, no urgency. She examines it, half-reading, before dropping it into a clear plastic bag that the man holds.

'And when did you say you received this?' the woman asks curtly. I had expected something closer to sympathy. So far there has been no warmth.

'Yesterday,' I reply. 'Wait. Yes. No. Yesterday. What day is it today?'

They exchange glances.

The man holds the letter in plastic, slides the seal and gazes at it like it's a weird insect. The woman opens her notebook and scribbles something. Just a few words. Nothing rushed, even as Lauren's cry for help suffocates in that airtight bag.

'What time yesterday?' The woman looks up. Sharp hazel eyes.

'I'm... not sure. Does it matter?'

Another scribble.

'It's just, it can help us establish how it came to be here.'

'I'm not sure,' a little more frustrated.

They look at each other. There. Stop, rewind, pause. That look. *Strange*, it says. Their eyebrows raised. An *all-is-not-what-it-seems* narrowing of the eyes.

'Why didn't you report it when it first came?' Another question hides within her half-friendly smile. A forward tilting of her body, as if needing to listen more closely.

'I was... waiting,' I say. 'For someone. And then they... came...' I hear the confusion in my own voice.

'"Someone"?' the woman repeats, playing the word back to me.

'My mother.'

'Your mother?' More focus in her eyes, as if trying to keep me on track. 'And did you have an argument?' She looks at my forehead.

My fingers stray there. It hurts, so I shift them away. 'No. No. This? I... don't know what happened.' Besides, the focus needs to be on Lauren, her letter, not on me. There must be no doubt, no uncertainty. 'I just... walked into a door.'

'Do you need to see a doctor?' Her eyes stray to the table, to the packet of pills, all popped out.

'Or we can take you to a hospital,' the man adds. 'Get you some help.'

I imagine the comfort of an ambulance, people around me. All those people. A safe place. Corridors, long and white. I'm on a trolley and they're wheeling me towards—

'No!' I insist. 'The letter. Just that.'

Another exchanged look.

'Do you think Lauren' – the policewoman refers to her notebook as if Lauren's name has already slipped her mind – 'that Lauren *is* being held by someone against her will?'

'Don't you? What does the letter say?'

Too attacking, a momentary invisible standoff. I need to be more cautious. These people are here to help me. To help us.

'And how concerned are you about Lauren?'

A flash of anger. Why would they ask that? My brow furrows. I wince with the pain of my head.

'It's just that it took you a day or two to report this.' They glance at each other.

'It was only yesterday... and I...' My mouth opens, my finger to my forehead. There isn't space for all the things I need to say, and nothing comes.

They don't believe me. Like Mum. They'll leave and nothing will come of it. It will all be my fault. Lauren will keep suffering because I can't make anyone believe me. The letter just another piece of paper buried somewhere, lost under a pile on a desk, in the system, misplaced or discarded, and no one will do anything. No one will join the dots with red string like they do on TV. No one will make that wall with Keele's house and Lauren's photo. No one will understand how Lauren has risked her life to send it. What he will do if he finds out. I think about showing them the necklace, the ominous engraving. Or the notebook. All clues, coming together.

'Lauren's file says she' – the woman coughs – 'that she took her own life. Sadly.' The last word such an afterthought.

I look up, my head snapping upright. 'What? No! That's not true.'

'The evidence suggested that she drowned herself in the canal, some of her things were found, and her body was most likely carried out to sea.'

'No,' more adamant, 'that's not right.'

'But the file states—'

'I don't care about your file!'

'And your *mother* confirmed that Lauren was upset when she left home.' That was true, she was. 'And she left a message, a note, implying she was going to...'

'A note?' I say out loud, shaking my head even if it hurts. What are they talking about?

My mind twists. Why would they say that? Why would Mum tell them? This is wrong. Wrong, wrong, wrong.

'There was no note,' I insist. She left a message, yes, to Mum in a book on her bed, but not a note. Not a *suicide* note!

'Your mother said that it was clear that Lauren had no intention of returning home. That she believed Lauren *chose* to go. That she was deeply troubled at the time. That this was her way out.'

'She's wrong. That's a lie.'

'Wrong that Lauren was *troubled*?'

Was that why no one went looking...? Why they gave up so easily? Just one more teen disappearance that suicide conveniently explained.

'Besides, we read about her in the paper, what her boyfriend said,' the man says. 'That she was deeply unhappy. That she was taking drugs.'

'Once! She smoked dope once. And you'd prefer to believe that? His words. Stupid things.' I turn to the woman. 'That's enough to give up on her?'

The woman leans back. She doesn't like being accused.

'This letter is proof,' I continue. 'She's alive. What more do you need?'

The man and the woman look at each other, a pause, like two synchronized gymnasts agreeing when to start the next phase of their routine.

'You're on sick leave, aren't you, Miss Fisher?' She consults her notebook again, as if it has all the answers in there. All except one.

'Sort of,' I reply. 'I have a... condition.'

She tilts her head. The comment confirms what they have already discussed outside in the car, in the warm, maybe with a smirk in their voices.

'And how would you describe your *condition?*' Raised eyebrows, as if that will help her to hear what I say.

'She's there, in hell.' I point to the letter. 'How would *you* describe my condition?'

'I'm sorry,' the policewoman says, sounding as un-sorry as she can. 'We just have to investigate all avenues.'

'All avenues except this address,' I blurt. 'Lauren is *there*, suffering. She's living through *hell!* You tell me how I *should* feel. Stop this bullshit, and act now.'

There are lots of small gestures: a distracted scratch of an ear, a turn of a page, a shift in their seat. The man coughs this time, as if he is in a doctor's waiting room.

'We're just trying to establish facts,' the man asserts. The woman smiles at him, maybe telling him to back down, she's got this.

'May I ask how many weeks you've been sick?'

This again, back to my illness. 'Six, maybe seven.'

'Weeks or months?' she asks with a blink.

The truth is my illness has been long but I don't need to tell them that.

'It must be quite boring,' the policeman dares to speak again, looking up at the female officer for permission. She doesn't stop him this time; in fact she nods a little encouragement, so he continues. 'I mean, stuck in here, all this time. Not much to do...' He scans over towards my desk.

'What *do* you do all day, if you don't mind me asking?' the woman asks, landing his question.

'I write.'

'Stories?' The woman raises one eyebrow.

'Things, yes.'

She repeats as a question. 'Things about... Lauren?'

'No. Well, sometimes.' *Because David told me to.* But I don't want to mention him.

The policewoman makes a note.

I imagine them laughing in the pub this evening. *Had a right one this afternoon.* He'll curl his finger around at his temple. *Curly whirly cuckoo,* just like the kids used to do in school.

'I'm not making this up,' I say, standing. It's like a bad dream in which no one will help me, screams that no one hears. 'Maybe I'm not well, but Lauren is out there being held by a cruel, vicious man... And we know who he is, where he is. This letter' – I point sharply at the plastic bag – 'isn't that enough now? Just go there.'

The woman looks a little confused.

'But the file says she...'

'She wasn't *suicidal,* and she didn't choose to be there. Why can't you just do your job and go and save her? What is wrong with you people? She was a child...'

I feel myself breaking. The tears of anger and exasperation juddering up within me. I can't hold in the pleading that is rising.

'We're sure you're very upset,' the woman says, looking away. 'We know you were last time.'

I stop.

'Last time?'

She smiles; it's meant to be comforting. 'And we will, of course, as we *always* do, take this matter further. We'll contact you just as soon as we feel the need for more facts.'

She is standing now, preparing to go.

'This can't be happening,' I say, infuriated. 'Wait. Let's try again. Please sit.' I pat the sofa. My arm hurts too. I see bruises on it. Do they? Maybe only shadows in the dimly lit room.

'She's there, with him. He's doing these things to her, and you refuse to investigate—'

'We've been,' the man says, cutting me off.

'What?'

'We've been. To this address. We've seen for ourselves. The last time you called us and told us.'

'And?' I look up and see something familiar in his face. How his eyes watch me with curiosity.

'You've made accusations before. Several times in fact. Do you remember?'

My fingers at my forehead. 'No.' I falter. He's trying to trick me. We haven't had this conversation. This is the first time. Fingers exploring my temple, as if I might find something there, but all I find is that bruise and it hurts even if I can't explain why.

'We're sorry, but the man at this address checks out. We've spoken to him and it's just him and his daughter.'

'*Cathy?*' I ask.

The woman speaks up now. 'There's nothing to see. No evidence of any wrongdoing. Just a man and his daughter, and his badly behaved dog.'

I seek out the light at the window, imagining in another world I could see officers pouring in around me, crowding the space, listening intently, agreeing a plan. I thought I would just say, 'Here's a letter,' and they would say, 'This is all the evidence we need. Bingo. We've got him.'

I think of them rushing back out the front door, up the stairs, shouting into radios, moving cars out on the road. Sirens and lights igniting, illuminating the icy fog. Heading to that address. A raid. Kicking in doors. Her being freed. I can almost feel it. *Hope*. Why can't I hold it, why can't I make that happen?

On the pavement, up there through the window, I will myself to see the hems of creased blue trousers, solid black boots, men and women, strong enough to kick doors in...

'Is there anything else you'd like to add?' the man asks.

'I...' I whisper, helpless tears filling my eyes.

He is standing too, straightening his clothes, muffled sounds of preparation for departure, closing notebooks, fastening buttons.

'Is there anyone we can call?'

I shake my head, a tear falls.

'Well, if you think of anything else that might be helpful, please be sure to contact us,' she says.

'Best not to wait next time, hey?' the man adds, almost jokingly.

They move into the hall, towards the door, looking around as they go. Scanning the walls, the pictures of Lauren, searching for anything unusual. More unusual than all these things, cluttered and strange. I see it now through their eyes. The paraphernalia and objects I have fastened on my walls, layered on my shelves.

'Please,' I beg, but I know I can't stop them.

They're up the steps, something so final in their departure. A few flakes of snow starting to drift, just like Mum said. Their body heat leaving with them. It's cold again with them gone.

But the woman is turning, a warm smile on her face. She's thought of something, realized the significance. 'Does anyone else know about this letter?' she says.

'Yes,' I say urgently. 'My mother. I showed it to her.'

'And what was her reaction?'

She's telling me something. The light of the day bearing down between us. More snow. Falling more quickly in my snow-globe porch. She wants me to know something I'm not quite grasping. That she waited until the end to emphasize. 'And she was convinced it was from Lauren?'

Seconds that feel like hours.

'Of course,' I lie.

'Right.' She nods. Nods again and then they go.

I wonder if they'll go to Mum, show her the letter again. Ask her if there's any chance she made a mistake. Or maybe a few. There was no suicide note. This is Lauren's letter. She is alive. Shouldn't they all just check? *Well, Mrs Fisher. We're going to go anyway. It's our duty to investigate every possible lead. Clearly, we're more concerned than you are. Frankly we find your lack of interest in this matter a little suspicious. That you implied she might have harmed herself a little misdirecting. Maybe we should have another little talk with you and your husband. Find out what you really know...*

'Don't give up, Lauren,' I tell her as I sit on the sofa, fingers knitted into the crochet of the blanket, TV dancing with light and sound in the background. Peter Gabriel and Kate Bush clinging to each other. 'I'm sorry I couldn't do more.'

'That's OK,' Lauren whispers back. 'You did your best. Next time will be different.'

Next time.

Next time.

Always a next time.

'Lauren,' I ask nervously into the empty room, 'how many times have there already been?'

'Too many,' she says. 'I can't remember anymore.'

THIRTY-ONE

LAUREN

Before

I knew when I came out, as he lifted me out, that bulb swinging overhead, burning my eyes. I saw the dog lying there beside the hatch. She didn't move. Maybe she was sleeping, I told myself.

The next day, I could stand a little better, stretch out my legs from that cramped space, had slept a bit, then Keele asked me to give him a hand. We squeezed through the kitchen into that space at the back and I saw the dog lying there exactly as it had been the day before, and I knew it then. Fur on skin on bones.

We put her in a bin bag, her stiff paw poking through the thin plastic. I didn't dare breathe, didn't want her to get inside me because I wouldn't be able to get her out. I knew he wanted me to see her. See that even his dog – that he said he loved – could be left to die like that if she made enough trouble.

I watched from the window as he put the bag in the boot of the car, and when I heard it slam I felt the tears rising. But I hid them when he came back inside. That dog and me, it was complicated, but maybe we had been friends after all. *Affinity*, I think that's what they call it. Something in common. The same master.

Keele locked me in the room upstairs with the shutters, and then he took her away, probably out into the woods.

As I sat there, I thought that one day, sooner or later, it would be me. Maybe the same thing had happened to his ex-wife or girlfriend... *Not known at this address.* And who was Cathy? I asked myself but I didn't like the question so I told myself to shut up.

That evening we sat in the living room, and I knew Keele was trying to be nice; trying to be sorry. His eyes paler, dark ringed. He looked tired. Maybe even sad.

I loved that dog, he said.

'I know,' I replied quietly.

You know... he hesitated. *It's your fault. You have to accept blame. Because of what you said when those people came. You made me... ANGRY. So I got a bit drunk and had to sleep it off. Which made me forget that she was there.*

And what about me? I thought. I was down there, lonely and half-mad from fear. I opened my mouth to say something, but closed it again. It wasn't just one night. It must have been days. What had he really been doing?

I just get so tired, he said then, and it was almost pitiful.

I nodded, avoiding his gaze.

Sit with me, he said, and he patted the sofa as if it was all forgotten. When I hesitated, he seemed to growl and said, *Not so tired that you shouldn't do what I tell you.*

So, I did.

You want to watch something, a little TV?

I was happy when he said that because he'd told me it hadn't been working for the longest time. Maybe that was what he had been doing, fixing it. I felt that buzz, the feeling I always got when I first came out of The Hole, and he tried to be nice to me, and convinced me that if I behaved well this was how it could be. Quiet, calm. No drama. No punishment. No hell.

Then the programme started.

'Welcome to *Real to Reel*,' the presenter said, and I was excited because it was something to take my mind off everything. Maybe it was Keele's way of saying he was sorry. Realizing he'd gone too far.

He handed me a glass with something like whiskey, and he nodded, and so I drank at the same time he drank with his head tipped back. Even if I knew the pretty pinks were inside and they never mixed well with alcohol. I was happy to have them in me, making everything swim.

The programme was running. At first it was about a disease spreading from animals to people. *Pandemic.* The word they said. From all those chickens in cages, farms in Asia.

Fucking with nature, Keele said then, then he laughed. *Sooner or later we'll be wiped off the face of the earth. Too many freaks, we're the virus on this earth. That's why the TV's better off than on, it'll only upset you. You want me to switch it off?*

He lifted the remote.

'No,' I said. I wanted to watch.

He paused, smiled, lowering it again.

The man on TV was standing in front of the *Real to Reel* logo in the studio, and he was saying:

'A report has found that the children of mothers who weren't able to breastfeed were more prone to depression in their teens. When a mother and daughter don't bond from birth, it can lead to devastating outcomes.'

I was thinking about the *pandemic* and all those poor animals in cages, and about the dog stiff in the plastic bag out in the cold in the woods under frozen soil. But the TV was showing a room – chintzy and perfect. Large lamps, striped wallpaper, a woman sitting in an armchair, and I felt that I recognized her. Some actress that I couldn't quite place. Some movie, I was thinking. Then I realized, it was Mum!

There was sweat in my armpits, prickling my skin. Palms cold and wet.

She lowered her gaze, coy as a princess, exactly how I remembered, and I could feel Keele watching me, prowling around the edges to see my reaction. *You want me to switch it off now?* he asked.

'No,' I said, but my stomach knotted.

Then the actress that was playing Mum said – 'I suppose I knew something was wrong, but no one seemed to listen when I told them how scared I felt. I should have seen the warning signs. It hurt that she didn't seem to want me. I felt rejected by my own baby.'

Something Mum had said years ago, drifting towards me like a car heading towards a crash. Any moment it was going to hit me. My head gliding with the drink and the pills, and me not long out of The Hole.

Was this even real?

The woman interviewing Mum asked, 'And how was your relationship with your daughter as she grew up?'

Mum closed and re-opened her eyes in slow motion. 'We never truly bonded,' she said bluntly. My stomach dipped.

The camera changed angle, filming Mum from the left now, her profile. Her lipstick, a soft muted pink.

'It wasn't what either of us expected, me and my husband. It was a shock. A painful shock. She...' another pause '... came between us.'

What? Did she say that? I was trying to understand, to hold her words in my head long enough to make sense of them, but they just kept slipping away.

The camera cut to the back of interviewer's head; she was nodding, as if agreeing. This faceless presenter, how dare she?

'And what about her father?' she asked.

'Oh, he was disappointed too,' Mum said, and it was like a punch in the gut.

Keele was staring at me, examining in detail, in the same way as the camera examined Mum.

You sure, Little L? he asked but I was transfixed.

'It took so much energy,' she said. 'Never a good day. There was never a day when it didn't hurt.' Her eyes darkened, heavily lidded.

Then she stared at the camera and said, 'With her. Never a good day.'

Hands sweating. Armpits stinging. Mouth tight. Stomach tied. I raised the glass to my lips, it clinked against my teeth, already empty. I'd drunk it all. I needed more, but then I would be sick. Everything Keele had said was true. They never wanted me. I knew, he knew. And now there she was on TV telling the whole world so everyone knew. Like Pete saying all those things in the paper. No one loved me, cared about me. No one except...

I wanted to cry. The flickering light of the television, Keele's eyes on me. He reached out a hand and laid it on my arm.

OK? he said.

I had been thinking about how much I hated him, my letter, someone coming, hammering on the door, demanding to take me home. Someone who would nod when I blinked three times, whatever name I said. Who would tell me how wrong this had all been as they led me away, all the way back home. Instead there was Mum saying that they never had a good day with me, that I had come between them, her and Dad, and everything I believed was true. She never wanted me, and he did. Or at least he was trying to make me better.

Mum blinked innocently. 'We'd done nothing wrong of course,' she continued. 'That was what she wanted. In the end we...' she paused '... were satisfied with the situation.'

Satisfied! Was that how they felt?

'And how do you feel now about your daughter?' the unseen woman asked softly.

'We thought, "It's over." A relief.'

I was surprised at her words. So blunt. Another cut away to a lamp on the desk as Mum spoke and then back to Mum with her head down. She fiddled with something invisible in her lap. 'We could finally get on with our lives.'

She stared into the camera, a glint of tears catching the lights, just enough to show she was a good, caring woman, a sensitive mother who had tried with her terrible daughter. And of course, she was a great *fucking* actress.

Something snapped inside me, and with it a burning river was running through me. I couldn't quite seize it or stop it. Shock, hurt, anger, disgust.

'Switch it off!' I shouted.

Keele hesitated, his fingers already poised on the remote.

I raised the glass, and maybe he knew I was planning to throw it at the screen. And who knew what hell would be unleashed after that. So he grabbed it, took it swiftly from my hand, and then he drew me to him, held me close. I remember he had once held me that way, that day in November by the canal, when he had given me that book. Said I could be his muse. Him in his grey coat, the dog jumping around in the dead leaves. It had felt wrong, and somehow... inviting.

I'm sorry, he said.

I shook my head, buried against his chest, nothing left to fight with. Nowhere left to go.

I guess I never realized how bad it was, until now, Keele said. *That she... she really never wanted you. I thought all this time you were exaggerating. I... doubted you. But you were right. She hated you. She always did. You never stood a chance.*

I thought I wanted to die. Stiff like the dog.

I always believed that someday they would try to see you, to convince you that you didn't belong with me. That I was bad and they were good. That they might... fight for you.

He held me away as he said it.

I wanted them to show you that they felt... something. As much as I do.

'She knew I was here, she never came.'

Isn't a mother's only job to love her child? he asked.

The room swam. He looked tired, drained, destroyed, the way we lived, because I was trouble. 'It's all my fault, isn't it?' I asked.

No. She was a bitch. I said that from the beginning. But then, all women are. Just like her. Except you. Better to be here where you're wanted. Unless, that is, you still want to leave... Do you?

I thought of him opening the door. Would I run this time? To where, to whom?

'She always hated me,' I whispered.

Shhhh, he said. *You're safe now. This is where you belong.*

THIRTY-TWO

RENE

Before

I wake.

I wake.

I wake.

Always the same shaft of light. The same sense that nothing will change. The same helplessness. Always a list that I have to cross out. Today's list.

- *To go out and exist.*
- *To be happier.*
- *To meet someone who holds me, loves me, maybe one day marries me. Maybe one day a baby. Sleep suits and plushy toys. Loving eyes and coos and that first smile. A blank slate that I can make things better for. Warmth and love. A fresh start.*

My phone jitters across the bedside table. 'David,' I say, relieved to hear his voice. He hasn't called me in days.

'How are you?' he asks, as if this could be any other conversation.

'There was a letter.' My head swims. 'From Lauren. But no one believed me. Not Mum or the police—'

'The police?' His voice drops. 'What did it say?'

I try to remember, but it's jumbled now, lost in the past.

'Terrible things. A hole, punishments. He's going to kill her. Why wouldn't anyone that saw it want to save her? Why can't I make anyone believe me?'

'But why can't she just leave?'

'He's a monster,' I shout. 'He won't let her leave! She's trapped there.'

'*How?*' David asks. 'How does he keep her?'

'Binders. A rope. A dark place he locks her in. He punishes her severely.'

'And what else?' he asks. His tone urgent as if he doesn't have much time.

'What else? She *can't* leave. He won't let her. And they don't want her back. They don't love her enough. No one loves her.'

I hear David tug in his breath. 'Wrong. They *do* want her back. They *do* love her. They always have. Don't ever believe those lies.'

'No,' I shout. 'No, they don't. They never did!' I scream and cut him off.

When my breath steadies and the blood stops pounding in my ears I hear a different sound. A scratching, shifting. I turn quietly along the corridor, to the front door. Something being pushed through.

Two white envelopes fall onto the carpet. I pick them up, dreading another letter, horror on the page. But they are only final reminders, nothing more. Then I think of Mum's words... *How could Lauren, who is being held by a crazed psychopath, make it all the way here, and then decide at the last minute not to ring the doorbell?*

I hear a rustling on the other side of the door. Unease creeps under my skin. Slowly, I raise my fingers to check the latches, four up its back and a chain. Then I position my eye cautiously over the eyehole and my breath catches as I see a man there. Maybe it's the police come back to say they've checked out the letter, the address. I was right. It's almost over. They've found her.

Instead, the person shifts, and I see it's a young man in a bright orange jacket. My heart sinks as I realize it's just the postman.

The postman!

And then I glimpse his face.

My fingers frantically work the locks, undoing them, pulling back the bolt, releasing the chain. Against my better judgement, I crack the door open. 'You!' I shout.

'Shit,' the young man says, throwing his joint to the ground.

'Pete?' I open the door just a smidge wider. 'Is it really you?'

He's apologetic at first, but it's too cold on the doorstep. Not for him in his big coat, but for me. I let him in, hesitantly. But I need to ask him something, so what choice do I have?

He steps into the living room; his high-vis jacket oversized for the small space. His face all chiselled and boyish, his hair which slides over one eye; he hasn't changed a bit.

'Would you like a cup of tea?' I ask, for want of a better opening line.

'Um...' He moves a little from side to side, an uncertainty on his face. Maybe seeing the state of my place, cluttered and disorganized, the scent of my unemptied bin. Maybe he's regretting the decision to step inside.

'Actually,' he says. 'Could I... erm... take a slash?' He points towards the bathroom in the corridor.

'Sure,' I say, a little unsure. I haven't heard that expression in years. Vulgar, adolescent. Same old Pete.

'And...' he says; I hang on for what he'll say next. 'I'd prefer coffee, all the same.' A flash of his youthful smile, those cheekbones and that shiny flop of hair.

'Sure.' I step aside, feeling the heat in my cheeks as he passes back out into the narrow corridor, his big coat making it even more awkward. Only when he's latched the toilet door do I let out my breath. Then I run into the bedroom, throwing clothes around in a desperate bid to find my favourite sweater. Then I glance in the mirror, rub my hands on my pale cheeks. Lick my lips and rub them together. No time for lip gloss. Still, I look bad.

In the kitchen, I look inside the cupboards for anything to make coffee. There's only that old jar, and I sniff it before chipping away at the dried granules, wondering if it will taste worse than it normally does. As the kettle boils, I run my fingers through my knotty hair and try to calm my nerves, wondering what the hell I have done. What the hell I am going to do.

A single thought looms: the letter. He must know how it got here.

Is it just a coincidence that he is here? That he's showed up like this and agreed to come in? Then this thought... What if it's *not* Pete and out of desperation I've invited a total stranger in, someone who just looks a bit like I remember him looking all those years ago?

'Wow,' Pete says, coming out of the bathroom and into the living room. 'I wasn't expecting to see *you*.'

It is him. My insides flip.

From the kitchen, I watch as he looks around, not making any attempt to hide his reaction to the state of my life. There's a stack of plates where I ate beans on toast several days in a row.

A tin with the spoon sticking out where I gave up on plates. Quite a few mugs with teabags wound round and welded to the handle. The blanket in a heap on the floor and Rebecca doll upturned in a corner where I threw her.

But it is as if something else is troubling him. He points a thumb back towards the bathroom. 'Um... you had a picture of me in your toilet.'

'Right, yeah...' I flounder, laughing it off. But, oh God, I'm dying. 'It's just I was...' I stir the coffee, desperately trying to dissolve the lumps, hoping his question dissolves too. I can't find a good excuse for the photo being there.

'Fucking cold in here,' he says eventually, rubbing his hands together and letting the question slide. 'Thought I could warm up in here, but not likely. What happened, boiler packed up?'

He looks towards my desk again, his gaze rummaging across my things. For the briefest of seconds, I think he's looking for something, his brow knitting as he does. Then he turns back to look at me.

'Coffee,' I say, coming out of the kitchen and handing him a steaming hot mug.

He sits, then hesitates. 'Look, I'm... sorry about what happened. The things I said... about Lauren. That stupid thing in the paper. It was—'

'Stupid?' I say.

We both smile, and I dip my head as a blush erupts. Lauren said they used to do that, finish each other's sentences. It was cute, until it wasn't. It's how she knew she liked him, until she stopped.

But Pete is not finished. 'He twisted it, you know?' he continues, more agitated. 'That's what those bastards do, those journos. Like that guy Lauren liked, what was his name – that arsehole?'

'David?'

'Yeah. That's it. David Prick-chard. Him too. All the same.'

He looks into the milk-less coffee. Lauren thought David was the best thing ever. Going to make all her dreams come true. 'Personally, I wouldn't trust him either.'

I watch him sip his coffee. I don't say anything. I listen long enough for him to say what he really thinks.

'Anyway, sorry about that. What I told them. Stupid. Hope I didn't burn any—' And then he looks up, our eyes meeting. He was going to say 'bridges' but in light of the making-out-under-the bridge-by-the-canal story it might not be the best turn of phrase.

But who reads or believes such belittling articles, made to make people think a young girl was *troubled* or less worthy after she went missing? Who cared about some sordid backstory, some questionable past? Society, the police, people in positions of power deciding that women or girls were in some way contributing to their horrendous fate. *The way she dressed. The way she behaved. The ways she lived her life...*

'No. No burnt bridges,' I say, lowering my gaze. Because Pete is only part of the problem. And today, he might just be part of the solution. I need to ask him about the letter.

I steal glimpses of him as he drinks his coffee. His young hands, his lean fingers. 'You still play guitar?' I ask. I've got time, his coffee is still too hot. He blows on it lightly. Those lips Lauren once loved to kiss.

'I was in a band for a while, Kill Your Heroines. Didn't make it big, but some fun gigs around town. The girls loved it.' He stops himself there. Doesn't need to say more. Then he showcases his orange high-vis. 'Got a new gig round town.' His grin slips. Is he disappointed with himself, where he's ended up?

But it's hard to ignore his face, how young he still looks, how fanciable. As if time has stood still for him. His sleek brown hair, his green eyes flecked like marbles, the bones of his cheeks with that mischievous lopsided grin. Pretty as a picture, he always was. Life hasn't been cruel to him.

'So,' he says, leaning forward. He sets his mug down, rubbing his hands along his legs as if for warmth. 'Mind if I...' He's going to leave. Not yet, he can't. 'Spark up?' he says, and he reaches into his pocket and tugs out a joint.

'Right. No, be my guest,' I say, pulling one of Dad's old expressions out of the bag. I cringe.

I watch as he puts the joint between his lips, how he reaches for the little yellow lighter, the one Mum left there the day of her tears and her confession. He lights the joint swiftly before blowing out a thick fragrant plume of grey smoke. Then he looks back at me, something glints in his eyes.

'Nice,' he says, nodding and settling back against the cushions. He always said that, as if nothing bothered him. Just a happy-go-lucky lad that Lauren thought was cool for a while. If only she'd stayed with him things might have worked out.

I tug my eyes away, before he catches me staring.

'So, I suppose you're wondering why I invited you in,' I say, sounding more like a crappy midday murder mystery.

'Me? *Nah.* Believe me, you're not the first woman on my rounds to invite me in *for a cuppa.*' He smirks, holds out the joint to me.

I shake my head. 'No, thanks.' But would women really do that? I think of Mum and Mr Colson, then bat the thought away.

He takes another toke, then nips the joint against the glass that Mum used as an astray; the end of her cigarette still sitting there kissed with blood-red lipstick. But unlike Mum, Pete doesn't clutter the gaps with needless conversation. He sits back casually, hands behind his head.

'What if I was a police officer?' I ask, trying to break the silence.

He laughs. 'You don't look like one.'

'Or a reformed drug addict, struggling to kick my habit.'

He raises his eyebrows, looking at me in my well-worn jammies and mismatched socks. 'I am *not* a reformed drug addict,' I clarify.

We both smile, eyes meeting, then gazing at the floor.

Silence unspools again.

'Pete,' I say, building up to my question about the letter, because I need to before he thinks about leaving. 'Do you... always deliver round here?'

'Mostly,' he replies.

'Mostly, or just sometimes?'

'Sometimes,' he says, then he looks at me and my heart tightens. God, Lauren loved his face, those mischievous eyes. A whole world of happiness in just stealing glimpses of him.

'Were you here a few days ago?'

'Yeah, 'spect so.'

'Did you post a letter?'

'Look, what is this? Twenty questions?' He laughs. 'I wasn't hanging around waiting to be invited in for coffee, if that's what you mean; this is terrible by the way.' He raises his mug. Then he sees my expression and something darkens in his eyes. 'Wait. I had no idea you lived here. Honest. I wasn't—'

'I know,' I say, holding up my hands to calm him. 'I wasn't suggesting you did. I just want to know about a letter. From Lauren.'

'Lauren?' His voice rises. 'But she's—' He stops himself.

'She's what?' I ask.

'Not much of a penpal.' His joke slips out and I can see he instantly regrets it. 'Sorry. I didn't mean...' He's such an idiot. 'I'm such an idiot,' he says, as if reading my mind. He fiddles with the lighter. 'It's hard to know what to say.'

'The letter,' I reiterate. 'Where would it have come from?' I put us firmly back on track.

'I just get them off the rack in the sorting office. Put them into the bag, into the van.'

'But this one didn't have my address on it. Not for here anyway. Or a name.'

He shrugs. 'I guess I didn't deliver it then.'

I gaze towards the window. *Hopeless.* There's no answer. Only the coincidence that it's him. But maybe this is more than a coincidence. Some clue I still need from him. Some question he needs to answer. Maybe it's not about the letter at all.

'Do you think of her?'

'Sometimes. I mean, yeah. I guess, wondering what happened.'

The words make me tearful as he fiddles with the lighter, turning it over in his fingers.

'Mind if I?' He holds out the joint again. *Nervous*, I think. He smokes because he's nervous. Maybe he always did.

He lights it and disappears behind another grey plume. A loose fragment of ash falling like a leaf, landing on his thigh.

'Lauren and me, we went down to the canal a few times. Nowhere else to go really, to be alone. We sat under the bridge. Talked, you know? She was young, very young. But an old soul, vivid thoughts, dark humour, searching for something. And I thought...'

What did he think of her?

'That she was different, something more to her, like there was another world trapped in there. And anger, hurt, resentment. Things that no one else could see. She said my music spoke to her, said she loved it. Especially my lyrics, my own angst and frustration. I guess I was flattered. Then one night she smoked a joint... it was her first. And she freaked out, said her heart was beating too fast. I tried to make a lame joke; told her it was just me. That I had that effect on women.'

She wasn't a woman, she was just a girl, I think. But his eyes are sad as if he realizes how stupid he sounds.

'I calmed her down, and then we...'

'Then you took advantage of her and then spread rumours about her,' I say more bitingly. 'Before selling her troubles to the world!'

'*No*. I liked her. I really did. It was her that dumped me, after she met David. Said I was just a "stupid boy".' He does quote marks with his fingers, his mouth slanted as he says it. 'Said she was more interested in someone more grown up, with something intelligent to say. All I did was smoke and muck around on my guitar. What she needed was someone who would take her places.'

He flips the yellow lighter. It sparks.

Lauren had thought that. Stupid, stupid, troubled, lost, naïve Lauren. She'd wanted someone like the Handsome Reveller to offer her the world. Especially after David had sent her packing.

Pete shrugs, something so nonchalant. But what he says next cuts deep into me, shocks me. The shrug was just another nervous mannerism, not a dismissal. He did like her. She dumped him.

'Lauren was going to be something. I wrote that in a song for her: "*One day she'll set the world on fire*".'

He sparks the yellow lighter between his fingers, holding the flame up, the light of it dancing in his eyes.

'Corny, I know, but she was going to be something.'

I think of the letter, the horror she described. A tear streaks down my face. Pete was not mean, just young and naïve and not really what she wanted, beyond being a cute guy with a pretty face. Nothing more. Cross him off the bad list.

Pete sets the lighter on the table and shifts over to the sofa and hugs me. Hugs me for the longest time and there's so much comfort in his youthful warmth. More gentle than I ever expected. His scent and his thin muscular arms. I think about him comforting Lauren the night she freaked out. Kind not cruel. Not like some.

'I'm sorry,' I say.

'Not as sorry as me,' he replies.

Eventually, we go into the hall, past the space where his picture once hung. Then at the door we stand close. I can smell his cheap aftershave, smoke on his breath, and the gum he's chewing now.

'Do... do you ever see Shirl?' I ask, more as a parting thought.

He smiles. 'Actually, we're getting—' He stops, shoves his hands in his pockets as if to stifle the cold. 'Um... I should get going.'

'Married?' I ask. They get to play happily ever after?

'You could come if you like,' he says, not sensing my displeasure. 'I'm sure you might recognize a few old faces.'

'No, I... don't think so.' I start closing the door behind him.

'All the more reason.' He sticks his foot in the door to stop it. 'Chance to get out, get back to your old life. You never know where it might lead if you just got on with things.'

I think of a floaty dress, a garish thing in my hair. A dull ceremony in a miserable church, chewing on jealousy for things that only happen to others. Not me, and never Lauren. A reception in a hotel that has been tarted up for the occasion. Getting drunk, too drunk. Dancing with some random groomsmen or uncle who isn't even an uncle at all, and not being Shirl's bridesmaid, and never being the bride.

'Well...' I say, cutting off my jealous thoughts. 'Stuff to do.'

'Likewise,' Pete says lifting his satchel that he's slung over his shoulder.

But he doesn't move, barely seems in any rush. It's cold out, he hasn't quite finished his joint. It's not because he wants to stay in here, close to me. Or help find Lauren. He's got a better life, with *Shirl*.

Icy drizzle fills the cold porch. He pulls his padded jacket around him, and I can feel the warmth push out from inside it. Then he leans down, kisses me gently on the cheek. A small wet circle left on my skin.

'See you round then,' he says, as he always did, before leaping up the steps two at a time. A thoughtless, harmless boy. Lauren's first love.

'You know where to find me,' I call after him. 'I'm always here. Right here...'

It feels good to let Pete go, to let him off the hook. He isn't the one I should be angry with.

Then I close the door.

THIRTY-THREE

LAUREN

Before

I was starting to play a new game. One where I wasn't in The Hole. You've got secrets, I've got some too. So, I was sitting cross-legged in the upstairs room, looking into that space under the floorboard. My place, my space, a hole, not like The Hole, not nasty and frightening, but a lovely place where I hid all my lovely, precious things. All few of them.

But now there was something new to add. I slid the photo down from my sleeve. The one I had found earlier. The photo of a girl and a woman.

I hadn't meant to find it, I wasn't snooping, not that there was anywhere left to snoop. Doors were locked, windows were barred or shuttered, fingers were burned that tried to touch things they shouldn't. And now Keele had said the place needed to be extra tidy, no clutter left out, in case he had visitors again. As if he was expecting someone. He made me put all my clothes in a box in the back room, and even made me paint over the bad wall with all the women and girls who didn't have people protecting them. I was glad about that. *Don't worry*, he said, *we can make a new one... later.*

We both seemed to be listening extra hard for something, not sure why. Keeping me upstairs most of the time, binder at my ankles, sometimes tape on my mouth. The slightest thing seemed to make him jump, and more often he found an excuse to put me back in The Hole. In and out, a few hours, a few days. He was waiting for something.

Or someone.

The Maybe-Police again, I thought. Or the lad from the post. Or animal services. Or maybe even my parents. Except, no, they weren't coming, I knew that now. That much was clear.

But maybe *Jacqueline French. NOT KNOWN AT THIS ADDRESS.*

So I was trying to please him, working hard, cleaning and wiping, trying not to put a foot wrong. Because now I knew that this was my only home, where I had to stay until I really was better, no one else wanted me. *And* not to end up like the dog. Meanwhile hoping that sooner or later someone would come. They'd have read my letter and believed my words. Soon.

I'd been in the living room that morning, wiping all around, removing all my sticky fingerprints which Keele always complained he could see everywhere. I accidentally knocked the frame over. Even though it wasn't new, Keele had just put it on the sideboard. A photo of him crouched beside his beloved dog. Arm lovingly round her neck. His beloved *dead* dog.

I had been wiping it carefully, I suppose I might have been looking at it, at her, wondering if I could still remember her bark, her smell, the times when she was nice girl not bad girl. And that's when it slipped.

Too many pretty pinks, Keele was generous with those these days. But thank God when I dropped it, it tumbled onto my foot and the glass hadn't smashed. And only for a split second had I thought about that: if it had, a great big shard of glass slamming into his fat jugular neck—

No. It was OK. I reached down and lifted it carefully, but still the back came off. The little latches swinging free, and I was putting it back – I swear – when I found the picture. Tucked behind the one of him and the dog.

A photo of a girl and a woman.

It was faded. But I thought the girl had a familiar look. Something in her eyes I recognized. Only afterwards when I peered in the mirror, I thought she looked a bit like me, or maybe how I had looked before, in the summer of fourteen. Back then...

Back then... it echoes back to me.

'Who are you?' I whispered to the girl in the picture, then I'd laughed at myself for trying to talk to her as if she might want to be my friend. I heard a sound and realized Keele would be angry that I'd found it; that I'd get into real trouble. Just a feeling. A big feeling.

'Shhh,' I'd said, putting my fingers to my lips to remind them to stay quiet too. Then I'd stuffed that photo into the sleeve of my jumper and put the frame back on the side with the dog showing, careful to remove all traces of my fingerprints. Keele must never know that I had even touched it.

But sitting upstairs, I had time to look at them more closely. To see the endless soft curve of the woman's hair tucked behind one ear, revealing a small gold stud. Her flattering green summer dress that stopped at the elbow, her left arm draped affectionately around the young girl. Young, but not a child. Nine or ten. Mother and daughter, had to be. The loving tilt of the mum's head, the way the girl sat obediently up close, her hands folded in her lap, not quite smiling at whoever was behind the camera.

Nervous, I thought. Something bothering her. I could *feel* it.

'Don't worry,' I told her. 'You're safe now. I'll look after you,' and I hugged them to me before lowering them into the space with my other special things. I know I imagined it, but I thought I saw the girl smile.

She was in the safe place now under the floorboard, along-side my articles that Keele didn't know I had, not the ones he'd given me, but others I'd found. The one with the name at the bottom – *David Pritchard*. I thought of him, his blond hair falling over his dark-rimmed glasses as he placed his hands under his chin, prayer-like.

'You're a good writer. You'll go far. I know it...'

How far, David? How very far?

I lifted out the other cuttings too, pictures from magazines and even the article David had written about a woman who had lost her daughter. An interview with the 'Missing Me' words. I imagined it was Mum talking to David about a lost daughter, and I had always hoped it might be her words about me. How loving they were. That was why I thought maybe one day she'd come. But now I knew the truth. It wasn't her. These weren't her words. It couldn't be because I had heard what she'd said on TV. We all had.

We all had, Sue Fisher.

Mum wasn't like the woman in the picture, sitting protec-tive beside her daughter. Or the woman in the 'Missing Me' article with the haunting words of loss. Mum wasn't any of those women, those mothers. Mum was Mum was Mum.

I had found the 'Missing Me' article in the newspaper a few years back. Lying under a car part I had been cleaning. It was only a fragment, the rest torn off. How I wished I could read the rest. But I heard Mum's voice in those words, and I reread them over and over until I practically knew them by heart. Held like a thread of hope.

After she went, I would sometimes get out her clothes, and her dolls and soft toys which she hadn't played with for a long time,

and I breathed them in. To find a little trace of her there still. I
was afraid to steal the last of her scent. As if it was all I had left
until she came back. But sometimes I just needed to remind
myself that she had ever been here at all.

It was stained with circles from a turps bottle and black
dirty smears, and tears I had cried. Good tears. Sad tears. But I
took it and folded it carefully, putting it in the space under the
floorboard. Next to the article about Pete, the one that Keele
had given me, a spark in his eyes. Almost glee. I'd told him I'd
flushed it away when he asked. But I hadn't. I'd kept it.

LOST GIRL WAS ALREADY 'LOST', SAYS EX

Pete Wise, the ex-boyfriend of the troubled teen, Lauren Fisher,
said she took drugs and had sex with him down at the canal in
the months before she disappeared. The same spot where her
bike was found abandoned.

'She already seemed "lost",' Pete said. 'As if she was
searching for something, for somewhere else to be.'

Asked if he thought she was suicidal, as was widely specu-
lated, he said, 'She wasn't happy with life. She'd distanced
herself from me and our friends. She'd fallen out with her best
friend and her parents. Become a loner. Got hung up on a local
editor, then something happened there too. She just seemed to
attract trouble. But she was special. She was—'

The rest was gone.

There was Pete's face, that picture of us from that party all
those years ago. That fringe I had grown out and regrown after
Keele cut all my hair. *Laid bare*, that's what Keele had said at
the time. *All your dirty little secrets laid bare*, his joyous laugh as
he handed the cutting to me.

See, Keele had said. *Giving away the goods too soon to that boy. He can't keep his tongue in his mouth, any more than he can keep his dick in his trousers.*

Still, I put it under the floorboards, just in case. Maybe if I read it one more time I would see something I had missed. Another reason, a message. Because David always said that the reason we wrote things, a message we wanted to get across.

Then I heard Keele on the stairs, and I pushed all the cuttings and pictures back in the space and the floorboard back in place. Shoved it down hard. Pete and David and the woman and her daughter. The lip gloss and the smear of blusher and a wad of wool from my most favourite jumper. Keele would never find them. Never.

Come on, he said, coming into the room. *Just need you to go back in The Hole for a little while,* and he used the knife from his pocket to cut the binders at my ankle.

'Please, Keele,' the fear rising. 'I can stay here. I'll be quiet. Don't put me back in there. I won't make trouble.'

He looked at me. *Like last time? All the fuss you made, when those people came.* He laughed. *You're kidding me, right?* He laughed like he was truly amused. *Come on. Get moving.* Then he growled. *Someone's coming. And I can't mess this up.*

I didn't move. 'Please, Keele. I promise I won't make a sound.'

Promises, promises. You've made me a lot of promises over the years. Kept none of them. And here we are. All you've brought me is trouble. Maybe it's time you left for good. What do you say, Little Girl Lost?

I flinched. Did he know I'd been reading the article? Had he seen me?

'Please, Keele. I'll sit here, quiet as a mouse.' I shrunk myself down small.

Why? What's so special about here? He looked around as if sniffing something out. I felt the heat rising, what if he saw the floorboard, found my things?

'I just meant... I could wait. No need to go down there.' But maybe I should just do what he asked. Not upset him. He'd win in the end, and I'd heard his words... *Maybe it's time you left for good.*

Then he hoisted me up.

Come on, we haven't got all day, he said.

'Please,' I whispered quietly, maybe too quietly. So quietly that even he didn't hear. Because if he had, he might have changed his mind.

THIRTY-FOUR

LAUREN

Before

When he finally took me out of The Hole, I was surprised. Everything had been cleaned. Cleaner than clean. Cleaner than I had made it. And that stench of bleach.

I told myself it was something to do with the dog. Maybe Keele had been worried because the dog had been sick – *pandemic* – that word dancing across my mind. Or maybe he'd done it for me. Fresh start, wiped clean.

But I was weak, and everything hurt from being in The Hole, and even if I wanted to ask, I swallowed the words. I just needed to lie down. I took my pretty pinks that he handed me, and a nice warm shower, and when I came down in my pyjamas scrumpled from where they'd been balled up and stuffed in the box, Keele had made dinner. Even the plates were set straight. He looked happy.

I sat quietly at the table, though my back ached.

I made your favourite, he said. *Lasagne. For being such a good girl. For being so much better. Because you are, aren't you?*

And now finally everything's going to be OK, Little L. Everything is all taken care of.

Something about him was different. Like his shoulders were down. Like a weight lifted. What was he up to?

But the smell of food was all around me, and I was so hungry and not sure if I could stomach eating all at the same time. Still, I sat slowly, looking at the crisp browned cheese stuck to the edges of the dish as he cut me a slab and laid it on my plate. I picked up my fork and poked it, making appropriate *ummm* noises, as if I loved it.

'Thank you,' I said, like the most grateful person in the world.

Keele's hand moved, and I flinched as I lifted my eyes. But his hand was on a book which he slid across the table.

It's for you, he said.

I thought of the book he gave me, that second time I saw him down by the canal. Autumn was in full swing, summer was gone, leaves turning pretty colours, that sweet decaying smell. Him in his grey coat, and the dog bounding around. I should have felt that gnawing fear in my stomach. That warning. Instead, he shone through against the fog of my anger at Pete and David and Mum and Shirl. Hurt. I was hurt. Heartbroken and alone. And along he came with his shiny dog and his bright excited eyes, and he said, *Fancy meeting you again*, like fate had played its part. Later, sitting on the wall, he handed me the book from his pocket. Said it was embarrassing really, because he'd been carrying it around for weeks just in case he saw me again. *Hoping*. He'd thought of me a lot. And my heart leaped, just a little. I should have known. I should have...

Maybe one day I'll be a writer, and I'll give you my book, he'd said. *I just need the right inspiration... the right muse... hey? Little L... mind if I call you that?*

It was several weeks before our paths crossed again. And I told him about David, how he'd told me my writing was good, and made me think it was better than good, something special. He told me to write, and I could show him if I liked. But that David was probably after the wrong thing. *Did he ever touch you? If he did, you should tell someone, that would teach him, hey?* And David hadn't but still I lay awake in bed that night, thinking... thinking maybe David did deserve to get in a little trouble, because he'd played games with me. I retracted it pretty quickly, and no one believed it anyway. Stupid thing to do. They made me see a counsellor at school. And even if Mum said she'd keep it a secret from Dad, that meant I owed her. Had to do whatever she said.

Then in December, because I'd been grounded, I was walking at the canal and I saw her. That dog – Girl he called her – and I thought that was affectionate then. I asked him where he lived, and he said out past the fields. The white cottage, did I know the one? *All my books and writing*, he said, and I said maybe I would go there one day and see for myself, and my eyes crept up to meet his. He had stubble, and sometimes he smelled of paint fumes and beer. His fingers not as clean as I imagined a writer's to be.

My old beauties, he said. *Classic cars. You can see them too. Just give me a call. Anytime. Anytime you want to talk.*

I asked him if he was married, and he hesitated. *Once*, he said. I saw a flicker of sadness pooling in the backs of his eyes. *I lost her sadly*. Then darker. A smile becoming a sneer. Then he reached out his hand and lay it on mine.

Thank you, he said.

'For what?' I asked.

For making me feel alive again, waking me up after a very long sleep, hey, like a princess.

And I said it was the princes who woke the princesses in those stupid stories. *Well, those stories were made to be rewritten by people like us.* He looked at me, then away again quickly and kicked a stone like he was almost shy. Then he stood up.

Well, one day, maybe when you're older. Our own little twisted fairy tale, hey, Little L. You'll be filling my head with so many wonderful ideas again. My muse. You are food for my mind and hope for my soul. Adventures, hey? Out in the great wide world. One day.

I longed then to see his white cottage. He made me feel that I could make someone else feel good. And that was all I wanted. Ever. And I wasn't very good at it.

Now, in his kitchen, with the lasagne turning rubbery on the plate, the new book lying there. All those lost years in between. Stupid, stupid, stupid.

You don't want to take it? he asked, his tone coarse.

I put my hand on top of it and closed my eyes, and tried to imagine I could smell that autumn day and I was back there at the canal, and I could get up and walk away. Could tell him thanks but no thanks, and goodbye and never see him again. Walk back home and close the door and lock it, go to my bedroom, safe and sound. Turn on my music, read a magazine, do some homework. Another reality, another life, we'd just slipped through a crack into the wrong one. But maybe this was the last time, he'd never do those things to me again. That that was the meaning of this gift. A fresh start. A reset. Back to the beginning.

Everything's going to be better...

I told myself that meant he was sorry.

But the dog was dead, and the house was cold, and The Hole in the ground was freezing now December was probably here. Things were getting worse not better. Dark days huddled on our doorstep. And it would never end.

'Maybe I'm not better,' I dared to say. 'Maybe you should take me somewhere, to let them... treat me. Make me well.'

Or maybe you should leave forever, he said.

Forever... and that was a mighty long time, as someone once sang. But I knew what he meant. My eyes flitting over to the title. *The Bell Jar*. And the thought came to me amongst all the other half-formed thoughts, in that kitchen with that untouched plate of lasagne. Maybe it *was* time. Because this would never be over.

But he lay his hand on top of mine, like that day at the canal. Some strange closure.

I knew you'd appreciate it, he said. *Because you understand things, messages. Because you're special.*

And then we ate.

He was nodding as I chewed. Enjoying that I was enjoying it. I lifted my head and tried to smile. I saw myself watching from across the room, disassociated as I drifted there, and I thought that anyone really watching from outside a window might just think we were a normal family or happy couple having a relaxing dinner. Me in my pyjamas, a book on the table.

But the light in the kitchen was bright, and the patterns on the tiles, the wood knots in the table, the flowers on the curtains, everything shifted. I told myself it was just my head, the pills, the stench of bleach. It felt as if I had emerged into a parallel universe.

Maybe this wasn't real.

Not feeling good? Keele asked.

I nodded, and he got up and opened the cupboard and popped out two more pink tablets. Slid them across the table as he sat. I looked up at him and fought a tiny smile onto my face.

'Water,' I said, getting up slowly.

The patterns danced with each step as I moved towards the sink. The light circled as if swinging overhead, and I found myself slipping. Everything closing in. A kaleidoscope of vision.

Knees buckling, falling down, days without food. Days without light. Crumpling down onto the floor, landing with a thud. The shock of the cold tiles against my cheek.

I lay there. In and out of consciousness.

The pink tablet had slipped from my hand and rolled out of my grasp, and away like so many things. Keele just sat there eating his dinner as if nothing had happened. He didn't move a muscle.

Eventually my eyes began to focus again, and I saw the tablet just under the cabinets. And that's when I saw it, the small gold ball right at the back against the skirting. I thought I was imagining it, but it glinted at me. I inched my hand out, touching the pink pill, before scooping up that gold ball into my hand.

A gold stud earring.

Keele never looked up, not as I pulled myself up. One hand on the cupboard door, one hand on the counter. My knees ready to buckle again at any second.

Then suddenly he was looking at me.

I felt the burning of my own fear. The earring in my hand. If he saw that I had found it and dared to pick it up, he would be worse than unhappy. I thought about dropping it, but it was too late. I was bound by my actions now.

I turned around and flipped on the tap and took a clean glass from the metal draining board all wiped clean. Not a single stain from half-finished tea. Cleaner than I had ever made it, as if something had needed to be removed.

I got the glass of water and opened my hand, and put it to my lips and swallowed the tablets. But Keele was quick, right by me then, gripping my hand.

What have you got? he asked. *Open your hands, both of them!*

I showed him my left and then reluctantly my right. Both empty.

Open your mouth, he demanded, and I opened it, flipped out my tongue. *Wider,* he said and he looked deep inside. Then he gripped my hand as if holding it to go for a walk. Tight.

Crushed fingers. He was moving my hand towards the hob, and he flipped on the ring, heating up quickly.

Tell me, he insisted.

He tugged my hand towards the hot ring of the hob. He wouldn't, he wouldn't. Then the heat touched the skin of my fingers and for a moment there was a brilliant white light in my head, almost godly, as if I had been struck by lightning. A scream burst out from me like fire.

But I never made a noise.

When he was sure I had nothing to tell him, he cast my hand away and went back to the table. Exactly as he had been before, eating with big thrusts of food into his ugly mouth. My brain pulsing with pain, and nothing could take my mind from it.

Someone had been here. Someone had lost a small gold earring on the kitchen floor washed clean with bleach. A gold earring that I had found and I had managed to swallow.

THIRTY-FIVE

RENE

Before

David stands at the door. He's wearing a thick brown coat, and his hair is damp from the low fog. He shivers slightly.

He goes to step inside, but I block his path. *I wouldn't trust him either*, that's what Pete said. But had he meant anything by it? Another throwaway comment.

'You OK?' David asks, a rasp of concern in his voice. 'Last time we spoke you were upset. Something about a letter and no one believing you.' He tries to step forward.

'And so you just *rushed* on over,' I say sarcastically.

His face makes a quizzical expression. 'I'm here, aren't I?'

'Only because you want her story,' I snap back. 'And why *are* you so interested in that? Why don't you just go back to your wife, your daughter? Go back to playing happy families...'

There's a pain in my throat, tight, as if I've been crying or screaming. My hand aches. I tell myself it's from writing, but I know that it isn't just that, I haven't written anything else. But my fingers throb, and I can't shut out the pain no matter how many pretty pinks I swallow. I just don't have strength for David today. His false enthusiasm and unclear motives.

He hesitates, 'Rene, let me in. I can explain if you do.'

'Then tell me here.'

He shivers slightly. His hair darkening with the damp. 'I owe it to Lauren. I let her down, we both know I did.' He shivers again. It's cold out, even colder than inside. But he looks drained, maybe even sick. 'I need you to hear my truth too, before it's too late.'

I think of Lauren coming home from school that May, saying she had met someone who believed in her writing. How excited she was, naïvely enthralled. At the Careers Fair, and she was going to be a writer.

Mum was dismissive, saying, 'I had wanted to be a writer once too. Could have been, but then I had you, dear Lauren. And like my mother always reminded me, children get in the way of everything.'

But David had encouraged Lauren. He wanted her to succeed.

'All right,' I say, stepping aside.

We sit on the sofa. Sip tea that I barely remember making. It doesn't matter any longer. This does. Because within David's story is part of the crumbtrail. A clue, maybe the last. I look down and see that my socks are matching. It bothers me a little. But I'm sure it'll be OK.

'Lauren meant a lot to me,' David begins, cupping his mug. 'More than she should, I suppose. I remember the first time I met her, the Careers Fair at school. It had been raining and I was soaked to the skin. She came up to me in the foyer and handed me some paper towels to dry myself.'

'She was probably just being kind,' I say, trying to dismiss it. But I know she wanted to make a good impression, or get his attention first.

'Afterwards, I got up on stage, presented my little set piece about working in journalism. I was nervous,' he smiles. 'Never a great one for big speeches. Hid behind my pen or my laptop most of my life. I think that's what all writers do...'

He shakes his head as if questioning himself, his life choices. Or maybe just knowing himself too well. I like that about David, those occasional quiet moments like he's reflecting on something deeper, and maybe even content.

'There was a marketing guy, rather confident. A chef, worked in one of those fancy places in town; never a seat and the bill always crippling. A game developer, so cool and innovative, carrying a blow-up shark for some reason. A lawyer, dull but rich. And a woman who had sailed around the world. *Twice*. She was amazing. Wiped the floor with the rest of us.'

He smiles at this memory, this game show lineup. The cast in a strange play. He takes another slug of tea.

'And then there was me. A local hack with two bad novels to my name. The mighty editor in chief of a dying local paper.'

As he speaks, I can almost feel the oppressive heat of the school hall, all those girls and teachers jubilant to see new faces, practically celebrities to them. The early May rain beating on the windows, intensifying the humidity inside. Row upon row of girls sitting cross-legged on the wood floor, hands in laps, all wanting to ask questions just to get attention. Loose, half-hearted clapping as each person finished. *No time for questions, girls*, the headmistress saying, because that's how it always was there.

I think of Lauren listening closely to Mr David Pritchard. She'd spotted his name on the wall a few weeks before and knew it was him she wanted to speak to. She'd read those bad novels. Both of them. Twice.

I think of her leaving the hall after all the speeches were done, eyes fixed on the ground as she walked the length of the corridor. Finding the room with the heavy door, where he was sitting for his discussion group. She knocked softly, and he looked up as she entered, his not-quite-dry hair falling over his black-rimmed glasses. His soft kind eyes welcoming her, and thin lips that looked very much like a smile.

'Lauren was the only one who came. It was awkward for both of us. But she told me about her passion for writing. A determination that I rarely saw, even in people far older. She showed me things she'd written in a notebook, and I had to admit it was good, complex, quite beautiful as if she saw the world... *differently*.'

But something is coming. I need him to tell me. His truth. What happened.

'I told her she had potential. That she should keep finding her voice. Keep coming back... to her writing. Maybe she thought I meant she should keep coming back to me.'

I think of Lauren that early summer, sitting under the rose bush that Dad had planted. Yellow roses, their fragrance intensified by the heat. Frantically scribbling. Her books becoming filled with stories and half-truths; made-up interviews, images, true-life news articles. She hadn't lived long enough to know enough to write about, so she stole ideas from places, things she saw on TV, in magazines; wove them into stories that sounded almost-but-not-quite believable.

'A week later the first bundle of her work appeared on my desk. A few weeks later, a few more.'

'And then?' I ask. He turns his head to the side, towards the window. '*And then?*' I demand. My hand hurts, but not as much as my heart. Because it's coming. The truth.

'She showed up at my office.'

I feel my brain firing, knowing what that moment had meant to her.

'It had been raining that day too; she was soaked to the skin,' he says. 'I wondered if she had done it on purpose, to create a connection, a symmetry. So that I couldn't turn her away.'

'You think that?'

'I don't think Lauren left anything to chance.' He almost smiles. Almost. 'So I gave her a handful of paper towels and I made her a coffee, saw how she screwed up her face as she pretended to enjoy it. There were others around, we were never alone. I swear. There's glass in my office window, and everyone could see us. At all times.'

Why does that matter? Why does he need to insist? But I know why. I know the truth is lumbering towards us, like a lazy unstoppable animal that can still devour us both.

'I saw how she watched me, how focused she was. She wanted something from me.'

'She wanted to write. That was her *dream*.'

'Yes, and I thought I was... helping.'

'*Helping*?' I repeat, a mocking tone invading my voice.

He shifts his feet, tucks them backwards. He's uncomfortable. Maybe he doesn't even want to go on. 'Her teacher had told me that she was a good student, but she'd been having "difficulties". A recent illness, problems at home, parents not getting along. Her grandmother had also died not long before; all of that. And I just thought...' He stops and breathes out. 'I guess I was the one being naïve.'

I see him push his glasses up onto his forehead, rubbing the bridge of his nose. Pain behind his eyes.

'So I listened. *Listened*, that was all.' His voice rises as if I am accusing him of something. 'Jesus, it's my job to listen. Journalism isn't about being able to write, it's about being able to shut up long enough for people to reveal themselves to you; to tell you what really makes them tick. Or what they've got to hide.'

'And what was she hiding?'

'She told me her mother was depressed, lived on a diet of pills. That they didn't get on, maybe never had. That her dad had been loving but had become distant. That her nanna had passed, and her mum had hated her too, or had until the moment she'd breathed her last breath. She'd sent me a piece about that. Another about a childhood doll and a miscarriage. Another about a postcard she'd found. Then she said she had this arsehole boyfriend who spread rumours, a bitch of a best friend who wanted to steal him. It seemed to her that no one really cared. No one listened. No one loved her. She felt... *lost.*'

He wants to stop. He wants me to tell him he did nothing wrong. But I shut up long enough for him to reveal what really makes him tick. To tell me what he did next...

'She showed up again, another bundle of her writing, and I gave her a coffee.'

'And you *just* listened, hey?'

Silence.

'David?'

More silence.

'Dav—'

'No!' he cuts in. 'I told her to write. Told her to get it down on paper, to use her imagination. To tell her story and maybe she'd see the truth in it. I thought it would help.' He's pleading.

'And?'

Because that isn't everything. I know it isn't.

He gets up, twists as if he's the one lost, doesn't quite know which way to look. He turns his back, stares out the window. 'I told her I was there for her. To call me if she ever needed anything. If she ever wanted... to *talk.* I gave her my number.'

'You *encouraged* her,' I say more forcefully. 'You made her *think* she was special. A girl who told you she felt like no one loved her.'

'I only wanted her to follow her dreams.'

'Why, David? Why did you do it if it was all so *innocent*?'

'Because... *because*... I... saw something in her. I saw... myself, as a kid. Needing someone who believed in me.'

'You were flattered by her attention.'

'Jesus, no! She was a kid.' He turns back quickly now. 'For

God's sake, we only met a few times – once at the school and a couple more times at my office. A handful of phone calls. It was nothing—'

'*Nothing?*'

'You know this!' His voice rising now, distressed to have to defend himself, to me of all people.

'She thought you liked her.'

'I did, but not like that.'

'So, you told her to go away. And where did she go?'

'This was months before she disappeared. I had nothing to do with that. I thought that was it.'

'And that's how the story ends, hey, David?'

Nothing.

'David!'

'No. You *know* it's not.'

THIRTY-SIX

RENE

Before

Suddenly I can see his anger. Those thin lips now without any hint of a smile.

'In November she reported me to the school... for trying to touch her.'

His breath in his throat, the sound of his hurt, confusion. I can hear the strain.

'But I didn't. I wouldn't have... you know that. I had a family! A wife I *loved*.' Tears in his eyes. 'I never...' He looks at me, pleading for understanding, then away.

I feel a sticky heat inside. Guilt, for Lauren, for what she did to him. He'd been kind to her, and she had done this. But Lauren has been the one who suffered. Lauren had paid the price for this. The accusation that muddied everything. Lauren quickly told the school there was nothing in it, and she was sent to the school counsellor.

'But it made things difficult for me after she disappeared. No smoke without fire,' David says. 'I was taken in for questioning then. My wife was pregnant with our second daughter.

We'd just started telling people about the baby. We were excited, and then—' He cuts off, fluctuating between pleading and anger. His teeth gritted now. 'Did Lauren ever think about that?'

He's angry; protective of his family, his own life.

'Did she understand? Well, *did* she?' His anger is rising, a spark in his eyes. He steps forward. He's scaring me. 'Her little made-up stories used against me.'

I stare at my unlucky socks. What will he do?

Then the anger shifts again, his hands open, pleading not for understanding but for answers.

'Why did she do it?' He moves forward.

Conflict knots in my stomach. Do I defend Lauren, or feel bad for David, or afraid of his rage just under the surface?

'Did she think about how it *destroyed* me? My marriage, my career? I nearly lost *everything*.'

'And Lauren?' My voice a whisper. 'What did she lose?'

More than just her dreams, her hopes, her aspirations. Her life.

He shakes his head as if he doesn't understand the question.

'No one believed her. The girl who cried wolf. We all know how that story ends. So you tell me,' I say. 'What did Lauren lose?'

David's mouth hangs open.

'She lost being trusted. She lost being believed. She lost being credible... even before she was lost.'

After the business with the school and Lauren came clean about her lies, Mum said they didn't need to tell Dad. *Our little secret.* But later she said if Lauren didn't do exactly as she was told Mum would be *forced* to tell him. Acting as if she was protecting her, but practically blackmailing her. Or that was how Lauren saw it. Mum saying if she wasn't careful, they'd have to get proper help. Not just the school counsellor, but therapy. Proper therapy. *You're out of control now.*

But it is still coming, the gaping absence in the heart of this truth. As I stand surrounded by all Lauren's things, and David wracked by guilt and hurt and confusion and anger. Because no one asked Lauren *why* she had said what she did. What made her lie.

Or rather *who*.

'Lauren never meant to make things difficult for you,' I say, getting up and putting my hand on his arm.

But David shakes me off.

Anxiety tightens in my throat. Poor David. And even more, poor Lauren. She was hurt by him, but she hadn't meant to hurt him this way. She had been manipulated. The power of suggestion.

'Someone *told* her to do it. To create layers of doubt.'

'To muddy the water,' David says quietly, as if reading my mind. Our eyes meet.

'He planned it all along, didn't he?' I say. 'Is that the truth? Is that what you wanted me to find? That he told her to say those things so they wouldn't come looking in all the right places...'

David has been desperately hoping for her to be found because he knew something terrible had happened to her, was still happening to her. That someone had manipulated her. But who would believe him? That cloud, that suspicion? Hanging over him, all of them. But not the right person.

Or maybe he just wanted to clear his own name. The thought enters my head. Self-preservation. To have his wife believe him again, to let him touch her at night.

'Listen,' David whispers, his voice dropping suddenly as if they might be overheard. 'Every day you're getting closer. Closer to the truth. But it's not that simple anymore. That isn't enough now. He knows that you're working it out. And in the end, if you know the truth, he will have to... kill you. Both of you.'

I feel a jolt of shock. 'Me? But he doesn't know about me.'

'I'm sorry,' David says, getting up and hurrying into the hall. 'I've said too much already. I've lost enough.'

He's at the door, working the locks, trying to get out.

'What do you mean, David?'

'Remember,' he says. 'Remember it all. And one day when you write it down, your story, everyone will see how brave you've been. How strong you are. This is your story.'

He steps outside, turns only briefly. His face looks worn, old. A last glimmer in his eyes behind black-rimmed glasses.

THIRTY-SEVEN

LAUREN

Before

I found that earring a few days later. The toilet had been scrubbed clean too, so I hadn't minded sticking my hand in, not for something so important. So precious. I washed it and my hands, careful not to lose it down the plughole. Then I wedged it deep in my pocket.

Keele was outside the toilet door when I stepped out. *You took your time*, he said, looking at me warily.

'Sorry,' I said. Nothing more.

Then I followed him along the upstairs corridor, to the back room. But then he was turning, and my hand was in my pocket; it had wormed its way in, like a tongue into a missing socket of a tooth. I couldn't resist. Couldn't stop myself. Touching that earring just to know it was still there. This little curiosity.

He turned quickly and he saw me. *What's that?* he asked.

I pulled my fingers out from my pocket and opened them obediently.

No, in your pocket, he insisted.

Split second. Truth or lie. 'I don't know what you mean,' I lied.

Show me.

'There's nothing, really, Keele. I promise.'

I tried to smile, and something in that made him know I was lying.

He scrabbled into my pocket, tearing the seam, snatching the earring out, and as I reached to take it back, he smacked me away with his other arm.

Well, well. Is that what you found the other day? Is that what you were doing in there all that time?

His hand rose again.

'No.' I cowered, but he caught me with his hand under my chin. A big hard crashing slap and I tumbled into the shelf behind. Crumpling to the floor, his foot connecting with my knee, and it was then that my leg shot out and kicked the bookshelf.

I thought maybe I had imagined it. That it moved, the wall moved because of the pain making my head fly – truly like white shafts into my brain.

Go on, he said, *kick like a donkey*, and he laughed, examining the earring.

But the bookshelf had come away from the wall slightly, some of the books had shifted, and a small gap appeared behind them. I knew it. Was that why it happened like that, so I would see? A space behind the wall. And what was in there?

But Keele dragged me into the bedroom and said, *You don't need this. Because you have other precious things. Other things you've been hiding from me. And you know I don't like it when you hide things, don't you?*

He clipped the cuff around my wrist.

'What?' I asked, not wanting to struggle but struggling nonetheless. Something tensed in me, drawing me back from the pain and the space I had seen, and the cuff at my wrist, tethered to the bed, and trying to avoid thinking of what he might do.

He crossed the room, over to the drawer.

When you're better, I'm good, he recited, sliding the drawer open. *And when you're bad, I can be a whole lot worse.*

He turned, smiled, then looked back, taking something from the drawer. Then he walked back towards the bed, and I shuffled back, feet grinding into the mattress, afraid of him now. The light in his eyes that shone as he sat. One hand held behind his back, the other he placed on my arm.

I smelled his smell – of alcohol and sweat and petrol and cheap aftershave – and I felt his adrenalin flowing along the muscles of his arms right down into his fingers and into my skin. I flinched, impeccable, unpreventable, but he felt it.

'I'm sorry,' I whispered desperately, bowing my head, even if I knew it was too late.

Shhhh, he said.

'I just found it. It was nothing. I just thought it was pretty. Shiny. It means nothing, I know it doesn't.'

Shhh, he said again. *That? Oh, don't worry about that. It's the other things you've been hiding from me. You know what I mean, don't you?*

Truth, or lie? Live or die? I dipped my eyes further so he couldn't see into them.

Look at me, he said. *Look at me*, he demanded again, and I did. I had no choice. No point making it worse. And then I saw his hand coming out from behind his back. The little bundle of cuttings and pictures, gathered over the years. Things I thought were safe under the floorboard. Had he found them?

I thought back to the day when the Maybe-Police had come, and I knew that I hadn't quite set the floorboard straight. He had seen it, but he hadn't said anything. Not then. No.

He had waited. Waited for me to put that picture inside. Waited until he could upset me most.

I swallowed, blinking back tears, realizing how much those things meant to me. The only things I had. The hours I had spent looking at them over the years. The woman's 'Missing Me' words, Pete's article about us, the stories David had written about other survivors as if sending me a message, the picture of the young woman on a bike by the canal, the woman with the red phone, the girl with yellow boots, the path that led to a beautiful tomorrow where one day I would go too.

'They're just rubbish,' I told Keele – as he held them in his hand. Even as I heard my voice rising and fought to hold it down. 'They're just scraps. I promise. Just to keep me entertained.'

His eyes shifted.

His weight on the bed made the mattress shift as he leaned forward, as he leafed through the cuttings and images, fanning them casually like a flip-book. Maybe he believed they were nothing. Maybe he would dismiss them as rubbish, just throw them away. My heart pounding as if it might burst, as I wondered what he was going to do.

I reached up with my free hand and touched his arm, trying to distract him.

'Please, Keele,' I said.

He pushed me away, playfully at first, and then more forcefully, and then his teeth snarled like that old dead dog, and he caught my hand.

What? he said. *What are you afraid of? That I'll find the little secrets you've been keeping from me? What does it matter, if they're only scraps?*

He was right. What did they matter?

If they're only rubbish. Light spit as he spoke.

He took out his yellow lighter and flicked it.

Little L, wants to raise a little Hell, doesn't she, he said, smiling, and he pulled out the old grey scrap of newspaper with the 'Missing Me' words that might have maybe been Mum. That I read when I wanted to feel that she was thinking of me, wishing I would come back.

You still want to believe that she cares, don't you? See, that's how sick you are. That you could think that, after all this time. After all this nothing from them.

He was laughing.

We always knew she was a good liar. Almost as good as you. Like mother, like daughter. But she was glad that you were gone. You told me that yourself, and then you saw it, just the other day on TV. I did her a favour taking you to look after. You realize that, don't you? Somewhere nice that you could recuperate. You told me all that, didn't you?

'Stop it,' I said, unable to control myself, reaching out to strike him, to grab my things. 'Stop it,' I screamed.

He pulled the bundle in his hand back above his head, out of my reach, and it only made him laugh more.

See? he said. *Maybe they're not just nothing. Look at you – like a wild animal. It's not going to change anything. But it'll stop confusing you about where you belong. About who it is that loves you most.*

He lowered the things again, flicked the lighter, the flames coming closer to the paper and dancing in the reflection in his eyes, the flame desperate to eat the old dry scraps. Tempting them to burn with each flick of the lighter. Maybe it *was* better that the lies were gone. Because they gave me false hope.

She knows exactly where you are, and still she never came. You know that. Doesn't it hurt? You always said yourself you left her a message that you were here, and you wrote. Those emails we sent. They didn't care. Glad that now troubled teen Lauren Fisher was my problem not theirs. You know that's the truth, don't you?

I half nodded.

Say it.

'That's the truth.'

Then he snorted, and it was cruel. Because maybe it was true.

Think what your father did, that last night. Remember? What they said? Or were you lying to me then too? His eyes flashed with fury. *I told you then that I didn't want you. That you should go home. That's true too, isn't it?*

I nodded.

Isn't it?

'Yes,' I said.

Yet here you are, after all these years. So why is that? Who still takes care of you? Who keeps you safe from yourself when you want to do crazy things? All these ways we have to live to protect you. Because you didn't want to be there, and now you don't want to be here. Ah, Little Troubled L, once a runaway, always a runaway. You don't even know your own fucking mind!

He edged up the bed towards me and his spit flew with the force of his words.

So what shall we do? You want to keep poor little Sue's lies? He held it out. *Lovely David's stories?*

'No,' I said.

What? I can't hear you.

'No,' I shouted.

He lit the corner. The old dry newspaper burning quickly, a flash of a blue flame, turning to ash, falling down and catching onto my clothes, the bed cover. I swatted them out. Then he got up, went across the room and lifted a metal dish he used in the garage. He placed all the pieces into the bowl and he burned them. Watching me as I watched them dancing down into ash.

Anything else? he asked.

I shook my head.

He cocked his, as if he was confused.

Nothing?

I shook my head again.

Still lying, he said. Then he reached into his pocket and in his hand was the letter. My letter. The one someone was going to read, and they were going to come and save me.

Blink three times. My name is Cathy.

Nothing, you say? and he looked to see how I would react as he opened it up and began to read.

The tears fell. I couldn't stop them. Slow. Fat. Lazy. They had all the time in the world and then the letter burned too.

Now, he said. *It's your choice, you want to make a fresh start? Wipe clean all that old history? Everything so clean now. Nothing left to confuse you and nothing left to bother me.*

'Yes.' I nodded.

Keele leaned across the bed.

Here's one thing for your new collection. One piece of news you might like to keep. His last.

And he held out a folded scrap of newspaper. I took it and unfolded it, and he tipped his head as I read it.

LOCAL EDITOR DAVID PRITCHARD COMMITS SUICIDE

I cried then as I had never cried before. Maybe Keele even felt sorry for me then. After a while he stroked my hair, tried to tell me it would all be better now. That he was sorry if I was too. And I let him console me, even as he revelled in my hurt. I let him feel my sorrow consume me.

I let him think I had nothing left. But that was a lie too.

My fingers sliding the little yellow lighter up my sleeve. Always something up there. And who knew what hell it might bring?

THIRTY-EIGHT

RENE

Before

Mum follows me into the living room, the last person I want to see, even if I'm grateful for company. She came without me calling; maybe that's a good thing.

'God, this place is a mess,' she says, looking around. 'And what's that funny smell? Have you been trying to cook?' Then she looks at the ashtray on the table, the end of Pete's joint. She knows full well it isn't cooking.

'It was a friend's,' I mumble as defensive as a teen. I scratch my thigh, nervous of my own lies. 'He came to see me...'

'Friend?' She narrows her eyes, watching as I try to come up with an answer. 'Don't tell me you've fallen in with those people again, smoking the funny stuff.'

I roll my eyes, remembering Mum arguing with Lauren over that. *What kind of child of mine hangs out in the woods, smoking drugs? Like a reprobate.*

It was just once, Lauren pleaded.

Once is all it takes to throw your life away. An accusation in Mum's eyes.

'Anyway,' Mum says, dismissing both our thoughts, 'I bought you some things; a few meals you might like, a couple of new magazines, some donuts. But I was in quite a panic. Did you know your phone's been cut off? I thought, what if I need to get through? What if something *awful* had happened?'

'And yet you still went shopping?' I can't help biting. Mum and snide comments are like strawberries and cream.

She hefts the bag down on the table. 'I rushed around the aisles, not sure if you'll like what I bought.'

She doesn't look glamorous today. Her hair is a mess and her nails are chipped. She's got on a black coat that's at least a decade old. Is it the one she wore to Nanna's funeral, has someone died?

But she lowers her eyes and pushes a strip of tablets towards me.

'I do try to help, in whatever ways I can. Let's hope this will soon be over.' Her eyes soften. She smiles. For just a second I want to reach over and hug her. 'It must be tough. Especially... now.'

I throw her a quizzical look.

Then she peers around the room, clearly troubled by the mess and the things that sit on the desk, on the shelves, on the walls. She doesn't like being here, surrounded by all Lauren's paraphernalia. I expect her to say something, to mock or deride it. Instead, she says: 'You're going to be OK. Because you're my daughter. My child. And you are strong.' She reaches over and grips my hand.

A pain runs through my fingers, and I flinch, pulling away. Yet, her touch. She actually touched me. I felt it.

'I was so sorry to hear about David.' It's fleeting and I could also have missed it.

'What about David?' I ask. A thud inside me.

She hesitates, tilts her head as if she's unsure she wants to be the one to bring me the news. 'You know that... he took his own...' She stops. What is she saying? 'Awful business. It was never his fault, was it? Still, the shadow hung over him, always did, for years.'

I stand up. 'He... *killed* himself?' A rush of panic, guilt, dread. *No, no, no.* Not David. It's not real. 'That's a lie.'

Mum moves across the room, goes over to the flamenco dancer on the shelf. 'He always talked about the truth, didn't he? He wanted you to know it. Tell me, did you find it? Do you know it now?'

I shake my head. It hurts so much.

I reach across the table and pop out a pink tablet, swallowing it down without water. My mouth and throat dry. I try to steady my breathing, but I can't. I want to ask about David, but Mum is thinking of something. Maybe there is truth in there too.

'Nanna brought me this,' she says, running her finger over the glass cloche of the flamenco dancer, her eyes far away. And I see a flicker of her smile. 'She brought it back from one of her extended trips, off with some man or other. Funny that you've kept it.' Her smile evaporates. 'Why *do* you keep all these things?'

I look at the shelves, the clutter, the mismatched objects. A magpie to a missing sister.

'To remind me of her life. Things that she loved. And she was always fascinated by that dancer. You would never let her touch it, or play with it.'

'Yes.' Mum nods, something glints in her eyes. 'And Lauren always wanted what was just out of reach. What she wasn't meant to have.'

She crosses the room, lifts her handbag, pulls out her white packet of cigarettes. I have that same feeling as before. Something coming, somewhere between fever and excitement. I watch, illuminated by the dull December light bluntly stubbing its way in through the window. Mum's hand is shaking.

'Mum, I...' I begin, my eyes on the cigarette.

'Well, you can't say you object,' she says, pointing to the half-smoked joint in the glass.

She plops herself down on the sofa and drags up the little yellow lighter across the table. She lights her cigarette and draws in. Still, I see her fingers nervously picking at the nail polish on her thumb.

'I tried to be a good mother,' she says. 'I really tried. And I know you think otherwise, but I did my best, under the circumstances.'

What circumstances? I ask in my head.

'When I was little, my mother – your nanna – was always away. Oh, she'd send postcards from exciting places she visited, and when we spoke she'd say she was doing it for me. Doing it so we could one day be a proper family. I'd finally get a new dad, a nice home, the promise of beautiful clothes and toys. But I didn't want any of that. I just wanted her.'

Mum's jaw tightens, her lips purse, barely enough space for her to take another drag. Tight lips, damp mouth, confined tears.

'I remember being small and standing in the harsh light of my grandmother's hall. My mother on the end of the big telephone, insisting that I tell her I loved her. But I could never say it, and Nanna would pretend to cry, to tell me how much her little girl was upsetting her. Those crocodile tears of hers.'

Mum gets up again, walks across the living room, back to the Spanish dancer under the bell jar. A memory of her childhood building inside.

'It always sounded so much fun at the other end of the line. An exciting world into which I could never go. Like I was the one trapped under a glass cover, waiting to be offered the chance to come out and dance. And I suppose, saying "I love you" was the only thing I had control over. So, I withheld it, in the hope that one day it might be enough to bring her home. But it never was.'

For the first time I see a genuine sadness in Mum's face. Have I ever seen her like this? Beneath the make-up and sharp words, stripped away like chipped nail polish, beneath her raw hurt and pain. Has David's death made her come closer to telling me the truth too? Or is it me, am I just finally ready to listen?

Listen to her...

'When Lauren was young, Nanna came to visit. I had asked her to come – told her I needed her. I'd had a miscarriage, lost a baby.'

I think of those spots of blood on the floor. Rebecca doll and the pasta sauce. Three red circles like red buttons at her feet.

'I'd asked for help. But she arrived months later, made one of her excuses. Lauren was still young, and when Nanna finally came, Lauren thought she was wonderful. Exotic. Her singing and her jewellery and her stories. Stupidly I agreed she could stay, just a few nights. But Nanna didn't want to leave; in the end she admitted she had nowhere else to go. She pleaded with me even as she lavished attention on Lauren, and Lauren kept asking if she could stay. *Please.* I knew she was manipulating Lauren for her own gain, not because she loved her. She was a master at that. All her exciting tales and her suitcase full of flamboyant clothes, costume jewellery and old make-up. To me, she was nothing more than a cheap travelling circus. To Lauren she was a world beyond ours.'

She's jealous, I hear Lauren whisper. *And Nanna says Mum has always been cold. Can't ever say 'I love you'.*

Mum wanders back to the dancer, and I watch as she lifts the glass cloche, and the hauntingly familiar tune begins to play. It's 'A Bushel and a Peck', the one Nanna sang. A smile creeping across Mum's lips as it plays.

And in the tune I remember Nanna's voice singing, 'I love

you...' Had I ever made the connection that it's the same song? A memory fills the room; Nanna singing to Lauren about loving her, and Mum coming in to find them cuddled up on the sofa. Mum walking over to Nanna and slapping her hard across the face.

Nanna standing. Gripping her cheek. The shock. The plate breaking. *Just get out!*

'I knew Nanna would tell Lauren that she loved her. And that hurt. Not least because I knew one day Nanna would leave and not come back, and Lauren would be heartbroken – just like I always was. I didn't want that to happen to my little girl. I was trying... to *protect* her.'

Her eyes find mine. Wet with tears.

Mum tugs on her cigarette, hasty, hurt, but I can see her eyes sparkle with fury now.

'Lauren came to me. Said Nanna had told her things. About how I wasn't a good mother. That maybe I couldn't love anyone. How I had struggled when Lauren was a baby, and that I had...' she swallows, words lost for a moment '... had tried to harm her. She told Lauren about me having to go away for safety. To get better. My "confinement", that's what she called it. That my trying for another baby was just putting our family at risk.'

There are angry tears in Mum's eyes now, teetering, waiting to fall. I almost want to go over and touch her hand now, to draw her to me. To hold her.

But her words burst out. 'How could my *own mother* use Lauren to hurt me like that? Lauren was so young, being used as a pawn in a very long game. That woman cursed my whole life; that *witch*. So, I confronted her. Told her at least I was around for my daughter, wasn't off chasing money and men. And she said of course I would throw that back in her face. She couldn't expect me to understand how difficult it was for her. "Don't worry," she said, "history will repeat itself". I had rejected her, and one day Lauren would do the same to me too. "Wait and see," she said. Almost like she wished it. Like a curse. Then I'd know. I'd feel it.'

My heart cracks like ice.

I hear the words, listening with Lauren at the gap in the door. Watching two grown women – mother and daughter – accusing each other of terrible things. I remember Nanna saying, 'Look at you, ending up in this little nothing life, at the end of a cul-de-sac, all stifled and frustrated with a man you don't even love and who doesn't really love you.'

Mum's lips twitch.

'She said it was obvious I wasn't happy, that I had never truly forgiven your dad for sending me away when Lauren was young.'

How dare you, I hear Mum shout to Nanna. *Get out!*

And suddenly, like a shaft of light in the room, I understand.

I not only listen, but I *feel* it. It bursts through me like lightning. Mum wasn't jealous, she was hurting, and she was afraid of Lauren being hurt too. She *was* trying to protect her after all. It was Nanna and Dad who hurt Mum. She couldn't help what happened to her after Lauren was born. It was an illness, no one's fault.

But swiftly then, Mum crosses the room, stubs out the cigarette in the glass on the table. It hisses angrily.

Her voice as faint as the last wisps of smoke. 'Nanna left that day, and we never saw her again.'

It's haunting to hear.

And also, a total lie.

THIRTY-NINE

RENE

Before

In the low light, I watch Mum. I want to tell her I'm sorry. That I never understood until now. But already she is shifting, like I can't hold onto this version of her.

'I know it's my fault that Lauren *went*. I couldn't tell her I loved her, and she was infected by my past, by the curse of my mother. By the lie she used. That I had wanted to harm Lauren and if I hadn't had proper help when I did, I might have done something terrible. I made a mistake telling Lauren that she needed help too. But I blamed myself for not acting sooner.'

I want to reach up, touch Mum. Draw her to me. Reassure her.

'Lauren didn't harm herself,' I say. 'Someone did this to her. They manipulated her. They used all this against her. They suggested she say things about David to the school. Made her behave in a way that she would look more troubled than she was. They *groomed* her. Made her feel they cared most, were protecting her. They were always planning to take her. And never let her go.'

I think of the necklace.

'Who? Who would do such an evil thing?' she asks, snapping her focus onto my eyes.

'Colson. It was him. Mr Colson.'

'The man who helped fix my car?' Mum asks with an incredulous laugh. 'Don't be ridiculous.'

Her head tilts, something almost mechanical.

'Is this another of your made-up stories?' Her face contorts; not the soft face she just had with the almost tears. 'Is that... what you write in your books. About me? That this is my fault? Didn't you hear a word I've said?'

'No... I just mean. Listen...'

But Mum is picking her lipstick out of her handbag, reapplying her perfect smile. Pumping her hair up from underneath, soft curls reforming. The tears entirely dried. As if it was all just to wring sympathy from me.

'Mr Colson was *nothing*. Why would you even say that?'

Because Mum brought him into our lives, out of her need and desperation, and she showed him how vulnerable we all were. She showed him that Lauren was alone, and that no one really listened to her. Or seemed to care.

But the old Mum is back now. Not the one with the broken heart. Not the one I almost believed could be hurt or hurting. Not the one that might listen to this. Here is the woman who preferred to think that Lauren took her own life. That didn't believe the letter. Who allowed the police, year after year, to give up on her own *troubled* daughter.

Finally, Mum takes out a small perfume spray, dousing herself lightly. 'You know, your dad's so sensitive to smells,' she says, almost a throwaway comment. 'I don't want to go home smelling of your *funny* cigarettes or *burnt* cooking, do I?' Her eyes shift to the ashtray. For a second I see just how naturally she lies.

'Mum,' I say as she tugs on her black coat. 'Mum, please.

Let's talk some more. I... need you. I'm not well enough to be left alone, and we can talk this through.'

'I wanted to help, but now it's too late. Too late to fix this. You'll always end up blaming me.' Then she stops, wistful almost. 'Remember, you chose this. You could have had *any* life, but you chose this one.' Bitterness woven through like beautiful thread.

'No, Mum, I—' But the door is closing. 'I... didn't choose this. Mum I didn't... I... love you.'

But those words fall into silence. It's too late.

FORTY

LAUREN

Before

Keele's not happy. Not gonna lie.
  Keele's gonna kill me,
  But I haven't the guts to die.
  A new earworm, dancing around in my brain. A growing suspicion that maybe he'd killed before. Blood on his hands, could it even have been his own family? Because he'd been hiding things. Very bad things.

Far worse than me.

Keele had been keeping a close eye on me. Too close. I knew that there was something I wasn't meant to find, but there was nothing I could do. Everything I'd ever felt about waiting was made double. You can't even try to measure it. Waiting for the school bell to say it's over, waiting for Christmas, maybe a new bike. Waiting to know if the person you have a crush on will show up, and they'll tell you they *like* you too. Waiting to be called into the headmistress's room to find out how much shit you're in.

Waiting for the day he's going to make you die.

He said I was looking for trouble again. *The last straw, Little L.* But I'd kept going this long by being me, submissive and smart and stubborn and crazy. Maybe it was time to finally give up, to admit defeat, to tell myself the truth, that I had been a prisoner all these years and he hated me, not loved me. He had groomed me and trapped me. Confined me within my own hurt.

I was upstairs in the back room, and he'd put on a binder between the metal loop on my ankle and the wall. The floorboard was gone and the hole was gaping and empty to show me that I couldn't hide anything, and he wanted it to upset me. I looked downhearted as he left the room. Always good to give him what he wants.

I heard him trudge back downstairs, and only when I was sure, I untangled the little yellow lighter from the hem of my trousers. The one I had taken after he burned all my things, and he was so busy pretending to comfort me and revelling in his psychopathic glee.

I looked at the binder and I thought, *Shall I? Shan't I?* and then I did; I melted that binder away. How the plastic danced like a writhing worm, disappearing into itself. I'd be for it when he came back, if I was still here, and I suppose I was past caring.

Free of the binder, I crept out of the room, and I could hear him moving around downstairs. I would never get past him that way, and all the upstairs windows were sealed, barred, shuttered or reinforced glass. I hurried to the end of the corridor, and I found myself by the shelf that I had seen shift. Was there something behind there? Another door, an exit? Dear God, let there be.

Sure enough, when I moved the books on the bottom, the back shifted as it had that day he had kicked me, and behind it was a space. You could smell the mildew and old perfume in there as if it was something that had once been living.

A narrow space.

Downstairs, I heard the shift of a chair in the kitchen. Keele was in a bad mood today. Maybe it was the wrong day to be so bold. Like there was a good day to be caught trying to escape.

But I'd done it now. I'd burned off the binder. I had no way to put it back.

Deep down I'd always thought he would never kill me. That we had made a silent deal. He would hurt me but he would never go that far. He wanted me there and I had nowhere else to go until I was better. But I was no longer convinced.

My heart pounded so loudly, but I was quiet as I shifted the books and made enough space to slide behind the partition. All the time thinking how I would get out and back in place if he came. Quickly. Could I? And how would he react seeing the binder gone? My throat so dry and my breathing nothing more than little crushed gasps of air, too afraid to go in or out. Throwing my life away just to be curious.

I crouched. I slid. I held my breath and wormed my way through as if being eaten alive by the wall. Each second further from where he should find me. Nearer to all hell breaking loose.

The space beyond was the width of the corridor, and twice the depth, made from where the corridor should have ended behind the wardrobes in the bedrooms. There was a pile of cardboard boxes, like Mum and Dad's attic.

I put the books back in the same order. Knowing time was ticking. Expecting to hear him any moment, and in my head I shouted in his voice, *What the* hell *do you think you are playing at!*

Inside there was just enough light from the hall. Otherwise it was entirely dark. But I was used to that.

My head was hammering with the thought that at any minute, any minute, any minute. What then? What then? Was I ready for that kind of pain? What excuse? But I was beyond excuses now. It was just too late for goodbyes.

Like a walk-in wardrobe, nothing more. Bigger than The Hole, bigger by far.

A pile of cardboard boxes, almost exciting, full with old junk. Dresses, clothes, handbags, jewellery, children's books, hair brushes, soft toys; their eyes so wide and sparkly that they looked quite insane in the thin light. And it all smelled like the inside of Nanna's old suitcase. Stuff that had been forgotten for a long time.

Then I saw a plastic box. Smaller and with a label on that said *Computer Stuff*, and it had CDs and DVDs inside, a bunch of tapes, cables, cassettes from an old old video camera, the tiny ones. I looked for the camera, but couldn't find it anywhere nearby.

I listened. Had to be careful not to forget myself.

Finally I found another shoebox, hidden behind a collection of matted-haired dollies, cheap imitations of Barbie. Inside was a tin opener, a roll of duct tape and a handful of binders. Had he used them before? I shuddered.

There wasn't anything else I could use. I took the binders and I knew I should just get out. At least I could fix myself back in place, which meant between the lighter and the binders, I could come and go. There was nothing else, except the sense that the girl and the woman in the picture he'd burned had owned these things. The same person who had worn the earring, who had caused Keele to scrub every surface with bleach? Another shudder. My things also stuffed in the back of the other cupboard like this.

In the handbag, I found an old perfume spray, all evaporated, not enough to squirt in his face. Nothing I could smash, nothing I could sharpen. Nothing I could use to escape.

I had to leave, get back, quickly. My hand on the box with the tapes as I pushed my way through, and there on the top was a disc. *Sue TV*. Was it... the show with Mum? Why had he kept it? How long had it been in here? This box was near the front so maybe—

And then I heard him.

On the stairs.

He was coming.

I was done for.

FORTY-ONE

LAUREN

Before

I tried not to breathe. Crouched, clutching my knees as if that would make any difference.

He was going to kill me.

Lauren? I heard him call.

Lauren? Lau—

He could see that I was gone.

Lauren! He exploded, thumping the wall, and I heard the chair crash across the floor.

He was in the hall now. Just out there.

Don't breathe. Don't breathe. Don't—

Where the HELL are you? Louder. And I thought of the woods. Of hiding when I was young, light between the trees, looking up at the sky and the lazy clouds and trying not to cry or giggle or make a sound. Knowing Dad was looking, hearing his voice getting more and more anxious. Except with Dad it was always a game. Or just practice for this.

Little L? Little L! Come out, come out wherever you are.

My ears trying to locate him. Any moment the bookshelf would come crashing down too.

I heard him go into the bedroom. Calling, shifting things, looking under the bed. I heard him go into the spare room with the nice bed for the guests that never came. Moving around like a great big monster. Not knowing how close he was just on the other side of the wall.

Little L. Little L. I'm going to find you...

A game, not a game. My heart in my throat. And then I heard him growl.

I'm going to kill you, and he slammed the door and thundered off along the corridor and down the stairs, his rasping breath fading.

If I was going to do anything, I was going to do it now. Now! But my legs refused to work and I realized I had wet myself. Felt it getting colder where seconds before everything had been only heat.

I shifted the panel, quickly, quietly. Pushed out the books, slid myself through. Quickly, I piled everything back, all the time drilling myself like a game show host. The clock ticking. Now! Now! *He's coming. He's COMING!*

I heard him cross the downstairs hall between the kitchen and the living room.

Lauren! he called out, and I froze. I looked over my shoulder to see if he was already there. Creeping up on me. Feeling the shadows of pain that he would inflict. The fear of pain shuddering through me. I shook, so much I could barely control my hands.

The last book on the shelf, I flipped it open, slid the *Sue TV* DVD inside, rushing down the corridor, into the room, over to the metal hoop. He was on the stairs.

Sitting. Legs folded. Pyjama bottoms wet. In my hand the other thing I had taken with me. A binder.

I looped it through the metal on my leg and the one on the wall.

Click, click, click it went as I pulled it tight, tighter, locking myself in place. Lamb to the slaughter.

My only hope.

I tucked my hair behind my ears and tried to steady my breath. *In, two three four. Out, two three four.* Head exploding. A strange euphoria.

I heard him. At the top of the stairs. At the doorway, hand gripping the frame as if he had just climbed a mountain. Eyes like those stuffed toys. Into the room.

Where were you? Where the HELL were you? he demanded.

I looked at him as if he was confused.

Tell me! he demanded.

'I...' I stammered, looking down at my leg and the metal loop and the binder. Did I dare? 'I was right here, Keele.' Sometimes he liked that innocent voice. I used it to buy me time. 'I needed the bathroom, but you didn't come.' My eyes on the damp patch.

I saw the flicker of doubt, the way it flew across his face, a flock of birds creating a shadow through his eyes. Swift, ominous, scattering.

He'll believe me. He'll kill me. Believe. Kill. The metronome back and forth. *Please* believe me. Please don't kill me. Tick tock, in time with the pounding of my heart, so loud I feared he'd hear it.

All that risk and nothing to show.

Nothing, except... a few binders and a disc hidden in the book on the shelf. Would I ever get the chance to retrieve them? What good would either do for me? What did *Sue TV* have to say now...?

FORTY-TWO

RENE

Before

I wake.

I'm in bed, my rose-pink room. The day not sure whether to be lighter or darker. December... who cares? The days slip by. The plants looking cold, unloved, barely surviving. My list.

- *David.*

No, not even that.

If only I could speak to stupid Red Lips and be told that David's busy or home with his family and she's *filtering* his calls again. Or I could force myself to go, open the damned door and make it to his office. See him sitting there at his desk like always with a coffee in his hand, surrounded by files and papers and cables.

Except he won't. He's gone. He's dead. Can't I just *imagine* him back?

I pull open the curtain, letting in faint light. The images on the wall still in shadow. I get dressed, pulling on jeans, the least wrinkled T-shirt from the pile. Out into the corridor, wondering if there'll be a letter. Or maybe Mum on the doorstep come back to upset us both, or Pete. Or someone I expect even less.

Like *Colson*?

I shudder. No. He wouldn't. He couldn't. Doesn't even know where I live. Not in here. He'll never find me. But I should go out. Find a really public place. Hell, I'll even go to school. Just for familiarity. And safety.

At the door, I touch the cold frame, how the chill runs up my fingers. I position myself to look out the eyehole, the small domed world beyond that I used to escape into but which now traps me. The porch thankfully empty. No visitors.

But there is something on the third step. A burst of misplaced colour against the drab concrete. A yellow rose, resting in a faint shaft of winter sunlight. Has it fallen from a bouquet up on the street? An unnoticed loss from a gift to someone else? No, it sits too perfectly placed, nothing accidental about it.

Lauren never left anything to chance.

I unbolt the door, turning the latch. Careful and unrushed, like slipping off clothes in a slow striptease. Holding my breath as I edge the door open, because whoever put the rose there might be standing at the top of the steps. I could hope that they hold the rest of the bouquet in their hand, ready to swing down and serenade me like a midday musical. Pete, realizing his feelings for me, come to tell me he isn't marrying Shirl after all.

I raise my hand to block the light, and see if there's anyone above, but the sky is white and blinding. My legs are cold. Something creeps into the corner of my mind. Fear. And the memory of the last time I saw a yellow rose. The night Lauren disappeared.

I creep out. Bare feet. No socks, lucky or otherwise. Chill through my toes. I reach the steps, the light spinning. The world above me thundering and vast. Any second. Any second. Something horrible. Fast and brutal. I coil my fingers around the stem which I grip, the prick of a thorn as I turn and run back inside. *Bang.* I slam the front door, the only barrier now four locks latched.

But I've taken a captive – the yellow rose.

Its soft perfume uncoils around me, and yet as beautiful as it is, its petals are browning. Already in the process of dying.

In the living room, I scoop up the glass that Mum and Pete used as an ashtray. The joint and cigarette butts create a tiny volcanic ash cloud as they rain down into the overflowing kitchen bin. I rinse the glass before filling it with water. Then I lower the stem and bring it to the living room windowsill, to drink in the most light I have to offer. Behind me the musical flamenco dancer plinks twice. *Plink, plink.*

Something about Nanna. And then I see a vase of yellow roses on a windowsill in the hospital. Mum had set them. *That* was the last time we saw Nanna. Not when Mum told her to get out. And there is another smell, unpleasant; it makes me recoil. The imminence of death, of urine and the scrub of disinfectant. A hospital room with Nanna lying on the bed, scarcely breathing. White sheets, white skin.

I need to capture this last truth. Why there was a yellow rose the night Lauren disappeared.

The last time we saw Nanna, Lauren was fourteen, and Nanna was dying.

Gone were the flamboyant clothes and jewellery, gone the layers of make-up and coral lipstick. Gone the lilting voice that sang to Lauren and told exotic tales. Or gave away Mum's dark secrets. She was gaunt, her hair a thinned white halo where colour had once been. Her flesh translucent and blue-veined like a dragon-fly's wing.

Her chest barely rose and fell. Her life departing a little more with each breath. A life that had barely been glimpsed in faded pictures and postcards, hazy and incomplete. Like Polaroids, morbid in their endless vanishing, just as she was then.

There was nothing private or dignified as the nurse came and went, ignoring the full bag of urine that needed changing, dangling like a vast amber gem under her bed. As if it didn't matter enough to anyone that for us her memory would forever be tainted with that smell. Was this what had become of the woman who traded everything to gain more? Who accused her own daughter of having amounted to nothing? The black-hearted witch now the white sleeping beauty.

This.

And Mum never took her eyes off her.

In return Nanna never opened hers, only occasionally did they shift beneath her eyelids that looked so delicate that they might split. Diaphanous.

I could hear the passing of starchy uniforms, rubber clogs. The clink and movement of a trolley in the hallway. Someone being wheeled along, mumbling, confused by medication, over-whelmed by pain.

Then I saw it. Nanna edging her fingers across the bed, like a snail in search of damp leaves; trying to find Mum's hand. Yet when they touched, Mum withdrew, retracted as if touched by something hot. Mum felt the need to brush invisible dandruff from her collar onto the floor.

She glanced up at the yellow roses on the windowsill, the only bright thing in the room. Her eyes made watery by the wet grey sky beyond. Then she dared to look again upon her dying mother.

Nanna's head shifted, and only then her eyelids lifted and a faint wisp of a smile broke. Her voice trembled as she spoke. A voice that had once told Lauren secrets. That we heard occasionally on the end of a telephone. A voice that had once sung about loving Lauren 'A Bushel and a Peck', and now it could hardly form a word.

'... We were together the morning you were born,' Nanna whispered. 'And now, at the end of my day, we are together again. Even if I wasn't there for you in the hours in between.'

A rattling breath. A sting in our throats. The terrible crashing of silence, a vast wave waiting to crush us.

Then her last words, 'I'm sorry.'

Her fingers reached out one last time to be held by her daughter.

Each second a battle of wills, like words withheld on a phoneline. Did Mum want to lean over, to kiss that cheek and say 'I love you', before it was too late? At the same time to hold firm to the resolution of her life defined in disappointment, to control this moment like few others. Sown in the vast emptiness of that childhood that we never knew or understood.

But Mum couldn't take her eyes off Nanna: in case the final moment came and it would pass and she would never have said what she was trying to say. Caught in her throat like half-swallowed pills.

Forgive her, I begged silently from the back of the room.

The cruelty of not offering a hand to a dying woman; I couldn't understand it. Couldn't accept it. We hated Mum then. Because we had no grasp of the hurt that she had felt. How alone her life had been. The word 'cold' levitating in the room.

Yet Mum's eyes were not willing this woman to die. Rather to live long enough that she could find the courage to overcome her own defences. To stop resenting Nanna, the only thing nurtured in all those years of absence. And Nanna never turned away. Never softened her mouth nor closed her eyes. She simply became unfocused, her chest fell. The silence settled on everything.

She was gone.

And in that space an accusation floated into the room. An eternal accusation that settled on Lauren, and she looked at Mum. This was the moment of the curse.

What Lauren saw was that Mum stood up, smoothed her skirt in that way that she did. No feeling at all. Only then Mum stepped closer to the bed and lifted Nanna's hand. The hand that had wanted so much to touch hers. Only then did she bring it to her lips and kiss it before lowering it to a motionless chest and placing it on her dead mother's heart. A final act of control.

'How could you?' Lauren whispered, stung and hurting, and Mum turned, as if only then realizing she wasn't alone.

'You'll understand one day,' Mum said, and her eyes were hollow and wide, searching for somewhere. 'One day, when it's time, I'll explain.'

Then Mum led us out into the hall, into the lift, out through the foyer. Past the clutch of smokers huddled outside the hospital entrance in the rain. Out into the car park, and we drove home. There wasn't a tear on Mum's cheek, but her eyebrows were raised, and her mouth was open, staring endlessly out that windscreen, as if an unending silent scream.

'Forgive her,' I whisper now, into the room, looking up at the rose on the ledge.

Forgive her, I tell Lauren. The curse that was passed down from Nanna to Mum to Lauren. Three generations of hurt.

Because the truth was that in the months that followed Nanna's death, Lauren turned fourteen, met Pete, fell ill, became obsessed with David, and one hot day in July she met a man called Mr Colson, who she thought might just show her something of the world beyond Meadow Close, and it started by meeting him almost by chance at the canal.

The rest was Lauren's dark history.

What's keeping her there? David asked.

He's exploiting you, Lauren. He's using your hurt. He's using what he knows. That there is no forgiveness.

I so badly want Mum to come. So I can tell her what I have worked out, and to tell her I'm sorry. Lauren would be too. Is too. We love her. Always have.

I sit alone and know it's colder, and darker, and the rose is already dying, and the truth is something so precious that I have to protect it above everything. That's what David was trying to teach me. The only thing that mattered. That we as a family loved each other.

Only that can maybe bring Lauren back.

FORTY-THREE

JANE

Today

Jane leads the thin man in the grey suit towards the girl sitting in her kitchen chair. She still has Jane's coat on her shoulders and blood in her hair, dirt on her feet. Her face is washed but in a way that makes it seem worse. The scars and bruises more visible.

'Here she is,' Jane says. She can't stop the sing-song tone, as if that will make everything all right, but her voice wavers.

The man steps forward. 'Hello, love,' he says, very quiet and low, his own voice not stable at all. Then he drops to his knees, crumples, no longer able to hold himself up. 'Oh God,' he says as if the girl is the Madonna and he must pray before her. 'Oh God, ohgodohgod...' it becomes a blur. 'Is it really you?'

He sobs, wracking whole sobs as if he is dissolving into himself.

Eventually he looks up, his face drenched. He rises, holds his arms out before Rene as if asking if he can hold her.

'Please forgive me,' he says.

Jane sees Rene's face. It is not fear but uncertainty. Then a very thin smile infects her lips, creeps from her mouth to her cheeks to her eyes. A faint glimmer. A wisp. She nods, and he places his arms around her, gentle at first, then gripping her as if he will never again let her go.

'Come,' Jane says, seeking out Dan's hand. She indicates with her head that they should leave, step away. They stand in the doorway, because while she wants to give them privacy, she also wants to stay close, to protect a girl who clearly hasn't been protected enough. She can't help the thumping of her heart in her chest, the not knowing what has happened, whether this girl is safe now, the idea that one day she may be called to give evidence about this very moment, to give testament to what she said or did, or even didn't do.

Jane realizes she's holding Dan's hand tight. She thanks God that this is not their daughter, and not Aidan and not Dan.

Rene's eyes look up to her father and then soften.

'I'm the one that's sorry, Dad. I made such a stupid mistake.'

He looks at her then. Looks and looks and looks. 'No. God, no. It's our fault. All our fault. We let you out of our sight.' His finger rises to her lip, trying to find something there, a scar amongst scars, but he doesn't quite dare to touch her. Something remembered.

Then his head tumbles back into her lap. His cheekbone against her knee, rising and falling. Sobbing as he grips her. Gripping her as if he can save her that way. Roll back the years and undo all the horror and loss. But it's too late for that.

'I'm so sorry,' he begs her. 'I'm just so sorry I lied.'

FORTY-FOUR
RENE

Before

The cold follows Mum in as she steps inside. She's wearing her sombre black coat again, with a black jumper and dark grey trousers. A dusting of snowflakes on the crown of her head glittering like a tiara.

'We went to his funeral,' she says. She sits down in the living room, crossing her arms over and rubbing lightly up to her shoulders as if she's cold or maybe more to comfort herself. 'I know that David meant something to you. You should have been there.'

I shake my head.

She can see that I'm holding all the hurt inside. Willing that bank not to break, so the flood doesn't drown me. But today I will be nice. Because now I understand her.

'I never thought...' I say.

Suicide. Such an ugly word. Neither of us say it.

Mum nods, looks towards the window. Outside, a little bird picks in the December snow for food, jittering awkwardly.

Then Mum sees the flower. 'Someone sent you a rose?' she says, her voice lifting as her eyes are drawn to it.

Then she looks back at me, her eyes widening in confusion.

Is she thinking about what happened with Lauren? The rose, on the day she left. Left in the snow. A mistake. One lie too many...

'Your dad used to send me roses,' Mum says. 'But that was a long time ago.'

She's thinking of Dad, and how they used to be. The journey that led them together and how bright they might once have burned. All I knew was lots of falling apart. Fragments of photos and postcards, matchbooks from hotels, birthday cards to *My Sue* from *Yours Endlessly, Jim x*. The story of their lives that didn't want the postcard of Nanna on a ship or the ultrasound of an unborn baby – eight weeks, five days. Those things that lived in a box in the back of a wardrobe. *Maybe their story didn't want Lauren either*, a voice in my head torments me.

'We should talk about Lauren,' I say. 'I think... we can find her.'

'She'd come if she wanted to. She'd find a way home.'

'No. She doesn't come because she thinks you never loved her. That you don't want her back. He told her that, and she believes it.'

Mum laughs that bitter laugh. 'Or maybe I loved her *too* much.'

Too much?

Mum pulls out her cigarettes, but this time she doesn't light it. She looks at the rose and then down at the lighter. My insides shift ominously. I feel... uncomfortably aware that something is about to happen.

'I wanted Lauren so badly. To be able to be that mother and daughter, to have the feeling I had missed my whole life. But then I got sick, after she was born, and I had to go away. After that your father seemed to be protecting me, as if I was something fragile, like that little Spanish dancer.' She glances to the shelf.

She's going somewhere. The rose has provoked it. I can feel it. The bird jumps agitated back and forth, as if it knows something is coming. Just around the next corner; the truth.

'Do you remember that holiday in France?' A light in her eyes.

I think of her dress with the sequins. Her warm skin. Lying beside her in the scent of suncream and perfume and listening to the waves on the little beach.

'That cottage by the coast. The garden that backed onto the sea. White sand. Blue skies. Lazy days counting the moles on my skin, feeling the warm sun. Like a beautiful dream.' There is something loosening, even as she rubs her arms. The story illuminates her eyes.

'In the evening, Lauren would watch as I put on my dress, my make-up. She was transfixed, she'd hover by my dressing table, and I would blush her cheeks and put pink on her lips, brush her hair and spritz her with scent. That closeness with my daughter, like the dream I had always longed for. And we'd go downstairs, and she'd twirl for her daddy, and he'd say, "Look at you, our very own princess."'

I can almost smell the burnt coffee that has sat in the pot all afternoon, lilac talc drifting in from the bathroom. The sound of distant waves through the linen curtains at the window, damp salt lingering in the air. A hint of lavender.

But then I see Mum sitting on the bed, sobbing into her palms. I remember this now. What had happened?

'I didn't want to go home. "A slow death". That's what I called it. Because that's how it felt, that life, back in Meadow Close. Your dad just said I needed to be careful, mustn't let it get a hold of me again. My depression. Said he could see me... "slipping". But he was wrong. I wasn't depressed, I just knew he'd stopped loving me when we were there.'

A tear traces along her cheek.

'I'd thought about leaving him. But I couldn't, not with Lauren. She loved him so much. She'd only have hated me more for leaving, taking her away with me. Or worse still, asking to stay with him.'

Mum lifts the packet of cigarettes again, but she sees that the glass she used as an ashtray is holding the rose on the windowsill.

'That holiday in France, those two weeks – the sun, and the light on the water. A love affair with my own husband, my family. I wanted that to be my reality.'

I remember watching Mum and Dad on the jetty at night, dipping their toes into the water, hearing their giddy laughter drifting up to my bedroom window in the warm night air, Mum's eyes stealing glances at Dad as she sipped her wine.

'Then we came home. Not long after we had a party, all that wine we'd brought back in the car. There was a woman there in a burgundy jumpsuit, a colleague from your dad's work. She was captivating, flirty, all the men saw her. And I was jealous. She wasn't tamed and domesticated. She wasn't someone trying to be a good mother, a good wife. She wasn't struggling.' Mum sucks in the side of her mouth, staving off the hurt. 'She wasn't... *me*.'

Tears flow now. Her lips are wet.

I remember the next day, standing at the bottom of the stairs in the debris of wine glasses and uneaten cheese, holding the banister with a swirl at the end, tracing it with my finger, pretending not to hear. Mum and Dad arguing, and I was singing to myself to cover the sound. *We need a holiday...*

'That bitch!' Mum spat.

'You're really out of control now.' Dad's harsh voice.

'Why don't you just sleep with her then?' Mum screamed. The sound of a wineglass smashing. A second of silence, and then splinters hitting the floor. I gripped the handrail. Mum running past. Dad catching her arm.

'I'm sorry,' he said.

'No, you're not!' She shrugged him off. 'You never loved me. She told me that. I might just as well not be here.'

I remember Mum opening the front door, and she was gone. For two days.

Yes, Mum ran away.

'But he didn't have an affair...?' I say tightly.

She bites her lip, killing her tears. She nods.

Dad *cheated* on her?

'And you were really going to leave him?'

I realize now what she is saying. She stayed with a man who didn't love her because of Lauren. Because Lauren loved him so much. She did it for her.

Or maybe I loved her too much.

Then what Mum says next shocks me even more.

'I discovered I was pregnant. The doctor gave me a scan, and I sat looking at it for hours. Imagining I could already feel it moving inside me. That new life conceived on that holiday in France. Would it mean another chance? Could I keep him with it? Hope is a powerful and frightening thing. It keeps you going, or rather keeps you coming back for more. Because you always hope it will get better. But it doesn't. It only gets worse.'

I think of the black and white cyclone photo: *eight weeks and five days*. The image that Mum kept in the box. The baby that never came.

'Your dad said he was afraid. What happened with Lauren, and the miscarriage before. I was mad to do it again. He didn't share my excitement. I said it was because of her, the new woman he loved. He said I was being ridiculous, it was because of me.' Mum's eyes are nervous as she looks up. 'I asked him, "Then I'll get rid of it? My baby." And that's what Lauren heard.'

They'd have got rid of me too if they could, Lauren had said.

'In the end, fate played its hand. In the end I miscarried again. Problem solved.' She smiles, but not a happy smile. Her lips still wet from tears. 'So I asked Nanna to come and help, and she didn't. Of course.' Another laugh. A little bitterness rising. 'And when she did... those horrible things she said. Maybe, in hindsight, she was right. She thought I should leave him.'

Mum stands, goes over to the window, touches the rose petals. As she does the little bird flaps up and takes to the sky.

'I couldn't forgive her. All those years later. I know that's what Lauren wanted me to do. And I should. But I failed.'

'The only thing you *failed* at was to not keep *hoping* Lauren would come home. That she'd be found,' I say.

'Lauren left me a note. A... *suicide* note. I showed the police. I told them.' The words stick in her throat.

'But that isn't true! She didn't. There was no note. Mum, why would you tell them that?'

At the window, her back to me now, her voice is strong, clear. 'It was my favourite book. *Lie Down in Darkness*. About a young woman who struggled with her mother and in the end... she... kills herself. She wrote the note in there. She left it on my bed the night she went. A single word on the first page—' Mum chokes on her tears. 'It said, "*Goodbye.*"'

'No!' I shout.

Mum turns.

'Why didn't you work it out?' I insist. My turn to be angry. 'That was the book that you told Mr Colson about. Don't you remember?'

'Mr Colson...?' Mum tips her head. Startled by my words as if she's forgotten that part of the story. Could she really have forgotten? Because it meant so much to Lauren.

'She was trying to tell you. That she was with him. That's what it meant. You were meant to realize, and to come looking for her. Can't you see? She ran away, like you, and she ran to him.'

Then we hear a knock. We both turn with a start, her eyes flitting off towards the hallway.

'Oh no,' she says. 'He's here.'

'Who?' I falter. 'Mum, who's here?'

She looks nervous. 'Don't worry. I'll let him in.'

Then she hurries out into the hall, and I hear her unlocking the door.

FORTY-FIVE

LAUREN

Before

Back in The Hole, and I was dying. All because I was fixated with that disc inside the book. *Sue TV*. I had to hear what she had to say. To know she was really glad to be without me. Those cruel words again, like poking a wound. I carried that disc around whenever I dared, whenever I thought there might be a chance. Hiding it behind here, behind there.

Then one day, he locked me in the living room and went for his shower. *Get myself clean for you, and while I am you can tidy in here.* I didn't smile or react, so he wouldn't think I was up to something. Inside my heart was jumping, prepared to pay the price.

Because he had changed since the day he'd found me sitting there in that upstairs room, and I could tell that that had messed with his head. Like I'd pulled some voodoo shit on him. It made him jumpy. He'd been different since the days of Squeaky Clean. The day I found the earring and all the hidden things I had. And then since I was there and then gone and then there again. All his confidence was unravelling. He jumped at shadows, and with that my confidence grew. Gave me some new kind of power.

How stupid I was.

For a while I thought all I had to do was say 'Are you OK?' and narrow my eyes with mock concern. He'd be gruff, mumble something, but he was worried. Inside he was freaking. He was thinking of the necklace and the letter and how sooner or later I was going to slip through his fingers. And he was afraid of what I could tell.

After he locked the door, and I heard him amble up the stairs, I switched on the computer and let it run through all its workings before it came to the screen with the password. I'd tried his name and then my name, the dog's name. Then combinations of numbers and house name. It was bound to lock me out soon.

Then I heard him coming, floorboards overhead. I switched it off, feeling defeated, deflated, as if he could see my fingerprints on the keyboard. Without a password it was nothing. Everything I had risked.

Then I had a brilliant idea.

Keele had given me a plastic mirror, before I'd stopped brushing my hair as too much fell out. I took it into the living room the next day, pretending I was trying to make myself nice for him. I don't know from where I got the idea, but I took that old cherry lip gloss I'd found, that had been there for years, all congealed and smelling a bit wrong. I smiled at Keele and set the mirror carefully on the side when I had finished applying it.

All right, he said as he stepped towards me, and I looked up at him as he touched my arm. I never broke his gaze.

That afternoon Keele sat at the computer, and I stood over by the door and asked him a question.

'What do you want for dinner?' I asked.

Whatever we've got left.

He started to type, then he looked up.

Go on then. Get on with it.

'Right. Yes. And would you like me to bring you a beer?'

Whatever, he said, which always meant yes.

I turned, and I could see his fingers on the keyboard. I just had to still be there at the moment he entered his password. I saw him typing, and I moved away. I'd be a genius if I wasn't such a fucking fool.

I couldn't quite get my head round what he typed backwards in the mirror and then trying to remember. Remembering these days was hard. Because I couldn't write this down. If he saw it, I'd be worse than dead. I could only try to remember.

CayCay15

I fetched his beer. 'There,' I said, setting it down. I smiled, thinking I had the key. Yes, if the key was to my own death...

It felt like days, I waited for him to lock me in again. It took forever for him to turn the key. Finally, I had my chance.

I switched on the computer, and waited and it whirred, and I tried what I thought I had seen. The screen pausing as it decided, then the box juddered. It had failed.

No!

The disappointment was crushing. How could I have messed up my chance?

Slowly, I put my fingers on the keys again *CayCay15*. I was shaking as I pressed enter. The computer left me hanging. A small circle spinning in the centre of the screen.

And BINGO!

Icons burst before me. I gripped the mouse and listened to hear him overhead.

Nothing.

I slid the disc out from under the computer where I'd been keeping it. Thought I could deny all knowledge if he found it there. That was my best chance. With it in the machine, I clicked a bunch of stuff. My heart running like a wild horse. My head buzzing. The silence deafening.

I found bank forms. Some incoherent writing. *Don't quit your day job*, I thought. And then I saw the folder. *CayCay+Jac*

Inside were files, numbered one to twenty-eight. Just like the tapes in that box behind the wall. Something Keele had organized meticulously. Almost too well.

I heard a noise. I panicked.

I closed the computer. It didn't want to shut down. *Come on, come on*, I insisted, hearing him coming down the stairs. Hearing the computer whirring. Heat where it had been working. He would notice that.

He unlocked the door, just as the screen went blank, and I threw myself across the room.

You didn't get very far, he said, as if tasting the air.

What if he switched it on? He'd see the folder still open, all those files inside I had clicked, as if I had strewn them across the floor. And nothing I could do.

I walked across the room and let him touch me, the only distraction I had.

Next time he went for his shower, I got into the computer quicker. This time I went straight to the mailbox and wrote an email. Calm, no hysterics. Not like the letter. The address of a Missing Persons email I had memorized from a magazine a while ago. And I wrote:

Please come. I am being held against my will by Keele Colson. Do not reply in case he sees. Send the police. I am about twenty something. My name is Lauren Fisher but I may give another name. If you do not see me I might be locked upstairs or under the rug in the back by the garage. I have been here for eight or nine years. I think. My parents are Sue and Jim Fisher.

I could not quite believe it.

I hit send. Then I deleted it and it was done. I was high. Like my lungs had finally opened. A game of only waiting now. This time they were coming. Coming. He couldn't burn this up.

But I was tempted, a new itch to scratch. The folders numbered one to twenty-eight, and inside files: *CayCay born. CayCay's birthday. Praia de Aviernos holiday. First day at school. Puppy. Camping at the Lake. Boat trip with Jac.*

Just a peek. To lift the lid, to see.

Holy shit! It was bigger than the space behind the wall. It was like finding an entire house in which people lived. Film clips of their lives in *this* house. The woman and the girl. Everything the same: the wallpaper, the furniture, all still here. Not so worn, much more clutter. Not everything taken away off every shelf in case I used it somehow. And there was this woman and this little baby with chubby legs kicking, then a tiny girl walking around in her mother's shoes. Ghosts that had lived here, goosebumps on my skin, smiling at them, as if they might turn and notice me. The girl and the woman in the photo. I had brought them back to life.

This *was* Keele's family.

I had the volume on silent, but I could watch CayCay on the recorder. CayCay laughing. CayCay dancing. A birthday party in the garden, bunting and a trestle table set with plastic cups and plates and decorations. CayCay in a long party dress. Her mother smiling and blowing a kiss to the camera. She had on a pretty dress too. A game of musical chairs. A cake with four candles. Then the garden was deserted, the bunting dripping with rain. Jacqueline standing by the open door. The children all gone. CayCay running up and her mother putting her arm around her. Just like in the photograph. Something protective, as if CayCay needed protecting. Eyes that didn't blow kisses at the camera now.

I heard the sound of Keele overhead. The creak of the

boards under the carpet. I was about to close everything down. Knowing that he was coming.

I waited. Heard the bedroom door upstairs shut, the creak of the bed as he sat on it. Or maybe the pills crushed in his tea had had the desired effect. Oh yes, the ones I saved here and there. Just in case. For me or him. For one of us one day.

But I needed to see that girl just one more time.

CayCay's almond-shaped eyes, almost sad and yet knowing. How much she looked like me. Or how I had once looked. I watched her mother's gently protective arm, never far from her daughter's shoulders. The way they held hands as they walked in the fields, as if alone in some tender world into which no one could intrude. Maybe not even Keele.

For a moment I could play God. I could make CayCay go from being a teen to a baby. I could control her life. She was blowing out candles, puffy cheeked and curly haired. She was riding her first bike. She was a teenager, annoyed at the person behind the camera. I could tell from reading her lips. *Fuck off, Dad*, she was saying. Her half-lit bedroom as he came in with the camera. Her pushing past as she walked out, some kind of scuffle, the tape stopping. I played that over. Something about him coming into the room with the camera and her pushing him away. It felt wrong, uncomfortable, an icky feeling in my stomach.

Then I could make her a little girl again, her innocence regained, playing in a paddling pool, naked except for a sunhat. Dancing in a pink leotard, concentrating on smiling and pointing her toes. Scratching her thigh and seeing what the gaggle of other little girls were doing.

And always Jacqueline close by, her proud mother. Jacqueline French. *NOT KNOWN AT THIS ADDRESS*. And now there wasn't much time left. Or maybe Keele was sleeping and I had all the time in the world.

I slid the disc out from under the computer and into the

slot. The machine whirred, a helicopter buzz as if about to take flight. Would he really be sleeping? What if he came down now?

On the screen the *Real to Reel* logo burst. There was that room, just like on TV. The show we had watched. There was the chintz and the lamps. And there was Mum. Of course I recognized her. Obvious now.

I touched the screen as if I could touch her, knowing she would speak of painful things. Of how much better life was without me. My fingerprints leaving a greasy mark on the screen, and Keele would find them and he would know. And now I realized that maybe I didn't care.

I turned up the volume. *Let him come*, I thought. *Let him see how smart I am. How I will never stop.* Fighting his rule until one of us is dead. I strained to listen as the interviewer said, 'How was your relationship with your daughter as she grew up?'

'She was always closer with her dad. But I tried hard. I was never sure how to be a good mother. Whether I was getting it right. I just wanted her to love me.'

Something... different. I leaned closer.

'We knew she was unhappy, but it wasn't what either of us expected. It was a shock. A terrible, painful shock. We feared for her safety every moment of every day. In my heart, I just feared every day that it was true what they said, that she might be dead.'

What? That wasn't what she had said before. They hadn't feared for my safety! Maybe I wasn't hearing it correctly because the volume was too low. I turned it up some more. Had to. *Let him come*, I thought then.

'How did you feel during the early days of the search?'

'It took so much energy. Every day. There was never a good day. Never a day when it didn't hurt.' Mum, tearful. But not tearful about me being bad – tearful *for* me. Missing me. Afraid...

'I understand the police questioned your husband, he was seen at the canal that night.' Why was Dad at the canal? Why was he questioned if they knew I was here? That was wrong.

'Yes,' Mum was saying. 'It was terrible. So many questions. We'd done nothing wrong. We just wanted our daughter back. In the end the police were satisfied with the situation. *Satisfied,*' she said, and then she laughed a little bitterly. 'We comforted ourselves that at least that part was over. He was innocent. It was such a relief for us. But we pushed them to keep searching. For our little girl... Our princess.'

'What about suicide?' the interviewer said. 'There was a strong belief that she might have taken her own life.'

'We hoped that she had just run away, that it was what she wanted. We wanted to hear her voice and have her tell us that she was OK. Then we could finally get on with our lives, knowing she was happy in hers.' Mum paused. 'The not knowing every day is an endless killer.'

No. She hadn't said that. Wrong wrong wrong.

Or... had Keele altered it?

He sat watching me watch Mum say those cruel things, and he had comforted me.

I heard him on the stairs then.

Everything was instantly sharp and bright. There wasn't enough time. I tried to eject the disc, or to stop it whirring, but it wouldn't stop. I couldn't use my excuse if it was spinning in the machine. Then I thought I heard him shutting the bedroom door.

I tried to shut the computer down. To kill it, knowing the disc was still inside. He would find it, and then he would know about the bookshelf and that day I hadn't been there in the room. That he was right all along. It was me fucking with his head. I felt everything crushing me, almost unable to move. Panting with panic.

'Come on! Come *on!*' I whisper-screamed. 'Pleasepleaseplease,' and it almost went blank and I was almost off the chair, and I saw the door opening. Keele was right there, huge in the doorway.

Well, well, well, he said. *Little L. What are you up to now?*

I couldn't breathe. I couldn't move. No chance to run. I could smell him, clean and close.

The computer was the first victim. Smashed across the floor in one arm's swoop. Slow and then sudden, and then I was next. Into the broken grey plastic and electrical innards, little blinking lights that no longer blinked.

You can't be trusted, can you? You can't be left for ONE FUCKING MINUTE.

I tried to get up, scrambling to rise... my hands out to defend me.

His shoe in my face. Once. Twice.

I begged him. Said I was sorry. I didn't say it, it exploded out of me. As he kicked me. Because those things might have saved me once.

You ungrateful bitch. You've only got yourself to blame. I tried to save you. Save you from yourself. Always in other people's business. Always stirring up trouble. How could you ever be trusted? Look how you treated your own parents. They loved you, and see how you turned on them. Tried to turn them on each other. And David, you destroyed that man's life.

Each sentence ended not with a full stop but a fist or a knee or a foot.

It got dark. Darker. And then I woke in utter darkness and I thought for a moment I was dead. But the pain told me I was still alive, back in The Hole. This time I would die in here. But at least I knew the truth. That Mum and Dad loved me, missed me. They wanted me back. All those stories had been constructed to twist my head. I had thought that his truth was *the* truth.

But the pain was too much and I knew I was dying. Soon I would be gone, and no one would ever know that anything had changed, after all the years of fighting and surviving and complying and believing and fearing. I would be nothing more than a question mark, forever left hanging. Like all those other missing people. *Where did they go?*

I was never going to get to say sorry to Mum. Or that I forgave Dad.

Now the pain grew and then it became strangely quiet.

I heard a voice, whispering in the darkness. Mum's voice. It was the end.

'*Do you remember that little cottage by the coast? The garden that backed onto the sea. White sand. Blue skies. Lazy days. Something magical there. In the evening, how you would watch as I put on my dress and my make-up. How you would hover by my dressing table and I would blush your cheeks and put pink on your lips, brush your hair and spritz you with scent. And you would go downstairs and twirl for your daddy, he'd say "Look at you, our very own little princess."*'

FORTY-SIX

RENE

Before

'Dad?' I say as he steps into the living room.

'Hello, love,' casual and soft, like always, as if no time has passed since we last saw each other. 'Your mum said you'd been under the weather. I've been starting to worry.'

'I'm fine,' I say, his proximity creating a maelstrom of emotions. After what Mum said – the affair. He'd betrayed her.

But he draws me to him, into his fatherly grip, a familiar feel and scent, and he kisses me on the forehead. 'I've missed you,' he whispers into my hair. Holding me, still with vague apprehension, even if I can feel he wishes to hug me tighter.

Still there's a feeling of resentment towards him. He is the reason Lauren went that night. He is the liar.

He holds me away and looks me over, searching for something in my face, raising his hand slowly. Running his thumb faintly over my top lip, his eyes darken, as if he sees something. A hint of a scar. Or a wound that never healed.

'I'm sorry,' he says, his voice unsteady, and it feels in that second as if we are both afraid of tears. 'I truly am.'

Somehow there's a shift. I can feel myself releasing Mum from the shackles of anger and blame. A fresh understanding casting her in a new light. But not Dad. Not so easily. What happened with Mum grew out of the years, it was the fabric from which hers and Lauren's relationship was cut. But Dad's was a swift strike that night she went. The shock that changed how Lauren felt about her entire life.

'What happened that night,' he begins as if reading my mind, 'it was a terrible mistake.'

He crosses the room, sitting down beside Mum. He takes her hand in his. Gone, her talk of affairs and unwanted babies, of daughters who took their own lives. Gone is the sense of heartbreak that this man caused her. The long, subtle betrayal. Yet the way he holds her hand, almost as if trying to reassure her, how she links her fingers over his, as if they are holding onto a promise they have made. There is something frightening in their unity.

'We both desperately want Lauren back,' he says.

Mum nods.

Outside, the icy grey and quiet world. Inside, the room which is warmer with them here. Thoughts that thump around in my head like feet overhead, not allowing me to hold them.

And Lauren is still there.

But they didn't mean to do what they did to her. They didn't want her to go. They loved her. And yet, no man has ever broken Lauren's heart as much as Dad did. No woman has made Lauren feel as unloved as Mum did. Dad is the one who finally sent her running towards Colson. Towards danger. A crack in the ice that our entire family fell through, because Lauren was vulnerable and went down the wrong path.

Sadness. Not sure I can handle it all.

'You know what today is?' Dad says, his voice brightening as if remembering something happier. 'December fourteenth. And you know what that is? Don't tell me you've forgotten.'

The day Lauren went. How could I ever forget?

'It's your mother's birthday!' he says instead, his smile growing.

Vague memories of years passed. Badly drawn cards, attempts at baking cakes, pocket-money gifts wrapped in already-used wrapping paper dug out from the drawer. A distant light in Mum's eyes as Lauren handed her a gift. But not that year. That year Lauren did something quite different.

'I'm sorry, Mum,' I say. 'I don't have anything for you.'

'Yes, you do.' Mum reaches out her hand and takes mine. She looks into my eyes and she's asking for something. 'Give us Lauren back.'

There are words on my tongue longing to be said but unable to form.

Suddenly, I smell mince pies: the sweet spice, cinnamon and warm fruit dancing through the air. A sense of home.

'I'll make some tea,' I say, standing swiftly, needing space.

I lean against the kitchen counter, my head reeling. I think of mince pies baking in the oven, their scent filling the kitchen in Meadow Close. My head sliding towards this day all those years ago. The day Lauren disappeared from everyone's lives. And Mum and David and Pete each held a piece of the puzzle in their stories that might bring her home.

And Dad. The final piece.

The man she loved more than anyone. The man she thought would always be there for her. The man who she had played hide and seek with in the woods by the canal, and had taught her to ride her bike, made her feel loved and proud. Who she watched matinees with on the weekend, and sitcoms as she grew. Who she waited to come in on a weekday and set down his briefcase in the hall, to ruffle her hair, *Hello, love*. He was the one with blood on his hands. That day all those years ago.

How could we ever forgive him?

Give us Lauren back.

'Listen,' Dad says, breaking into my thoughts as he calls to me from the living room. 'Mum and I have been talking.'

He gazes around my flat, all my things, all the mess. Everything I've clung to, the stacks of notebooks and magazines, photos on the walls, objects on the shelves, collected and curated. All here to keep me going. All made-up with no place to go.

'We should never have let you live like this. We could have been more insistent, made this stop sooner. But we... failed.'

'But we can still help now,' Mum interjects, tears in her eyes and a soft smile that she shares first with me and then with Dad. Their fingers intertwined. 'We can do this, together. As a family. Because, it's... time.'

My head tightens. They don't understand what they're asking for. What might happen...

'You know the truth,' Mum states, rising. 'You knew it all along. But it was buried. *He* buried it,' Mum says.

Colson.

She lets go of Dad's hand and comes over to me. Takes my hand now.

'You understand that we're sorry about Lauren, don't you?' Dad says. He goes over to the windowsill, touches the browned petal of the yellow rose. 'That what happened that night was... an accident. We only wanted to make her see...'

Mum's birthday.

December fourteenth.

The smell of mince pies in the oven...

It's coming. I can't stop it.

It's going to kill me.

A yellow rose on the doorstep that night. My fingers rising to my lip, where Dad had touched me when he arrives. The scar he was looking for. Except it wasn't mine. It was Lauren's.

Mum and Dad stand around me now. The heat rising within me. The heat of fear. Déjà vu. Because this has all happened before. This was how it was that night. The night that Lauren ran into the snow never to return. Blood on her hands, and his, the man she loved most.

'We'll get you the help you need,' Dad says.

This is it.

'Whatever it takes, we can do this. We're stronger together,' Mum says.

My stomach twists. They're surrounding me. History repeating itself.

'That's right,' Mum says, shifting a strand of hair from my eyes. The warmest smile.

'Come,' they say together. 'It's time for you to go...'

FORTY-SEVEN

LAUREN

Before

In the darkness, gripped by pain, I found myself drifting into it, standing on the threshold of that night. The night I went. The dark night I disappeared. When it would have been better to have drowned.

The clock in the hall said 16.07. December fourteenth, Mum's birthday.

It was cold out, but we were inside baking mince pies. *I'm too old for that*, I'd protested, but it was her birthday, and I caught a glimpse of her disappointment that I couldn't even try. So I join in, dragging myself with unnecessary reluctance. She did most of the work, I cut out a few half-hearted stars for lids, painting them with a lick of egg yolk, and then she placed them onto the tray and slid them into the oven.

The doorbell rang.

I watch Mum open the door, and there on the doorstep was a yellow rose, wrapped in plastic with a small note. Mum looked at it, her head tilted. It was her birthday after all.

Suddenly I was there. 'Well, is it from Dad?' I asked, suspicion woven through my voice.

'Yes... of course,' Mum said, but she faltered as she read the note.

'You're lying,' I said. 'It's from someone else, isn't it? One of your lovers.'

'Oh, don't be ridiculous,' Mum rounded, laughing as she dismissed the accusation. Still, she took the rose into the kitchen, placing it on the counter, touching the petals as if a hint of something in their softness. I thought of the day Nanna died. Had she been thinking that too? A hurtful barb that I hoped she would feel. Then Mum went to check on the mince pies, their warm scent filling the room.

'I'm telling him,' I said as I followed her into the kitchen. 'I'm telling Dad when he gets home. That you're having an affair.'

Mum looked at me, her eyes seeking something, almost as if she didn't recognize me.

'Lauren, please,' she said wearily. 'You don't know what you're talking about.'

'Well, it's not from Dad, is it? Is it an affair?'

I saw Mum's pinch of concern, emotion in her eyes. As if she knew something. 'Look,' she raised her hand to my fringe, the one I didn't think suited me anymore and was going to grow out. 'Let's just throw it away. It's... obviously a mistake. A stupid one. No need to play games.'

But I had turned away. I was running upstairs, two steps at a time. I was foolish, jealous, silly, grinning as I went. Thinking I had won some game. Because I already knew who had sent it.

When Dad came home, he set his briefcase in the hall, with no idea what was about to unfold. He yanked his tie sideways, as if to free himself of his day, and already I was there.

'She's having an affair,' I blurted.

'Who is?' Dad asked, somewhere between amused and confused.

'It's all lies. All of it. Everything she says.'

'What?' he began.

'You can't trust her. Nothing she says... she'll say anything.' Because I didn't want Dad to believe her words over mine. About what had happened at school, about David, or smoking at the canal. Someone had told me – and now we know who that someone was – that no one should have that level of control over me. *When people know your secrets, they can use them.*

I thought *Colson meant Mum.*

She appeared in the hall. 'Jim, please—' Mum shook her head, her hair curled for her birthday, bouncing gorgeously even with her anxious response.

'She got a rose from a lover.' I was tripping over my words. 'So you can't trust anything she says.'

'A rose? What, your mother?' His eyes flipped towards Mum. 'Sue?'

So many questions in the way he said her name.

'It's not true,' Mum said quietly, her lips thin and pale. 'You know it isn't,' and there was something deep in her voice. 'We should talk. Alone. Without Lauren.'

'No! Whatever she says, about me, about any of it, you can't believe her. She's a liar,' I insisted.

'Shut up, Lauren,' Dad snapped, which surprised me. 'I sent it,' he said. Which surprised me even more.

I stepped back, uncertain, confused. 'Why are you lying? Why would you lie, for her?'

'Saying that I love my wife on her birthday? That I sent her flowers? Jesus, Lauren. You're out of control now.'

That expression. He'd said it to Mum years before. Now he was saying it to me.

He stepped forward. For a second, I felt I was afraid. But I couldn't stop myself.

'It wasn't flowers! It was *a* flower.' A laugh in my voice that wasn't happy. 'Now I know you're lying.' But my eyes shifted, trying to find something to hook onto.

'That's enough!' Dad said exasperated, running his hand through his hair. 'Is it drugs? Is it boys? Someone telling you to say these terrible things, to do these strange things, is it? We're a good family. Were... and you're just a child. Too young for all this. What the devil has gotten into you?'

'See, Jim,' Mum said, her voice sounding exhausted. 'I told you, she's looking for attention. Your attention. So why haven't you been here, hm? Why don't you tell *her* the truth? Tell her which one of us is *really* having an affair?'

Dad looked at Mum. His eyes went wide. 'Sue, not now.' A fierce whisper. 'For Christ's sake, this is *not* the time.'

'Why not?' She blinked, a small triumphant blink. 'When *is* the right time? Because clearly you don't see the damage you're doing.'

'Dad...?' I flicked between then. 'You can't be... having an...'

'No, Lauren,' he said, stepping towards me. 'No, look. She's just confused,' something cruel in his voice. 'And besides, it's you that needs help.'

He was having to think on his feet. He was flustered.

'We'll get you that help. Whatever it takes. Counselling. Medication. Whatever you need to get better.'

I took a step back.

'You'd send me away?' Shocked. 'Is that how you'd deal with me? Like you did to Mum. You... think I'm like her? You think I'm crazy like she was?'

The storm whips up inside our small suburban hallway.

'That's enough,' Dad shouted and he raised his hand.

'Jim!' Mum was at his side, reaching out to catch his wrist, trying to protect me. Mum's eyes wide, everything falling apart, and from the kitchen the scent of mince pies burning in the oven.

Dad's hand fell. I saw it, more than felt it. My head rocked backwards, my hand rushing to my lip. The clock in the hall.

18.23.

I turned. Turned and ran upstairs, fury and confusion twisting my face. And a small victory. I was in my room, I was rushed and confused and everything was bright and yet undefined. I grabbed my bag, already packed and sitting on the bed. For a moment like this. The excuse to run, to punish them. I hurried back down the stairs. There were voices in the kitchen, Mum and Dad arguing.

'Why did you... you should have... I never would... How could you!'

I slipped out the door. Glancing back only once, seeing the time on the clock by the light in the kitchen, the moon on a string that once swung back and forth in the days when they had said they were proud of me.

18.28

The last moment I was ever home.

I slung my backpack over my shoulder.

Outside, the dark had consumed the driveways, Christmas lights twinkling in windows of the pretty houses on the cul-de-sac of Meadow Close, where nothing ever happened. All the children safely inside for dinner, and no one saw me leave.

I got on my bike and began to pedal, feeling the horror and joy of delicious freedom. The question ringing endlessly in my ears.

My God. What have I done?

FORTY-EIGHT

RENE

Before

Mum and Dad are standing either side of me, holding me up by the arms. My body hurts, I need to take more pills. Yet I feel disorientated and afraid. Everything shifts.

'It's going to be OK,' Mum says faintly. 'Don't worry.'

They begin edging me towards the door.

'But... my things,' I say, 'I can't leave them.' I try to wrestle myself free.

'You won't need this anymore,' Mum says. 'We have everything you need.' Seeing my head lolling, she grips my chin. 'Just listen to what we're about to tell you.' She holds my gaze, nodding and guiding me to nod too. 'You need the medicine I gave you; the extra strong stuff. And something to drink. A bottle, the big one of Coke. You know the one. That'll give you just enough fuel to keep going. OK?'

Extra strong medicine...

A big bottle of Coke...

Just enough fuel...

I nod.

'Come on, love,' Dad says. 'No more time to waste. Just stay with us. OK?'

I nod. 'OK.'

They lead me out into the hall. Dad going first, stopping at the picture of him and Mum and Lauren on the pontoon in France. 'Ah my little princess. That's a smashing picture.' He touches it, and his head turns back to me. He nods.

Smashing picture.

My head is vague, I can't concentrate. Too much pain to do this. Dad starts unbolting the door. Four small locks up its back that have protected me from the real world for too long.

'Where am I going?' My voice drifts.

'We're going to save Lauren.'

'Yes,' I whisper.

'Oh, and one more thing.' Mum reaches into her bag, holding out the little yellow lighter. The one she used, and Pete did, in all those moments during conversations that unfurled like smoke. Confessions, stories. Finding the truth at the heart of it all. Mum's heartbreak. Nanna's distance. Dad's betrayal. Pete's immaturity. David's misguided attempts to offer help.

Everyone's fault. Everyone except the one man who had used all those weaknesses to make himself strongest.

Keele Colson.

Always one step ahead.

I look at Mum, taking the lighter from between her fingers, a question asked with only my eyes.

Extra strong medicine...

A bottle of Coke...

Just enough fuel...

Smashing picture...

Little yellow lighter...

'You're going to need all of them,' she says.

Then she takes my arm, and Dad takes the other.

'Just remember what Pete said about Lauren?'

How could she know about what he'd said?

'Say it,' Dad urges.

And I answer with what feels like my last breath. 'She was always going to start a fire.'

FORTY-NINE

JANE

Today

Jane wonders if she should call the police again. It's been nearly an hour. Waiting is horrible, only eased by the fact that Rene seems to be pleased that her dad is here. From inside the kitchen she can hear the muffled sounds as they talk and cry, as they tell each other they are sorry, as they cling to each other.

When Jane glances at her phone, she sees there's a missed call from Alice. Strange that she should have called. Perhaps she knew just how much she was thinking about her. Sixth sense. She's not even sure how she missed it.

Jane also knows that despite being right at the centre of today's drama, she still doesn't know anything really. The truth of what happened. The girl, the notebook. She steals quick glances back to the man in the loose grey suit and Rene with her bruised face and Jane's coat still draped on her shoulders.

They've shifted to the sofa, Rene has Alice's blanket on her knees too, and her father, Jim, is cradling her, stroking her face.

And that's when she hears it. The name.

'Lauren.'

It is Jim who says it.

Jane freezes.

She takes a step forward. 'Lauren?' she asks. 'Do you know where Lauren is?'

Jim looks at her. '*This* is Lauren,' he says, and his eyes are red raw from crying, his smile is wonderful and damaged.

'This is Rene?' Jane asks. And the sirens get closer. *Now they are rushing*, she thinks. *Now, finally, when it is almost too late.* Dan enters the room from the hall where he has been waiting and pacing. Staying out of the way.

'They're here,' he says, almost excited. He searches Jane's eyes, then frowns, seeing that she is unsure.

Jim turns and looks up at the girl. He grips both her hands, tight. '*This* is Lauren,' he is saying.

The siren crescendos then stops suddenly as if sliced with a knife.

'But then, who is Rene...?' Jane asks. 'She told us her name was Rene.'

Jim looks at Lauren, gives her a comforting smile. 'Rene was... Lauren's imaginary friend,' he states. 'She always blamed her for things when she was little. That's how I knew...' he says.

'But I don't understand. When we called... you said.' Jane looks back at Dan in the hallway by the door, for reassurance. For understanding.

Jim says, 'There've been so many prank callers over the years. Terrible cruel things; who would do that? But that's how I knew it really *was* her.' He pauses, turns back and smiles at Lauren. 'Only you knew about Rene.'

The sirens are silent. Suddenly there's a knocking at the door.

That's why there was no mention of Rene when I searched, Jane thinks. *That's why I could only find Lauren's name online. It makes sense now. There was only ever one missing daughter.*

Lauren was missing, and Rene was... 'trying to keep Lauren alive'. That's what she said.

She hears Dan answering the door, talking to the police, inviting them in.

Jane is aware of her mouth hanging open. She looks at the girl-woman who is not Rene but Lauren and the man who is not Jeremy but Jim, in a home that is hers but was once theirs, and contains more of their story than it ever will of hers.

There's the sound of heavy footsteps entering her house. A relief, an end to Jane's responsibility, to the game of patience; trying to work out what to do or not do since the moment she gazed out her window and saw something there in her bare January garden by the rose bush.

Her eyes drift away from the bruised face of Lauren, and only then alight on the notebook that she is no longer holding. It sits on the side table. The thing that brought her to Jane's garden, to her kitchen, to her home. To this very moment.

What does it say? Will she ever know? But the girl sees Jane looking, and she scoops it up, holding it even more tightly. She still wants to protect it. But their eyes meet, and Lauren smiles.

A brief and grateful thank you.

FIFTY

LAUREN

Before

I knew the moment was coming. I knew it.

After he took me out of The Hole, and I reassured him every day that it was all my fault. Lesson learned, forever this time, I promised. That I would never, ever touch anything. Or try anything. That our secret was going to be safe with us, forever and ever, Amen. And they all lived happily ever after.

I'll be good as gold, I promised.

My leg was bad, I could hardly walk, let alone run. Still, he dressed my wounds, and though my jaw was the worse, I made him keep me alive. Spoon fed. Mush. Like a baby. Hand to mouth. One moment at a time. Reborn. And I was. He would never know who this new child really was. *I am Rene. And I have everything I need now to get away from you.*

Some pills I took. Some pills I hid. I healed, bit by bit, and I tried to cook, tried to keep house. I lay with him, feeling nothing and everything. Because I had to. Because I was holding onto something precious.

They love me.

I wouldn't let him tell me anything else ever again. The truth was going to set me free. I held onto it like a magical golden thread that I could follow home.

Then one night he cried. Cried at what he had done. That made me afraid. That he was going to do something bad, worse. That this was the end. *Don't leave,* he begged. Maybe he saw the new me in my eyes. Maybe he guessed that there was a new fire inside me now.

'I won't,' I promised, fingers crossed behind my back. It scared me a little that I was still the liar I had always been. Can a lie ever be good? Lies destroyed lives. Like mine.

I was just a boy, he said. *Uncle Ray, he made that hole. He punished me the same. I know how frightening it is in there. You can get crazy down there. You can imagine all sorts of things. Voices, faces, terrors. I know what I've done. I will never, ever—*

'Sh,' I told him. I opened my mouth to say it, 'Maybe, if it would make you feel better, you could...'

I was going to say, 'you could let me go'. He could unlock the door, let me walk free. I thought of crossing the fields, about the woods, to the canal. And beyond, the posh gated houses and the cul-de-sacs. To Meadow Close. Temptation crawling up my throat. Those words waiting to run faster than I could now. Back to my family who I knew were missing me after all.

'You could...'

His fingers flexed, because I had promised. He would know I was still lying.

What are you trying to say? he asked.

'Nothing,' I replied. 'Nothing.'

I could feel that infection spreading in my leg. I felt worse. Worse. Day by day, he gave me more pills to numb the pain that was not willing to play anymore. It throbbed and my head got crazier. And little by little, I hid them away. He might want to kill me, but he didn't want me to die this way. He nursed me back so he could kill me first.

When the pain was so bad, I swallowed a few down, knowing it would mean my plan would need more days. A trade. Rid my pain for a few hours and be stuck here longer. Maybe too long.

Then one night I begged him to take me to hospital, all full with fever, and the throbbing that raged, *pleasepleaseplease-please*, hallucinating that I was with Mum and Dad, and they were holding my arms and saying it was time to go home. Even with all the pills he gave me, and most I took, it would not stop.

Little L. I can't. I can't! Ask me anything, but not that. He stroked my brow. *Not now. Maybe later. Yes later. I can take you to the hospital.*

Some part of him must have known how bad it was, what he had done, that he would never be allowed to leave with me.

He told me the doctor would come soon. No one came. He scoured online and tried things with vinegar and salt. How bad it stung. I thought he'd wanted to let me die, put me in a bin bag like that dog, and take me to be buried in the woods, finally like I should have been eight years ago, under decaying leaves, or worse still, thrown into the canal to wash away to estuaries, never to be found. But always he promised he'd never put me in The Hole again. If I lived...

It was the last time, he said.

When I was really twisted with fever, he even said he would fill in The Hole with concrete. He whispered for me to get well. *Don't leave me alone. Don't ever leave me.*

'I won't.' I nodded. I dreamed that he put me in it and filled it with concrete and buried me alive in that hole.

Then just like that the fever broke. I woke and the sweat and raging were gone. Had I said anything in that madness? Had I told him about my plan?

That Sunday afternoon, I was better, and I hobbled around

the kitchen and made him lasagne, and afterwards I served him a beer. I had crushed pills in both. The rust-smelling froth on the top of the can the only sign that something was brewing. I knocked it against the table, and it fizzed over the lip.

'Sorry,' I said, making it seem like my leg had given way, making me stumble. I was clumsier than ever, but I glanced down at my feet, my mismatched socks; because that was lucky. Froth streamed down from the beer onto the table. He eyed me suspiciously. Even that was creeping back in now I was getting better. 'I'll clean it up good,' I said. 'Don't be mad.'

Get the cloth, he snapped, and I went off and got it.

After we ate (more pills), he went out onto the driveway. Went to tinker with his cars. He came back in, and the kitchen was all tidy. He hadn't seen me go into the living room and smash the picture. Hidden a big old shard of glass inside my leg bandage, all the time thinking why hadn't I done it before, before, before? And I could tell he was slowing, see it, like a tired man plagued by a fly at night. He swatted at his head, as if trying to clear it. It was December cold out and I could see it had slowed him down too. His lips a little blue.

Get me another beer, he said.

'Sure. You want me to help?' I offered.

Out there. No way. He laughed, as if it was the most ridiculous thing.

'Why not? Not like I can run.' I pointed to my leg.

Not an answer. More of a growl.

'But I know how to clean the parts like you showed me. And you can pull the garage door down. I just want to be useful, be close. Together. Like we used to be. Please.'

I should get an Oscar for playing that role.

He smiled a little, lifting the corners of his mouth, but something bothered him. *You up to something?* he asked.

'Just trying to make you see things are better. I'm better.' I touched his arm, as if the fever had changed me. That troubled him, like something he couldn't quite remember. The person I was. The person he wanted me to be.

You'll sit at the back, where I can see you, he said. *And no funny stuff, OK?*

He frisked me down, and my heart thundered at the idea he would find the shard of glass. But when he was sure, he brought me out, and I sat in the shadow as he dragged down the big metal door. He lumbered around from shelf to hood. *Don't even think about screaming.*

'No, sir,' I said, and he even smiled.

Slower he was, like a fairy-tale giant, staggering from shelf to bonnet. In the corner was the big old Coke bottle, filled with turps. Like the one he had given me in The Hole to drink that time he thought it was a joke. I shuffled over and lifted it down and took a swig. Then I spat it out, a great big mouthful all over the floor, and he laughed then.

Stupid thing. What are you doing? Give me that. He was laughing. Thought it was funny as I choked and spluttered.

I went over to him on my bad leg, spilling more as I went, and then I handed it to him. He set it on the side of the car and put his head back under the hood, and I slammed it down onto him, as hard as I could. And that stopped him laughing.

Oh, that stopped him all right.

He growled and shifted, and the bottle fell, the fluid glugging around his feet as he came out and he grabbed at his skull.

What the? – and that's when I slashed him with the piece of glass. *Smashing picture*, words in my head from the fever. The shard in my hand now glinting like ice and tipped with his blood like stained glass from a church.

I thought it would go deeper. I had hoped it would.

A moment when everything waited. Even the world held its breath.

And then I started to panic. *What have I done? What have I—*

He tried to focus on me. His hands going to his neck which was bleeding, pulsing, pumping. But he smiled as he saw his blood-covered hands, the red river flowing through his fingers as he tried to stem it. When he smiled, he snorted from his nose, shocked and hurt and the muscles of his belly contracting under his shirt, so confused at what was happening. Didn't know whether to laugh or cry.

So this is how it ends, huh, Little L? he said slowly as he came at me. No rush in him. *Some people never change. Some people NEVER FUCKING learn!*

'Stay away from me,' I shouted, my hand outstretched, glass in one hand. I backed up as far as I could go, against the wall. No further.

He came at me then, lumbered towards me, got me by the throat. Instantly I couldn't breathe, I struggled, grappled, his other hand gripping my wrist to try to get my hand to pop open and drop that shard, gripping it until it hurt so much I thought he would wrench my hand off. But I didn't let go. So he kicked my bad leg and the lightning exploded. Not standing then. Everything bursting white. I dropped the glass onto the ground, and I heard it break against hard concrete as it landed. My legs folding, only held up by the throat. Then he lowered me to the ground and lifted his leg to sit astride me.

Oh Little L...

He knew I had nothing left.

Oh, Little Little.

He held me there, and I could see him straining. His breath short and hard as bull snorts. The wound in his neck not as bad as it could have been, but the pills, they might not let it stop, not clot. But that would take forever.

His hands had the strength of everything in them, and I had none. He had stolen every last drop. Drinking it in day after day. I was never going to win. I should have always known that.

Like he said, I was stupid enough not to ever listen.

It all went slow then as he started to lean forward. As if that day at the canal, approaching for that first kiss.

Little L, he whispered, and his voice was hollowed out, hard breaths, a fleck of spittle. But I wasn't going to be fooled; he had enough left. More than me. My fingers trying to get his hands off my throat. Strangling me, I couldn't breathe. This was it.

My eyes bulged, throat ached, crushing, trying in vain to pull his fingers away, no light coming. Entering the blackness. Feeling the pulse of each second in the blood at his neck, and the black-white patterns in the corners of my eyes, converging, pulsing with my leg, the life throbbing out of me.

'You know,' I said hoarsely as the room faded to only darkness and shadow and the smell of oil and dust, and his furious sweat. 'You know... Pete told me...'

My hand fell from trying to wrench his fingers from my throat. Loose at my sides, giving up. Too late. Writhing at my side, by my pocket. I pulled out the only thing I had left, one last trick. A final hidden thing.

'Pete said... I was always going...'

But my thoughts were wandering. The patterns were joining. What had Pete said? What did I need to do? Drips of Keele's blood on my face as he slumped heavily over me. Not letting up on my throat.

'I was always going... to...' My fingers holding something. Flick. Whoosh. '... to start a... fire...'

I sparked that little yellow lighter.

Woof, went the turps I had spat out, up in flames.

Boom, went my head as he struck the back of my skull against the garage floor. The flames burst from that patch I had spat out, and I wondered if it was enough to reach the puddle under the car, or to follow in his footsteps from his fuel-soaked boots. Only thinking that after all those years of surviving, this was how I was going to die.

Little L, burn in hell. No one would ever find me. Would

they come when they saw the smoke? But by then it would be too late.

Because I was always looking for trouble.

And finally,

Oh yes.

Finally, it had found me.

FIFTY-ONE

JANE

Today

It happens fast then.

A man and a woman enter the kitchen, the man hangs back while the woman approaches. Almost instantly she speaks into her radio, and Jane feels a heatwave of guilt as the policewoman calls for an ambulance to Meadow Close, as if Jane should have done that all along; the first thing before even calling Dan.

Then the man approaches Jane. 'Can you tell us what happened?'

Jane flounders for words, realizing the quiet-noise buzz of it all has been broken with the sudden business of the kitchen, now they are six in this shrinking space, busier than when the kids were still home. The girl and her father, the policeman and the woman, bulky dark jackets and big boots, and Dan and her.

'I... found her. In my garden. She was...' Jane gazes towards the window. How to describe it? She finds her finger pointing and then she drifts over to the window. The policeman stays close to her, not wanting to let her get too far out of his reach. 'She was *digging*.'

Jane almost wants to laugh, the word sounds ridiculous as she says it. Her head dips and she realizes she might just be in shock. The magnitude of it. If this is Lauren then she has been missing for eight whole years. And Jane has found her, right there in her garden.

She laughs, but it crumbles through to tears. Her face collapses and the policeman reaches out a hand to touch her arm for comfort. Then Dan is there, beside her, scooping her into his arms and she's so very glad he's there. The relief in that moment.

'Dan...?' she says, seeking his comfort.

'It's OK, Jane,' he says.

'No,' Jane insists. 'That poor little thing.' She starts to cry.

'She'll be OK. It's all OK,' he whispers into her hair, as if he too cannot find words, and she realizes then how much tension he has been holding as he paced and busied himself in the house this last hour. 'She's safe. She's finally safe,' he says, over and over.

Jane finds herself glancing around the room. This room, in her home, where she knows so much of her own life has happened. Realizing that so much of someone else's life happened here too. Terrible, sad things. Loss and pain. A tragedy she cannot comprehend, or dare to imagine. She's so grateful for the life she's had. Her children, grown and healthy and happy. And safe. Her marriage, steadfast and constant. Dan, her rock that she calls and he comes. A house they filled together with laughter and care. Her eyes trail over to Aidan's birthday picture, the scent of lemon zest, never far from her mind.

Dan looks at her. 'I love you, so much,' he says, and he holds her as if he's forgotten to say it, how wrong that is. She feels his body wracked with his own tears.

'I love you too,' she says, leaning her head against his. And more than ever, she realizes how much she truly means it.

FIFTY-TWO

LAUREN

Today

I am nothing more than flotsam carried along by this sea. I am hoisted onto a trolley. I am in a vehicle, surrounded by moulded plastic. The siren is loud and all around.

'What is your name?' they ask over the sound.

'Lauren,' I say as if I cannot believe my own name.

I am Lauren.

I am no longer missing.

A mask, cold air. A needle. My eyes fluttering closed. Except this time, inside the dark, there are no dreams or nightmares, no fear of waking, there is no shadow sister, in the dark, underground, keeping my story alive. No Rene, no voices. It comes quick, and I am far gone.

I enter the hospital through doors, and more doors. A corridor. Another corridor. A lift. More doors. Bursting through. Bursting. Everything surreal and bright and garish.

I see lights passing overhead like I am a plane about to take off. The place rushes past, or I rush along within it. The nurses and doctors talk to me, but I can only hear my own breath in the mask on my face. The oxygen so clean after all that smoke. The mask on my jaw which is still painful, my mouth dry and sticky sweet from the Coke the kind lady gave me.

I never even asked her name.

I want to feel elated, but everything is too distracting. I can't hold my thoughts. I can't remember anything the second after it has happened, each thought passing with each ceiling light. Where is Dad. And... where is Mum?

I raise my arm to look at my wrist. A tag that the nurse has placed there; *Lauren Fisher* it says. Hands push my arm back onto the gurney and we trundle along the endless corridor which gets brighter. The thump of opening doors. Still my arm snakes up again. I'll remember this afterwards, out of everything. How ridiculous it seemed, but I wanted to be sure that I am Lauren Fisher.

It could still be a test.

Keele is clever like that. He knows how to plan. Always one step ahead. He wouldn't let this happen.

'Where is he? Where is Keele?' I ask, tugging the mask off.

People in blue uniforms bustle around me. My eyes cannot follow them. Too much movement, I feel nauseous. I raise my arm to look at the wristband again just to be sure. *Lauren Fisher.* They lower it again. A woman pats my wrist. A mindless affection, thrown away but to me it is treasured. The woman did the same in her kitchen, patted my arm. Maybe I will never forget the woman whose name I didn't remember to ask.

This endless corridor. Where are they taking me?

'It's OK, dear,' the woman says. Then another injection goes in. Cold in my arm. Liquid that creeps and stings. 'It's OK,' she says again, and lifts my wrist to feel my pulse.

I drift into the blackness that I know only too well.

My only thought: *He'll come looking for me here too.*

FIFTY-THREE

LAUREN

After

When I wake, I am lying in a stark, white room. The mask is gone but there is a tube running to my nose and another into my arm. My leg is in a cast and raised. I have vague memories, but nothing I can shape enough into recall.

As the room comes into focus, I see it is not all white. It has a door with a metal frame, grey venetian blinds, a clock with blue hands, and a wall of cupboards and an empty shelf. Beside me, as if standing guard, is a thing like a hat stand with a bag that runs into my arm. In the corner, a beige chair.

A woman sits. Not the woman from the kitchen or the woman from the corridor patting my arm.

Where am I? I think or ask. And if this is real, then where have I been? I think backwards past the injection and the wrist-band with my name, the siren and the kitchen, digging in the garden for the notebook, digging for the truth, and back to the smoke-snow falling. Heat and ash. I am hurtling backwards and into the moment when I did what I did. In that garage. His weight crushing me. Forcing out my last breath.

So where is he? He wouldn't be so careless as to leave me alone, or unfinished.

'Don't worry,' the woman says, seeing how I contract each time the door opens. 'No one can harm you here.'

'What about Keele?' I ask.

'Especially not Keele.'

'Is he here, in this hospital?'

She moves to the side of the bed, checking to see if I am OK with her proximity.

'He's... dead.'

'In the fire, which I started?' my voice rises. A terrible pulse of guilt.

'No,' she says. Something hesitant.

'But then how can you be sure... How can you know he—' I remember coming around in the garage with the flames everywhere, and looking for him. He was not there, and I was. I scrabble to sit up. He could be here, anywhere, about to—

'He can't do anything to you, Lauren. I promise. We found his body.'

My head whirring. Promises can be lies.

It's a trick. A test. I mustn't believe her.

'Keele Colson is dead. I trust the person who told me. You will never see him again.'

I cry. Not tears of relief. Tears of guilt. Unsure how I really feel. *I killed him. It was me. Blood on my hands.* Because of what I had done.

'I did a bad thing,' I say.

'No,' she reassures me. 'Keele was a... he did... he did a *bad* thing. And he knew he would be punished for it. For a long time.'

'But he was there. He was with me... in the fire.'

'No. He left. He took a car, went into the woods and... they found his body. He'd killed himself.'

'He left me there?' He left me to die?

No, he was bleeding. The fire. He couldn't. This is wrong. He isn't dead. They're lying or confused.

'You've nothing to be afraid of,' she says. 'You're in safe hands now.'

But he told me I was in safe hands before, I want to protest. Keele *wouldn't* have left me to die. He wouldn't have taken his own life. Even if I tried to kill him. Or maybe because. So it was my fault.

Still, in my head I will come back to this. Time and again. More and more doubtful. He left me there, knowing he could have survived, and so could I. Knowing he could live if he chose. He didn't want to stay and die with me. But he didn't want to – or couldn't – live without me.

'It will take time,' she says.

You will never understand, I tell her silently.

Nothing hurries here. Everything is purposeful and slow.

When they talk, they are hushed and slow. When I eat now the tube is gone, I eat little and slow. When they take my vital signs, they are silent. Each of them delivering their care with warm-milk smiles, topped with a chocolate dusting of pity.

When I close my eyes, it rushes at me. That day at the canal with the book. That day in November when Keele first told me that he liked me, cared for me, needed me in his life, his hands holding me, and he said if we were good and made a plan we could help each other, be together. If I wanted.

I remember the shimmering grass along the bank. The day when he stopped being Mr Colson and started being Keele. The day he reached over and kissed me and I thought that...

He loves me.

As if magic had come back into my dark world.

After that, every moment I was helping him weave a prison for me. Knitting the metal bars from my own words and confessions. Thinking he thought I was special in a way that no one else did. Telling him every secret, every truth. During those walks, and those first days at his house. Did he really know that one day he would do those things to me? Was that always his plan? Until the day I realized I could not leave, not escape. Maybe something in me made him a monster. Some chemistry between us that I sparked in him. Perfume that smells bad on some skin.

Because in the end, I was the one that killed us. Not the other way around. I was the one who brought trouble to us both.

'No,' the counsellor says. 'You were fighting for your life. You were prepared to do anything to survive. Anything. He wanted you to believe this was your choice. Your doing.'

I'm afraid to sleep, to let them sedate me. I am afraid when I open my eyes I'll be back there again, him standing over me. That this is just a dream or a nightmare, or both. I'll be back in that damp, dark hole in the ground, waiting to die, playing the game, trying not to scream, listening for him to come and punish me again. Thinking of Rene, another attempt to escape by any means possible. Through any sliver of light.

I hold up my arm and see the white name band.
Lauren Fisher.
Only then I close my eyes.

Dad comes to the hospital.

There is a policewoman behind him. He comes towards me as if to hug me again, and there is amazement and dismay and disbelief just like the first time I saw him in the kitchen that was ours but not ours. His face is haggard. So thin. His eyes lost. He's been crying again, or is still.

He waits to touch me, and then he grips me as if he might

drown without me. I retract myself, and the policewoman steps forward.

He stops and his hand rushes to cover his mouth as if he is afraid of what he might say. Or as if my form shocks him more than his does me. Beneath his wrinkles, his grey hair, I see his face. I see my dad's eyes. How afraid he is, as if I might break. He slowly raises his fingers to touch my face. My lip. The scar he is always searching for amongst all the others.

'Lauren,' he says.

I see the dull light in his eyes and the years engraved in his face. Have I done this to him? Also my fault. His face shows me just how much time has really passed.

'Where's Mum?' I ask. I asked him in the kitchen but he didn't reply. Now he turns to the counsellor, and she shakes her head.

'Where's Mum?' I insist.

'I'm sorry, love,' he says, and he is not crying, he's holding it, but I can see it is only for my sake. 'It was... it was only recently.' He can hardly speak. 'She... she tried to hold on. She... she wanted so much... would have loved to...' He turns back to the woman, and now she shakes her head again. 'I'm so sorry,' he says.

He cannot continue anyway. The tears consume him.

In all those years, all those conversations I imagined Mum had with Rene, I never thought that she would ever go. That she could die. She was so strong. Too strong. Invincible. I thought nothing would ever break her.

Until the end when I knew she was always broken.

I think of Nanna's fingers, reaching across the pale hospital sheets. A bed just like this. I look at my fingers, thinking of Mum kissing Nanna's hand, but only after she was dead. The regrets, floating into the world. Regrets, when it is too late.

That curse.

I was so angry at her. So hurt. Maybe I hated her. But in the end, when I was hurting so badly in The Hole, she came to me and spoke softly to me. She soothed me as I sat dying, or maybe it was her that was dying.

I think of her talking to Rene. Rene who kept Mum with me until the end. Kept her close to me. Because she always knew, saw what I could not, or refused to see. Rene was always the good one. The one I couldn't be.

Rene brought Mum back to me.

Over the days and weeks we talk about what happened. The counsellor is cautious and never asks me to go on. We don't speak as if it is an ordeal; we talk as if we're discussing casual things.

'Tell me about The Hole, if you're OK to,' she asks. 'How did it make you feel?'

I pause.

'It was easier after Rene came.'

'Rene?' she asks.

'My sister. I thought of her and her life, and she was a connection to my family, my old life. She showed me what was happening, what people were doing, she made happy lists every day. Went to school, got a job.'

'She showed you... what was going on, out there?' she asks, taking notes.

'Yes. Her life, how it might go. She had little adventures. She took a job with David. She wrote stories. She was a good writer.' I trail off.

'Lauren,' Joanne asks quietly, 'do you *have* a sister?'

I pause a very long time.

'No,' I say, hanging my head. 'I don't think I ever did.'

'And Rene, would you say you imagined her?'

'No. Not really. She... was... it was as if she imagined herself.'

'"Imagined herself"?' she repeats.

There is another man in the room now. Maybe this is not the same day. Maybe this is weeks later. Time is fragile. He has introduced himself as Dr Arpen. The counsellor glances at him. I am not in a bed. I am sitting in a chair. There is a table. There is a tape recorder. I've told her all this before.

Dr Arpen is a specialist. He's very curious about Rene.

'I thought of her, and what she might be doing. And then, after a time, she just... did things. She was full of ideas, places to go, people to see.'

'Where do you think she got her ideas from?' Dr Arpen asks.

Memories, or things I'd read, things I'd seen in magazines...

'Where do any of us get our ideas from?' I reply instead. They are always asking me questions, so I ask them some back.

Dr Arpen makes a few notes. 'What are your earliest memories of Rene? When would you say she was "born"?' he asks.

'She was there when I was young. I played with her. When I got lonely, when Mum was unwell.'

I thought of how we'd sit in the garden, and we'd play with Rebecca doll, tea parties and picnics, and I'd read her stories. Later things I'd made up myself. My little audience. She always listened.

'Was Rene always there?'

'No, she went away. For many years.'

'So later, at Keele's, when he put you in the dark, she came back?'

'Yes, when I was frightened in there, at first I thought *of* her. But then I couldn't stop her coming, or what was happening. What she was doing. Things went off sometimes in... unexpected directions.'

'You weren't controlling it all?'

'No, it was like a film, running in my head. A cinema. I could only watch. The bad things seeping over.'

Dr Arpen and the counsellor go to the back of the room and talk for a while. Later, next time I see him he hands me a printed document. It talks about a man in Afghanistan who Dr Arpen had been studying. He was put in a hole for weeks on end by his captors, held hostage, and he describes his hallucinations and conversation. How he spoke of endlessly folding a piece of paper, and how he wrote letters in his head to people he knew, and even some he didn't. How he had entire conversations and correspondences. He explained how at some point he stopped being in control of it. How it took over and became beyond distractions and obsessiveness.

The report refers to his condition as The Prisoner's Cinema. That the mind needs sensations, and that during sensory deprivation it finds them.

In the dark, the mind fills in the empty spaces. The holes.

FIFTY-FOUR

LAUREN

After

The counsellor tells me that they have found the body of a
woman and it's been identified... it's Keele's ex-wife.

'Jacqueline?' I say.

'Did he ever speak about her or meet her?'

I think of the videos on the computer and her things behind
the wall, feeling as if I knew her, and CayCay. I worry about the
girl.

I tell the counsellor about what I found behind the wall. I
know the house was largely destroyed by the fire. The fire I set.

'His daughter?' I ask.

'Catherine? You knew about her?'

I lower my head. 'CayCay...'

I smell bleach. I think of the clean kitchen surfaces. The
mouthfuls of lasagne and the pills in my hand. Me falling to the
floor. The small gold earring there by the skirting. I think of the
innocent little girl. Blowing out candles. Blowing a kiss to
Daddy. Pushing past him, wanting him to leave her room.

The counsellor says, 'Catherine never came back from

Spain. She was fifteen when she and her mother, Jacqueline, left him. His finances took a dive, and he lost his teaching job, became a supply teacher. Jacqueline never formally accused him, but there were reports that he was controlling and aggressive. Abusive. She told the authorities she was afraid and took Catherine to live in Spain.

'That was a year before you went missing. She left and took their daughter, which seems to have triggered something in him. He most likely saw you as a *substitute*. Wife and daughter.'

Did I become the wife and child he wanted to take back under his control? One complete package. It was never about me.

They continue, 'Then Jacqueline reappeared a few months ago at the cottage, looking to have him finally settle his debt, their divorce. She must have told him he needed to sell the house otherwise. Or maybe she became suspicious. Saw your things. It seems she... *never left*. She was reported missing in Spain but never traced to here.'

'Was she... was the body... was she wearing a gold earring?' I ask.

The counsellor looks at me quizzically, tilting her head. 'I'll try to find out,' she says.

Later she tells me she was. 'But only one. Why did you ask?'

I look at my fingers, scars where I was burnt on the hob. Knowing I had found the other and swallowed it, trying to keep it.

I don't feel sorry for Keele anymore, only sometimes when I think about him and how he was abused by his uncle Ray, as a boy.

My counsellor calls it Stockholm Syndrome. She explains that an abductee often comes to empathize with someone as a tactic to improve their chances of survival. It's why older children are more prone to be found after many years in a captive situation, and younger children are... less fortunate. They are less able to adapt.

Was I fortunate or not? I wonder.

Then one day a woman comes. I recognize her, the woman from the kitchen in Meadow Close. My home, but not my home. I never even asked her her name.

'Jane,' she says, and she extends a nervous hand which I shake. Strange, after all, we have met before. That day. The day of freedom.

She sits down and we talk. She tells me about Aidan and Alice, and her husband Dan. There is sadness in her, but also happiness. I thank her. Then she looks at me, and asks me, 'What was in the book? The notebook that you dug up in our garden.'

It's still here, in a drawer. I lift it out. Soil-damaged and warped.

I open it slowly, still smelling its smell of earth and must. And some other hint, of hairspray and body mist. There are scribbles and stories, ideas for David. Doodles and love hearts. The last thing I had written is this:

The Fairy Tale

Once upon a time there was a beautiful princess. She loved to sit beneath the rose bush at the bottom of her garden. Did her father remember that he had planted that for her? Did he remember that he once loved her? She was worried he did not.

Because sometimes she felt alone, and sometimes she felt sad. And why did her mother hate her? Why was everything she did a mistake? It was all so hard. Was that her fault?

So one day – when she no longer felt that she was their beautiful princess – she decided to write her parents a note, and to bury it in their garden. And after she was gone – because she would go for a short while – they would find this and realize how sorry they were, how much they had loved her. And they would miss her. How careless they had been to lose her like that.

And only then they would beg her to come back and be a family again.

Maybe then they could live happily ever after.

'And you came back for this?' Jane asks.

I nod.

Because inside I had stuck a picture of Mum and Dad and me. It is faded, but we are smiling, standing on a pontoon in France, lit by the sun. Mum in that dress I loved, with the iridescent sequins. And Dad had once said it was a 'smashing picture'.

Or maybe I had just imagined that.

Hard to remember. Memory is fragile.

FIFTY-FIVE

LAUREN

After

I can write the end of my story now.

It is July. Warm, not hot. Not like it once was on the day I met Mr Colson. Dad and I are standing at Mum's grave, and he turns to me, he lays his hand on my shoulder and says, 'I want to say something about that night...'

'Dad,' I say, trying to stop him. I feel the heat rising in me, pricking at my cheeks, my armpits.

'No,' he tells me, not forcefully but determined. 'That night. I never meant to hit you.'

The day is bright, but Mum's grave is grey. Except for the yellow roses I have lain there. Yellow roses that I now know mean hope.

My leg aches. It never set right after Keele broke it. It's always cold from the pins they put in it. As cold as the marble stone in front of me, the one with Mum's name on it.

Sue Fisher.
Wife, Mother, Daughter.

'Your mum sent me after you that night. She told me to come and get you. To bring you home. She pleaded with me. She was afraid what you might do. That you might harm yourself. But I was angry. I was so fed up with you arguing, and I didn't understand why.'

I stare at the sunlight on the headstone of Mum's grave. I don't want to go back there. To remember... that night. Not anymore. But he needs to finish this. He needs closure too.

'She said we had to put everything aside. That you were what mattered most. We had to make sure you didn't do anything foolish. To protect you. And she said you'd listen to me, you'd come with me, not her. If I just said I was sorry. She insisted I go.'

His head is low, his mind far away. Back there, the horror starting all over again. I can feel it growing.

'So I followed you,' he says. 'I took the car. You rode down the alleys, and you were gone.'

He was seen out, driving the car, blood on the steering wheel. Another reason they didn't look in all the right places. Suspicion everywhere. David, Dad, Pete, the canal. But never Colson... so close but not close enough.

'I wish I could have caught up with you. How many times I have wished...' He tries to hold his sob.

I focus my eyes only on Mum's grave. *Wishes*, I think... wishes are for the future, not for the past. Wishes for the past are just regrets by a prettier name. I *wish* I had had the chance to say goodbye to Mum. I *wish* I could have had all those conversations with her and not just in my head. I *wish* I had understood her better and known she loved me then. I *wish* Dad had found me at the canal that night and told me he was sorry. I *wish* we had never met Mr Colson on that hot summer's day. Or had a crack in our family that I could fall through.

My mind follows Dad to that place, even though I don't want it to. Let this be the last time. Let us free ourselves.

'I had arranged to meet him,' I say quietly, picking up the story. I stare at the headstone, as if needing to tell this to Mum and Dad together. Maybe that is why we are here.

I close my eyes and in my head he is coming. Keele is on his way. I had thought that it was a good thing, after I called him from a payphone. That excitement that it was really happening as we had planned. As he had told me. This would be good for us both. We'd show them, hey? *Little L.*

'I stood on the wall at the towpath. I waited. He said I should. That was where I should stand and wait. I was worried, the wall was icy. It seemed like a long time. I was hurt and confused, wanted to come home, but didn't. I threw some of my things in the canal, my jumper, my notebook, my keys. To spite you. To make you question. To frighten you maybe. I thought about what Mum had said about your affair. That you would leave us, and I hated you so much.

'I even thought about jumping. I stared into that freezing water and I wanted to just disappear, to follow my things as they sank. To make it all stop. Deep down I felt it was all my fault. But he was coming, and... I believed he was going to make it all *better.*'

Dad reaches out his hand. Places it on my arm. 'You don't have to say anything more,' he says. He's afraid of what he has started. Of what is coming.

I shake my head. I must. I must finish this.

'I saw the headlights of his car, so I got down from the wall and I rode towards him on my bike. I couldn't even wait. But he came at me. I heard the dog bark inside the car, and then the car ran straight into me. My head hit the bonnet, and then the road...'

Woof went the dog.

Boom went my head.

Splatter went the blood-rain.

'You don't have to,' Dad says, trying to stop me. To save me, all over again. He doesn't want to hear it. How he stole me. But I need him to know why I always believed that Keele wasn't going to hurt me.

'He pulled me up, lifted me to my feet, and my head hurt and I just couldn't understand. I was confused. And he... was backing away.'

Dad's hand tightens on my arm. *Still time to get away.* But there wasn't. There never will be. It will always be too late.

'He was drunk. I knew by the way he spoke,' I say. 'And he shouted at me, "Go back to your bitch mother, and your father. Your happy little family. I'm nothing but trouble," he said. And he started to cry.'

I can't turn to Dad. Can't see the horror that I can feel is flooding through his face as he hears this.

'I told him I needed him to take care of me. I couldn't go back, you were going to send me away. That you were a liar and a cheat. And I needed to get better. I told him how mean you were. *Cruel* I said. But he refused. He said, "Go home. *Please*," he begged. "Before it's too late."'

I swallow hard. Because he must have realized what he was capable of.

'Then he got back into his car. And he drove away...'

A tear trickles down my cheek.

'But...?' Dad starts to ask.

The sun is strong as we stand there but I am cold as ice. As cold as that December night. I stare at the grey shingle on Mum's grave.

'I should have waited for someone to come. You might have found me and taken me home, and we would have talked and everything would have been all right. Eventually. Another life. But I didn't. I knew where he said he lived, and I started to run. I thought...' Choking on my words now...

I am there in that moment where all the bad things start to dance. *He loves me. He loves me not. Dandelion seeds.*

'I remember looking at my hands, the blood on them from the wound on my head. I ran through the woods in the dark, the fields beyond. It's a long way. It was freezing, and the snow made me wet. I'd lie down because my head hurt and I was confused, but I would always get up. I kept making myself get up and keep running...'

I turn to look into Dad's face now.

'I was running to him, but really I... was running away from you.'

I taste my tears in my mouth. Thick salt tears. And blood. Blood on my lips.

Breath escapes us both, an implosion, as Dad drags me to him. As if he holds me tight enough now it will undo everything, all those years. In that moment I realize the difference between the small trouble of home and what I ran into. The love of my family, and the hate of that place.

Dad loosens his grip. We step apart, but I have one last part to tell. One more lie to be free of. To preserve the truth.

'It was me who sent Mum the rose,' I say. 'I was angry and spiteful and my head was turned by crazy things, things Keele said or told me to do. And I wanted to make you doubt her and what she had said about me. So you wouldn't trust her. But you saw that rose, and instead...' I can barely say it, it eats me.

It eats me.

'You said it was from you. You lied to me. For her.'

Dad touches my cheek, down to my lip where he struck me that night. A non-existent scar, or at least less visible than all the rest.

'I loved her,' he says. His hand falls away and he turns to Mum's grave. A sadness crosses his face, and I finally see all that he has lost. Like distant stars dancing in water in his eyes. 'Always will,' he says.

We stand there and look at her grave. *Wife, mother, daughter.*

Then after a while, we turn and walk slowly back to the car.

FIFTY-SIX

Dearest Lauren,

I don't care what they say. We'll find you. They say I do not have much more time, but I won't give up, not until there's no more breath in my body.

What does 'terminal' even mean? I know what it means. Terminal is every day not knowing what really happened. Terminal is every moment that I accept that I won't ever see you again. Terminal is a life without you. The idea that I will never hold you again, my precious little princess.

I do not fear my own death. Losing you forever is the only thing I fear. What else is there for a mother to dread?

I hate myself for how we struggled. All that wasted time. And I know it was my fault, caught up in my own past. Sorry, sorry, sorry. But I will make it up to you. You'll see. Because I know, in my heart, in every inch of this stupid cancer-riddled body, that I love you. Even when I couldn't say it. Even when I didn't like the things you said or did, or the way you looked at me or doubted me. I didn't realize it was all such a cry for help. A cry for help from me. Like I'd always heard it. Ever since you were a baby.

Sometimes I believe that you're off on some adventure, living the life you always wanted, that this is what you chose, and that one day you'll call or just come home. Step inside my kitchen door, stand there in front of me and tell me all the wonderful things you've been doing all this time. And if that's it, I'll accept it, I'll be happy for you. Just to listen to your stories, your wonderful colourful stories. I'd like to think that that could be the truth. Please...

Until then, I'll keep hoping and praying that soon you'll be home. For that day when I can hold you, and tell you how much I love you. Because I do, I always did. More than anything else I've ever known.

With all my undying love, Mum x

This book is dedicated to David Pritchard, who inspired me to keep going.

He used to say 'everyone has a story to tell'.
This is mine.

Lauren Fisher.

A LETTER FROM THE AUTHOR

Please let me take a very quick moment to say thanks and share my gratitude for you reading *Lauren Is Missing*. This is such a special book to me (see my reasons below), and I hope you felt hooked into Lauren and Rene's story (and Mum's), and their journey to some form of freedom.

If you want to hear more about my other books, new releases, and bonus content, you can sign up here! I have more to share and would love to keep you updated.

www.stormpublishing.co/sj-king

A quick note, reviews are so important in helping an author like me find their readers. Even a few words can make all the difference to people discovering my stories. Also, for me to hear what you thought and how you experienced this book. If you are able to post a quick review, thank you! Five stars ***** to you for finding time to share *Lauren Is Missing* with others.

And now, why this book is so special to me.

It evolved from my own fears. I was pregnant when Madeleine McCann disappeared. As I watched in horror and heartbreak as her parents' story unfolded, I thought how terrible it must be for someone to not know what happened to their loved one, especially their child. Their disappearance hanging like a forever open question mark, colouring the rest of their life.

Grief, without end. And fear. The idea taunted me, until Lauren's story was born.

This book unpacks the intergenerational trauma that many of us inherit and unwittingly inflict. I know that no matter how hard we try as mothers, our children see us as something other than what we are; as we did our own mothers. How much we hold in. How much we hide. How vulnerable that can make us. There are those that exploit such sadness, in women and girls. The most important thing is to talk, to each other, before it's too late. As this book has emerged over the years, my own children have grown, and as a mother of a teenage daughter now, I see this cycle.

The journey to publication was not easy for this book, even though so many people loved it. In the beginning it was raw, poetic, abstract, and ultimately confusing. I needed to contain it to do justice to the unpeeling of the emotional onion, whilst keeping the balance between a heartbreaking story of hope, and a horrifying pulse-racing thriller. Because I wanted Lauren and her mother's story to reach and touch as many people as possible. Including today you.

I hope it did. Thank you.

SJ

www.SJ-King.com

facebook.com/s.j.king.author

x.com/sjking_writes

instagram.com/sjking_writes

tiktok.com/@sjking~writes

ACKNOWLEDGMENTS

Some years ago, on a whim after reading *The Happiness Project*, I sent this book to the incredible agent that is Madeleine Milburn. She called me back within the hour. When she said I had just sent her something and that was why she was calling, my first thought was that the file must have been corrupted or contained a virus. Nope, she asked to see the completed novel (it was not even completed!) and within the coming days offered to represent me. The following week was London Book Fair. With her immense enthusiasm, *Lauren Is Missing* was on submission.

Despite Madeleine being a powerhouse in the publishing world, the book was not ready, I know that now, and it did not sell. She has remained a kind voice in my publishing journey, though not my agent, and this book was shelved. I wrote others. Another agent later put Lauren out on submission again, such was the belief in this story. Publishers were praising but no one quite bit. It's a competitive marketplace and the book was still not ready. I wrote more books and did more writing courses.

After a rework some years later, I sent Lauren on another whim to Storm Publishing. Again, it drew attention, and that was how I met Vicky Blunden, my incredible editor. She signed me, and revived this story that I have loved, laboured over, and longed to see out in the world. Her guidance to hone this book from manuscript to published work is a gift. Her instincts for crafting great stories that satisfy many readers are calmly presented but impressively astute. She is quite literally my partner in crime-fiction! Supported by Oliver and the Storm Publishing team, I have been blessed with my book journey so far. Thank you, Alex, Anna, Elke, and the many who work to make our Storm books fly. Such caring and professional hands to be in.

I do also want to thank Emma Cooper, who through her mentorship with Jericho Writers taught me things that I finally applied to this book. And even though she never worked on it with me, without her teachings, encouragement and friendship, I would not have given Lauren another try, or found Vicky and hence a way for Lauren and my other stories to finally escape into this world. Thank you. *Cheers!* My monthly Fridays are only truly complete when I get a moment to chat to you. So nice that talk authorly things now. Keep inspiring me, and many others you mentor.

To Matt, who read this along the way and left a comment in the document: 'You are a genius.' Thank you, I have carried that little positive feedback in my sea of writer's self-doubt for many years. I have way more gratitude than you have olive trees! Still, I am jealous of your way of life.

To my mother, who was one of the first people to read this (after Madeleine offered me representation, I felt I should). My mother's first question was 'I hope I am not the mother.' Yes you are, and no you are not. Although Mum in this story is as vulnerable as she is strong, and as misunderstood as a teen daughter can make her. So yes, some parts are us. But we have been able to stay close and remain dear friends throughout our lives. We have been able to share our stories. And tell each other we love each other, many times.

Deeply, I thank my husband Johnny, who has been Lauren's biggest champion for years and years. And mine. You are amazing. You never gave up on her, or me. You dreamed my dream with me. Lauren and I are profoundly grateful for that Halloween night in Hong Kong, and all the journeys and words that followed. To my son, who has heard about this person Lauren his whole life; a sister he never lived with but she was always there. (*Read me,* she says...)

And then, to my dearest daughter. It is in the fear and love that you being born brought to me that Lauren and Rene's story emerged. And that of being a mother. Everything I learn from you and your needs, teaches me things about my own life. You complete this cycle for me, making me a mother as well as a daughter. Never doubt how very much I love you and champion you, and I hope that gives you more freedom and self-confidence to be fearless and bold in all your life brings you. That is the happy ending I will always wish for.

Printed in Dunstable, United Kingdom

64404113R00190